MW00946911

The Old Bentley Schoolhouse

VICKI MARGO STUVE HUGHES

WESTBOW
PRESS®
A DIVISION OF THOMAS NELSON
& ZONDERVAN

WestBow Press books may be ordered through booksellers or by contacting:

WestBow Press
A Division of Thomas Nelson & Zondervan
1663 Liberty Drive
Bloomington, IN 47403
www.westbowpress.com
1 (866) 928-1240

ISBN: 978-1-5127-3923-7 (sc)
ISBN: 978-1-5127-3924-4 (hc)
ISBN: 978-1-5127-3922-0 (e)

Library of Congress Control Number: 2016906607

Print information available on the last page.

WestBow Press rev. date: 05/24/2016

Dedicated to Robert Douglas Bishop,
a teacher born, not made.

Chapter One

Andrea Michelle Hogan

Her mother's heart told Andrea that the call on her cellular phone was coming from the best Christmas present she had ever received; her son Will Roger Hogan. Her heart, and the fact he had programmed her phone to play *Allegro in F Minor* whenever he called. Born late on that Christmas night in 1981, he had been the light of her life for all of his twenty-seven years on this earth. "Hi, Will!" she answered. "I was just about to call you!"

"Mom, guess what?" he asked excitedly. "I got that job with the public radio station here in Austin! You are now speaking to the new voice of WKMT, 99.9's 'Saturday Night Alternative Music!' I start in two weeks! Can you believe it?"

"Oh, Will, that's great! You've wanted to work in radio for so many years."

"You can't say I was ever at a loss for words," he acknowledged. "Of course, this isn't full time so I won't be leaving my day job at Whole Foods, but my boss assured me that she won't ever schedule me to work on Saturday night. Although… it would be cool if we could do a live remote from the store one night!"

"I can't wait to tune in through my laptop. I'm so glad you made me buy that gadget; I can stream WKMT any time I want to, and if you're on the air, I'll want to!"

"I'm glad to know I'll have at least one loyal fan! I can't wait to introduce these Texans to Will Elliott Whitmore."

He sounded so happy that she was reluctant to interrupt with her own good news. Or was it good news as far as Will was concerned? It certainly put a crimp in their tentative plans for her to spend the winter with her friend Connie in Fort Worth. Her news would put all long term plans on hold for at least five years.

"So Mom" he inquired. What's up with you? "Did you finally start that novel you're always threatening to write?"

"No, no novel this year," she admitted. "I'm probably going to be pretty busy starting this fall when I begin teaching Freshman English and Composition at BGM Consolidated School System in Marshtown, Iowa."

"Whoo-hoo! This is the day for news in the Hogan family!" he crowed. "Mom, I'm really happy for you if this is what you want to do. Looks like your plan to substitute teach in Des Moines took a giant left turn!"

"I thought that was my plan too...right up to the time that I hit 'Submit' on the online application to teach at BGM," she admitted. She went on to tell him about the job and how her young friend from UNI, Trish Wilkins, had encouraged her to apply. When she had returned to UNI two years ago to complete her secondary education certificate, she had not planned to teach full time. This was to be her retirement job—substituting from time to time in the Des Moines school system to pay for that blasted necessity: health insurance. Winters would be spent somewhere warm—preferably in the same state as her boy. But along the way she had been bitten by the teaching bug and after all those hours studying, writing papers on the latest teaching techniques, and finally the four glorious months in the classroom during her student teaching she had been hooked. She loved the smell of the classroom, the perfume of the dry erase marker, the sight of all those desks lined up so carefully. She knew she could not be content hopping from one classroom to another, one school to the next. She wanted her own classroom. More than that, she wanted her own students, young people who would challenge her mind and hopefully learn a little something about that quirky language known as English.

Could she get a full time job at the ripe old age of 58? That was the question. What school system would want to invest in a teacher who already qualified for the AARP restaurant discount? Certainly not the Des Moines School District where substitutes bounced from school to school for years before achieving the all – important full time equivalent status. No, if she was to have her own classroom, it would be in a small rural school or at a teacher – starved district in the middle of Houston. All in all, the rural Iowa district would be the better choice for her.

When Trish told her about the opening in the district where she was being hired, Andrea decided to give it a try and let the Lord and the system decide if this were to be her new home and career. Trish had had many offers with her new credentials in math and science, but had chosen BGM to be near her elderly grandmother, Susan Duggan. Andrea and Trish had become friends despite the significant age difference while they were both entrenched in Education Methodology and Classroom Management Techniques. They had worked together on a joint project for Class Room Management and found that they were a good match—Trish could handle the computer graphics while Andrea supplied the words.

Andrea was surprised but pleased to receive an e-mail from Craig Seeley, principal of BGM, shortly after she submitted her application, requesting that she call him to set up a time for an interview. It had been a somewhat disconcerting conversation as she recalled.

"Seeley here" had been the response at the other end of the line when she called the BGM phone number on a muggy early July afternoon. She had forgotten that the secretary would not be working in the middle of the summer—but no such luck for the principal. "Mr. Seeley, this is Andrea Hogan. You asked that I give you a call to discuss your opening." There was an alarmingly long pause, and then she heard, "Refresh my memory, are you calling about the 9th Grade English or the 10th grade Biology position?" Her reply had been hasty as she laughingly informed him, "Considering that I almost flunked Biology when I took it forty some years ago, I think we'd better talk about the 9th grade English position!"

"Sorry about the confusion, Mrs. Hogan. It's pretty crazy here right now. I remember you, you're Trish Wilkins' friend."

"Yes, that's me," Andrea assured him. Thank goodness Trish had given her an advance recommendation when she had interviewed for her job at BGM. Mr. Seeley at least had a glimmer of recognition now, but it would be up to her to make the glimmer turn into interest and the interest into a job offer.

"I've been talking to and e-mailing so many people about our open positions that I'm afraid I may hire a physical education teacher and expect him to teach calculus," he admitted. "But I think I'm on the right page now, Mrs. Hogan. So when can you come visit us down here in scenic southeast Iowa?"

"Please call me Andrea, and I can come down whenever it is convenient for you. How long does it take to get to Marshtown from Des Moines?" she asked.

"Oh, we're a good three and a half hours from Des Moines. There are no interstates in this part of the state," he said.

"I have some friends in Keosauqua I'd like to visit anyway. Shall we say next Monday afternoon?" she asked.

"That's fine. I'll be here in the office all afternoon. How about 2:00?" He asked in return.

"Two o'clock, it is. I'm looking forward to meeting you. I take it I won't have any trouble finding the high school?"

"No," he admitted. "As in most small towns, we're pretty easy to spot. Just come into town on Highway 2, turn right on Main Street and we are about twelve blocks ahead on your left. You can't miss it. I'll see you next Monday at 2:00."

"Thanks for the opportunity, Mr. Seeley."

"You're welcome, Mrs. Hogan. You come highly recommended."

He hung up before she could even think of a reply. Highly recommended? She hoped that Trish had not oversold her abilities. Sure, she had the wisdom of years of experience in the public sector, but her teaching experience was very limited. Still, she remembered her friend Janice's first evaluation as a teacher and that coveted phrase, "A teacher born, not made." She had certainly wanted to be a teacher for a very long time. Would that be enough to get her the job?

She thought about the choices she had made when her marriage ended in her early 30's. Will had been just three years old and the thought of being a single parent AND going back to college to become a teacher had seemed overwhelming. She had enjoyed her position at the Legislative Service Bureau, and there had been stability, good benefits, and a pleasant working environment. Raising a small child alone seemed daunting enough. She had decided to take the safe route and stay in her position with the State.

4

No, she had not been unhappy with her choice, just a little nostalgic about the what if's in her life.

That had been six weeks ago. Craig Seeley had called yesterday and offered her the job. Four sections of Freshmen English and Composition, one Study Hall Monitoring, and one blessed prep period! She was a teacher! Craig had been very surprised when she accepted the position without even asking about the starting salary. Her "Yes!" had been blurted out in sheer excitement and relief. She truly had left it in the Lord's hands and had not applied for any other positions. The starting salary had not been anything to write home about, but with her State of Iowa retirement, she would be very comfortable.

After she had hung up from her phone call to Will, she made a cup of tea and settled in her sunroom to think, and plan for the upcoming months. She knew that she would not be selling her home in Des Moines. This was where Will had grown up and where he returned for briefer and briefer visits. His world now revolved now around life in Austin, but return he did. She wanted the familiar home to be here for him.

Her dear friend Sally had unknowingly resolved the problem of what to do with her big old Victorian while she was residing in southeast Iowa for the next few years. Sally's niece Sue would be moving to Des Moines from Wichita, Kansas, to attend law school at Drake in the fall. A nontraditional student in her early 30's, Sue had graduated from Wichita State in the spring after attending college for the better part of twelve years, taking one or two classes a semester while she worked full time as a secretary in a small law firm. Now she was taking the plunge, quitting her job, taking out a student loan and tackling law school. Andrea had offered to share her lovely old home on the east side of Des Moines with the young lady for a nominal rent. Andrea would have the assurance that her home was well cared for and Sue would have a quiet, safe place to live and study during her law school days.

Once again, it was Trish to the rescue when it came to a place for Andrea to live in the BGM area. When she had called her earlier to tell her the good news, almost the first words out of her mouth had been, "Oh, and I've even found a place for you to live!"

"Wait a minute, Trish!" she had declared. "I haven't even gotten used to the idea that I have a new job. I'm certainly not ready to think about where I'm going to live!"

"Well, you'd better get ready, Andrea! I'm here to tell you there isn't much of a choice in any of the small towns around Marshtown!" Trish warned. "In fact, the place I rented last week was the next to the last one available at the Bentley Schoolhouse Apartments!"

"What in the world are the Bentley Schoolhouse Apartments?" Andrea asked incredulously.

Trish laughingly informed her, "It's the lame name of one of the coolest places that I will have ever lived!"

"Well, I can figure out that it's in Bentley—but what else is cool about it?" she inquired.

"It's actually the old Bentley elementary building, and Coach Samuels just finished renovating it into apartments," she informed Andrea. She told Andrea that Coach Samuels had used some of the money he had earned while playing briefly in the NFL to purchase his old elementary school after the center had closed in 2005. "He couldn't stand the thought of that beautiful old building being torn down or turned into storage for Shearer Heating and Cooling, the county's heating and air-conditioning company," Trish explained.

"He bought the building for a song, but I hear he has put over $100,000 into the renovations," she continued.

"How did he manage to carve out apartments from an old school building?" Andrea asked.

"It's a neat old building with the wide center hallway, with three classrooms on the main floor and four classrooms upstairs. He converted each classroom into a one – bedroom apartment with the living, dining, and kitchen space wide open. It feels lots bigger than 600 square feet. The ceilings are very high and he refinished all the hardwood floors. On the main floor he converted the principal's and the secretary's offices into a neat library complete with floor-to-ceiling shelves and a wood-burning fireplace. Andrea, it is just way cool, and it would be so neat to have you living in the same building! You could feed me on a regular basis like you did when we lived in Cedar Falls! Oh, and the gym, kitchen, locker rooms, storage and furnace room are all in the basement. He's not planning to put apartments down there. He'd like to see some sort of a community center. Bentley doesn't have much going for it now that the grocery store and Laundromat have closed."

"That is certainly a rousing endorsement of the town!" Andrea replied somewhat sarcastically.

"It may not be much of a town, but it's the only one with any decent apartments!" Trish reasoned. "I know—I looked everywhere in Marshtown—and if you're looking for a tiny, poorly insulated, one bedroom apartment on the outskirts of town, then I can pass on a phone number, for what it's worth!"

"Don't worry. You've convinced me of the worthiness of living in Bentley, Iowa! I'll call the coach right away. Oh—what was his name again?"

"It's Scott Samuels, and you can reach him on his cell phone; here's his number. Don't delay," she warned. "The apartments are great, and the last one won't be hard for him to rent."

And delay, she did not. As soon as she hung up, she dialed Coach Samuels' cell phone number. Again she heard an abrupt greeting when he answered his phone. What was it with these men who worked for the BGM School District?

The voice that greeted her was just as abrupt, but younger. "Samuels, here!"

"Here we go again!" she thought, but plunged on anyway. "Coach Samuels, this is Andrea Hogan calling. I've just been hired at BGM to teach Freshman English."

"Oh," he replied. "You're Trish's friend, aren't you?"

"Why, yes I am! It seems she is laying the groundwork for me wherever I go!"

"I take it you're calling about the last apartment at the Schoolhouse?" Scott asked.

"I've been praying that it hasn't already been rented," she replied hesitantly.

"Well, actually it has sort of been promised to someone, but since you're the person I'm holding it for, I think it will all work out fairly well," he replied. He laughed at her silence on the other end of the line.

"I don't understand, Coach Samuels. How did you know that I would even need an apartment? I just found out that I was being offered the position a few hours ago!"

"Well, you may not have known until a few hours ago, but I knew last week. Knowing how hard it is to find good housing in this area, I decided I'd better hold this one for you for a few days," he explained.

When she still didn't respond, he softly reminded her, "It's a small town, Mrs. Hogan."

"Indeed it is, Coach Samuels!" she finally managed to sputter. "I guess I shouldn't even bother to ask about the rent, since I'm willing to pay whatever you are charging. Just curious…what is the rent? Oh, and please call me Andrea—or Andi works just fine, too."

"Then Andi it is!" he replied. "The rent is $400 a month, but that includes all utilities."

"That's more than fair, Coach Samuels. I can remember paying $400 for my first apartment in Des Moines more than thirty years ago!"

"Well, you may have heard that I'm doing this more as a labor of love than to become a landlord. Renting the four apartments will more than cover my expenses. By the way, it's Scott or just Coach. I'm a pretty informal kind of a guy."

"Then Scott it is! That's my brother-in-law's name, and he's one of my favorite people on this earth!"

They agreed that she would move in on August 10th, two weeks before school started on the 24th. He explained that each apartment was about 600 square feet and featured an open floor plan that included a kitchen and a living/dining room. There was one good-sized bedroom, and one bedroom that wouldn't hold much more than a computer and a single bed. That sounded perfect for her. No big house to keep clean, no empty old house to keep filled with good spirits. Her home in Des Moines would be there when she wanted to visit, or more likely when Will wanted to visit, but for the next few years she could see calling a cozy little apartment home.

Her tea had grown cold as all the changes in her life whirled around her. What a difference a few weeks could make if you let the Lord and luck guide your path. In just a few weeks she would pack up her living essentials and transfer her home and life hundreds of miles from where she had lived for the better part of 58 years. Of course, she had gone to Cedar Falls for her undergraduate degree and back there the past two years to complete her teacher certification program. To leave Des Moines and her oh-so-comfortable life here, that *would* be a little scary. Was she up for all this change at the ripe old age of 58? She was sure to find out.

Chapter Two

Patricia Elaine Wilkins

Math had always come easy to Trish. She had always smiled when her friend Andrea explained to someone that until she was thirty years old, she had not known that what you do to one side of an algebraic equation, you have to do to the other side. Now her math skills had brought her to the first rung in her career ladder, a fulltime teaching job right out of college.

Actually she had known since her junior year that finding a job as a math teacher was not going to be difficult. The difficult part would be deciding where to teach. She could move back home to Lancaster, Pennsylvania, to be near her father, his new wife Becky, and kids Ian and Jessica. She could also move to Mesa where her mother had recently relocated after marrying a very nice man who was five years older and already retired. Or she could teach in southeast Iowa in one of the many rural school districts around Marshtown where her Grandmother Sue lived. She loved southeastern Iowa with its hills and valleys and the beautiful Iowa River running through the heart of it. It reminded her of Lancaster where she had grown up. It amused her to see the Mennonite buggies in Cantrel, and the Cantrel General Store could have been swapped for the Lancaster Mercantile – lock, stock, and bulk storage bins! The Amish of Lancaster County and the Mennonites of Van Buren County may have held different beliefs about rubber tires, but they still dressed and lived in a very similar manner. She felt comfortable there, as comfortable as she felt anywhere these days.

Still, when she considered moving to Lancaster, there was a knot in her stomach. Did she really want to live near her father and his new family? Face it: his life had never revolved around her. He had left her mother when she was thirteen. He had left her as well. Sure, he tried the Weekend Daddy routine but just never felt comfortable with it. His new condo was not conducive to hosting teenagers, and the weekends had fallen away as she became more and more involved in school and church activities. Finally in the last two years of high school their time together had been reduced to the occasional Sunday night supper.

Then he had met Becky. Her father had never been a demonstrative man. His hug when he saw her felt forced and without warmth. No wonder he had been attracted to Becky. A nice enough woman, but very plain, pencil thin and without an ounce of humor. She was also thirteen years younger than her father. Becky was an accountant with her father's firm. She had certainly been on the far side of spinsterhood when she first took a position in the advertising agency where her father had toiled for most of his career. Whether they were attracted by their mutual loneliness or some unknown chemistry, the romance had been swift. It had resulted in a quick ceremony in Las Vegas when Becky discovered she was pregnant with their now six-year-old son, Ian.

They must not have learned much about birth control from the unexpected birth of Ian. Six months after Ian was born, Becky discovered she was pregnant again. Trish had figured that Becky's biological clock was running pretty rapidly and she had decided to finish her family propagation as neatly as she added her columns of numbers. Fortunately, the next half-sibling to arrive was a girl. They named her Jessica, and her father's new family was complete. A quick vasectomy later and her father would not be a new father again.

His life was busy now with soccer games, dance classes, and school programs. She tried not to be bitter about all of the soccer games, dance classes and school programs that he had not attended during her childhood.

Trish was very close to her mother, but, she had little interest in inserting herself into her mom's and her stepfather's lives in Mesa, Arizona. She was happy that her mother had met Mike while doing volunteer work at her church in Lancaster, during Trish's freshman year in college. Mike, five years her mother Gloria's senior, had just retired when they met while sorting clothes for a homeless shelter. Their mutual interests in the outdoors and their love of playing bridge bonded them almost immediately. A mere six months later, the two were planning a quiet wedding and a move to Mesa. Trish's mom had worked hard to raise her alone with only minimal support payments from her dad; she was especially pleased that her mother could retire, perhaps not in luxury, but certainly not in need.

So where did that leave Trish? She had pondered that question over many a cup of tea, many of them shared with her new friend, Andrea Hogan. Andrea was a woman in her late 50's who had retired early from her career in state government so that she could pursue her lifelong dream of being a teacher. They had first met in a methods class and had cemented their friendship when they prepared an oral presentation on "The Efficacy of Time-Outs for Third Graders." Andrea had been a whiz at the words, and Trish had handled the Power Point with ease.

Andrea Hogan had actually been the first person to propose that Trish stay in Iowa after graduation. Andrea knew that her indecision came from no longer having a sense of place. Trish's childhood home was long gone, replaced with an adobe ranch on the outskirts of sprawling Mesa, Arizona. Her father John's home had never been hers, and since the addition of the latest child, did not even contain a room for her to sleep. No, she needed a place to call her own, and she needed it soon! Returning to Van Buren County in southeast Iowa where she had spent the last two summers began to seem more and more appealing.

She had sent out half a dozen letters of inquiry in early spring before graduation and was only a little surprised to receive five letters inviting her to submit applications online for upcoming teaching positions. She had interviewed in all five districts and had received offers from all five! Talk about feeling wanted! In the end, the pay had been similar between the five districts, and she had chosen BGM. The consolidated district included the small towns of Bentley and Grimball, along with the larger community of Marshtown.

Before she even graduated, her position was secure. Finding a place to live had been a tad more difficult. Of course, her grandmother had immediately offered to change her own plans and remain in her large house in Marshtown, instead of moving to the senior citizen apartments on the edge of town. Trish was touched by her grandmother's generosity but knew that her grandmother had been looking forward to downsizing for quite some time. "No," Trish thought. "I'll stay with Nana through the summer and help her get ready for the big auction in August, but I'll find someplace to live on my own in the fall."

It turned out that was easier said than done! Trish has scoured every inch of Marshtown for a one or two-bedroom apartment and had come up disappointingly empty. In a town of 5,000 there were only three apartment complexes and just a dozen or so residences with apartments as a part of their architecture. She had dutifully looked at apartments in all three complexes and had decided that if she really had to settle for what they offered, the complex near the city park was the least objectionable—but it was still pretty objectionable.

Her luck had changed one day in Olson's Hardware Store when she had blatantly eavesdropped on a conversation. Mr. Olson and a nice-looking young man were discussing door pulls for kitchen cupboards. She had stood behind a keg of roofing nails as she heard the two talking about what seemed to be a major construction project.

"Now, Scott," Mr. Olson had begun, "I can order these pewter ones for you, but I just don't see the need when I've got these perfectly good gold ones just going to waste in the back room." Scott had studied the two styles of handles and suddenly a smile broke across his face. "Mr. Olson," he began. "I know you've had these gold handles in your back room since the Carter Administration. Isn't it about time you were willing to cut me a deal on them? After all, I'm going to be taking enough off your hands to outfit five kitchens." Mr. Olson had smiled as well and agreed to what he felt was a fair bargain. "I'll tell you what, Scott. You buy enough to outfit three kitchens, and I'll throw the other two in for free. I guess if you weren't converting the Bentley Schoolhouse into apartments, that place would just end up a blight on my home town."

"Mr. Olson, you are a man among men! Thank you very much for your generosity. Now, just add five cans of pewter spray paint to my bill, and we'll both be happy!"

While the two men were settling up, Trish had quietly slipped out the door. She was conspicuously loitering outside of the hardware store when Scott left with a large box topped off by spray paint cans. She knew she had

13

to be bold or risk living in a dump, so she quickly approached the stranger. "Excuse me," she began. "My name is Trish Wilkins and frankly, I was just eavesdropping on your conversation with Mr. Olson."

He fixed her with a quizzical look and asked, "Don't tell me you get a thrill from hearing about gold drawer pulls?" "No," she assured him, "But I do get very excited when I hear about five renovated apartments! All I've seen for days are apartments with threadbare carpets and refrigerators that *also* were manufactured in the Carter Administration!"

"In that case, Miss Wilkins, I think we'd better find a place to sit while I regale you with my life story. I promise you I'll eventually get around to five renovated apartments complete with spray painted pewter drawer pulls!"

Chapter Three

Scott Eugene Samuels

After he stowed the box in the back of his very large pickup truck, Scott and Trish walked over to the town square and found a bench under a century-old maple tree. It was one of those precious days in June when the temperature and humidity are both in the comfort zone, and they settled in companionably as Trish invited this athletic-looking man to tell her his life story.

He did not hesitate. He started by telling her that his name was Scott Samuels and that if she took a look at the trophy cases at BGM High School, she would see his name on a dozen or so trophies from the early 1990's. He had played football, basketball and baseball. He went on to play football for the University of Iowa where he was a First Team All Big Ten running back. He was drafted in the third round by the San Diego Chargers. He had played four years for the Chargers, starting in seven games in 2004. He went on to explain that in a playoff game against the Seattle Seahawks, he jumped above a defender for a game-winning touchdown catch. When he came down in the end zone, that same 220-pound defender landed on his knee. Scott barely remembered being carried off on a stretcher, and never played another down in the NFL. It was a long and difficult recuperation, but he had used the time wisely by completing the teaching degree he had started at the University of Iowa. He had begun teaching history and 9th grade social studies at BGM in 2007.

He even told her that he had lived with his parents, Jane and John Samuels, while the renovation of the Bentley Elementary School project was being completed. Scott had further explained that he had financed the renovation and remodeling with savings from his salary as a football player. He had spent six years as a student in the building and hated to see it torn down or used as a warehouse of some kind. He was proud that he had actually done some of the work himself. Most of it, he had to admit, was done by his brother Steve, who owned a small construction company. Scott told her that he and Steve were very proud of the work they had done on the old school building. They also hoped it might become something of a community center for the small town of Bentley, Iowa – population 284 if you counted the cats and dogs!

As Scott talked about the hardwood floors and the huge windows that were now double-glazed and energy efficient, Trish could not hold back her hopeful enthusiasm. "Scott, please don't tell me the apartments are all spoken for! They sound like just the kind of place I want to live!" she had implored.

"Actually," Scott admitted, "there are only two apartments spoken for at the moment. There is mine which is a double unit, and the one that I'm renting to my parents' friends, the Swenson's. Do you have a few extra minutes? I'd be happy to show you around. It really is just down to the drawer pulls and a few pieces of hardware."

Trish was on her feet before he finished his sentence. "Let's go!"

Chapter Four

Scott's Schoolhouse

It was clearly a construction site, but the majesty of the old school was still evident in its solid, inviting façade. The old Bentley Elementary School sat at the end of Vine and State Street surrounded by century-old trees and 1950's era playground equipment. Its cornerstone proudly displayed the year it had been built—1905. The Superintendent had not even had the decency to let it stay open for one hundred years, but had closed it after a mere ninety-nine years of educating the town's children.

The two story brick building was as long as it was wide. The front steps were still as inviting as when hundreds of Buster Browns ran up and down them. Scott opened one of the double doors for Trish to enter, and she could smell the distinct odor of refinished wood and many gallons of paint. As she walked up the five steps that led to the main floor, she saw a gleaming hallway that must have been at least fifteen feet wide. The light fixtures clearly dated back to the Art Deco era when the building had been electrified. The polished nickel base with the stenciled shade allowed soft yellow light to fill the hallway and light the way to four doors that looked like they were straight out of a Victorian mansion—which was exactly where they had started their lives.

Scott explained, "There were great doors already here from the original building, but with two-foot square windows in them, I thought the residents might want a little more privacy." He went on to explain, "I found these doors in a barn outside of Marshtown. The old farmer who owned them had always planned to do something with them, but just never got around to it. When I explained where they would be used, he insisted that I take them all for free. I've run into that so many times as people learned about this project—just like Mr. Olson at the hardware today. Of course, free to me didn't mean free to the project. After painstaking stripping and staining, these free doors cost well over $200—but still, a pittance compared to what they're worth."

The wide hallway had four doors, three of which proudly displayed their new apartment numbers…1, 2, 3. The fourth door was not the highly carved Victorian of the other three apartments, but it was the original door that had led to the former principal's office complete with the lettering to prove it. When Scott proudly opened the door, Trish saw that the room had been converted to a warm and welcoming library, complete with empty bookshelves, two leather chairs, a comfy couch filled with pillows and a fireplace that looked ready to warm up a room full of people. Scott beamed with pride as he explained, "I kept this room as a kind of library or meeting area in hopes that the tenants would enjoy getting together, either to read or talk or maybe even play some cards. I know it's something that I'd like to do, and since I'm living here, I figured I'd better provide the space to make it happen!"

Scott was clearly excited to continue the tour so Trish reluctantly left the warm and inviting space and followed him to Apartment #1 across the hallway. Scott unlocked the door and invited Trish to enter before him. When she did, she was enchanted by gleaming hardwood floors and a large open room with a line of cabinets and appliances against the back wall. When they shut the front door, Scott immediately opened another door which looked in on what had once been the cloak room but was now the tiniest bedroom she had ever seen—and her dorm room had been miniscule—or so she thought. "Is this the bedroom?" she asked, worry filling her voice.

She was relieved when Scott laughed and said, "It's a bedroom—but there is another larger one. I just converted the cloak room into a tiny bedroom in case someone has a guest."

"Well, that's a relief! I already know I'm going to beg you to rent me this apartment—even if this IS the only bedroom!"

"Then I had better show you the rest of the place," he replied, the pride still fresh in his voice. He opened a second door to show her a very nice bathroom with gleaming white fixtures and a modern medicine cabinet with pewter colored handles. "I see why you bought the spray paint—you want the kitchen handles to match these, don't you?" she asked.

"You've got it!" he agreed. "Now, let's see what you think of the size of this bedroom," he said as he opened another door.

Inside, the gorgeous hardwood floors continued into a bedroom that, while not huge, was of a decent size. There was plenty of room for a queen-size bed, a dresser, and even a desk. Another door within the room revealed a closet big enough for at least one season's clothes.

"I know the closets aren't huge," Scott admitted, "but there is an entire storage room in the basement that people can divide up and use to store their winter or summer wardrobes. You'd be welcome to my space as well, considering that the difference between my summer and my winter wardrobe is a couple pairs of long underwear." The moment the words were out of his mouth, he regretted them and turned a peculiar shade of pink.

"Thanks for the offer, but that's about the difference between my summer and winter wardrobe as well!" Trish assured him. It was Trish's turn to blush.

"So, what do you think? You're actually the first person other than my family to see the nearly-completed project. For me it's been a labor of love, so I can't really see it objectively. I love this old building, and it just hurt my heart when I heard that it would probably become a warehouse for the Shearer Heating and Cooling Company. It wasn't hard to outbid old man Shearer when they auctioned it off last year." He chuckled as he recalled to himself how Mr. Shearer had called his plan pure poppycock—the strongest language Scott had ever heard come out of his lips.

"I'm very impressed, Scott!" Trish assured him. "Are the upstairs apartments just the same as these down here?"

"Not exactly," Scott admitted. "Would you like to see them?"

"Try keeping me away!" Trish enthused.

They proceeded up the ten-foot wide marble steps to the second floor. The same gleaming floors greeted them, but there were only two of the refinished Victorian doors on this floor.

Trish looked at Scott with questions practically bouncing out of her eyes. He saw her consternation and quickly explained.

"I put pretty much my whole saving account into this renovation so I figured the least I could do for myself is to make myself a place to call home." He opened the door to Apartment #4 which ran the whole length of the hallway. Inside, there was no wide expanse of hardwood floors as could be seen on the lower floor. Instead, a pleasantly neutral, but ultra thick carpet greeted their footsteps. Trish's immediate urge was to remove her shoes and sink her toes into the deep pile. She laughed when she saw Scott begin to remove his shoes, and she quickly did the same.

He saw her remove her shoes and quickly assured her that she did not have to go barefoot. "I'm just so paranoid about tracking in dirt while I'm still renovating that I've just gotten used to slipping in and out of shoes in here."

This apartment, while large and pleasant, was not as wide open as the three apartments below. A nice sized living room led to an archway where a chandelier hung just waiting for a dining room table to be positioned beneath it. To the left another antique door led to the master bedroom and bath. It was clearly a man's idea of graceful living. The walls were off white and the carpet was beige. The original ten-foot tall windows allowed light to pour into the room on two sides. Clearly this was a man who did not sleep past dawn very often. When she stepped into the master bathroom, she saw that it was designed for a man, but with a woman in mind. There were two separate sinks and cabinets, one taller than the other. The glass enclosed shower had three rain shower heads, and she noticed that it was also one of those fancy new steam models. The spa tub was quite easily big enough for two, and the turbo jets would be marvelous after a long cold football game.

Back in the living room he led her through the archway into the dining room and the kitchen beyond. This kitchen was not open to the world, but held gleaming stainless steel appliances, and plenty of granite countertop space, and more cupboards than one bachelor could ever fill.

"I decided to keep the kitchen enclosed here in my apartment since I'm not the neatest of cooks. To the right of the kitchen, a hallway led to another bedroom and a full bath. Also along this hallway was another small room that could be whatever a person wanted it to be—except perhaps a bedroom. There was no closet in sight.

"I'm going to use this room to store my sports equipment, but it would also work as a small den...or even a baby's room. Not that I'm planning on having one of those anytime in the near future!" he assured her.

"Is the apartment across the hallway the same size?" she asked with curiosity.

"It is, but without the extras. I've actually designed it with the idea that my folks may move in there when they want to give up their big house and huge lawn. For now I've rented it to the new head of the English Department—Rich Knight. I had thought maybe two people would want to share it since there are two baths and plenty of space to spread out, but Rich snapped it up before I could tell him the amount of the rent. He said that he wanted the extra space for when his kids visit him."

Finally, Scott showed her the large gymnasium/cafeteria/common room in the basement of the old schoolhouse. The Civil Patrol Air Raid stickers were still clearly visible on the walls and the doors that led to this space. During the Cold War, the area had been every bit as important to the school children as the oft-practiced, duck and cover. The space, the same as the upstairs without the walls, echoed as they walked across a hardwood floor. It was polished, but clearly not newly-refinished.

Scott explained, "These floors were really in pretty good shape. I know for a fact that nothing but gym shoes were ever allowed in here no matter what time of year it was." He went on to tell her that when he had been a first grade student here in 1982, he had walked in on the first day of school and had been practically knocked over with by the smell of polyurethane. The janitors had stood guard at the doors to inform the little children that no one would EVER be allowed to wear street shoes in the gymnasium. And no one ever had.

So, the space felt as if it were in a time warp. Children from the turn of the century had played in the same space as Scott's parents and, eventually, so had Scott. Now the floors waited for their next adventure.

Trish was immediately intrigued by the big empty space. "What do you plan to do down here?" she asked.

"That's a good question. There's a great kitchen on the other side of the room. It was remodeled in the late 1970's, and all of the appliances, and refrigerators and freezers still work. There are even pots and pans in the cupboards and nifty plastic trays stacked under the counter. I bought the place lock, stock, and barrel—I just didn't realize that the barrel included divided plastic trays!"

He showed her the kitchen and explained that he had hopes of the basement becoming something of a community center for the small town of Bentley. "Ever since the grocery store closed," he explained, "there just hasn't been a decent place for folks to gather."

"I've got a storage room full of eight-foot banquet tables and industrial strength folding chairs. We could feed the whole population of Bentley in one fell swoop—if the cats and dogs stay home."

"Scott, you've taken on quite a project here!" Trish commented.

"For now, I'm concentrating on getting the apartments rented and putting on the finishing touches. So, does all this meet with your approval? Shall I reserve one of the apartments for you?"

"Absolutely!" she exclaimed. "Which one can I have?"

"The Swenson's will be in # 2 and I'll take #4, Rich will have the two-bedroom across the hall from me--#5... so I guess you can choose #1 or #3."

"I think I'll take #1, I like the way the light comes in the living room in the afternoon," she decided. "I suppose I should ask about the rent," she admitted, realizing that she would absolutely melt into a puddle of sorrow if it turned out that she couldn't afford to live in this lovely old building.

"I'm renting the main floor units for $400 a month—but that includes all utilities," he quickly added.

Trish did some quick adding of her own and realized that the worst apartment in Marshtown would have been more expensive than these, when you included the utilities.

"Count me in as one of your tenants!" she happily announced.

They shook hands and she felt the rightness of this move down to her toes. The Bentley Schoolhouse Apartments would be a place she could call home.

Chapter Five

Richard Daniel Knight

He sat back in his desk chair and starred out at the sparkling blue water of Lake Redfern. He wondered how in the world his life had gotten so out of control in such a short period of time. How could he be divorced, when just last summer he had been happily married? Wasn't it just last summer that he, Sally and the kids were sitting on the deck of this lake house, talking about the future and all it held in store for them? Had Sally not participated in the conversation? Was her new life so firmly entrenched in her mind by then that she could not see that they were a happy family? They were happy. He could have sworn it. No fights, no money woes, no sharp philosophical differences. They even both supported Obama from the very first day he announced his candidacy.

Then why, on that late summer night last year had Sally told him that she would not be returning to Belgium and the Supreme Headquarters Allied Powers Europe (SHAPE) community school with him to resume her teaching career? He remembered her calm, cold, matter-of-fact statement that still managed to cut him to the quick. "Rich, I'm going to be telling the kids tomorrow that I've decided not to return to Belgium with you."

The sudden jerk in his heart had physically hurt, and his reply had been confused. "What do you mean? You've got to go back with me on Friday. We start teaching on Monday!"

"No, Rich," she replied. "I won't be teaching at SHAPE this next semester. I resigned last spring."

His dumbfounded look finally thawed her chill just a little. "Listen, Rich," she explained. "You must know that for some time I haven't been happy. It was fine when we had the kids to keep us busy and occupied as a family. These past few years with both of them so busy with their own lives, I've just felt lost within myself. I know I'm not explaining it very well. Trust me, Rich. This is for the best—for both of us."

He had just sat there, wondering how this had happened to him. Sure their lives were busy with work and their theater schedules—but they were both busy, weren't they? She directed almost as many plays at the middle school as he did at the high school each year, didn't she? They were happy, career-oriented people—weren't they?

Apparently they were not. She had finally confessed that she had been planning to leave him for well over a year. She had made all of the arrangements without him knowing a thing. She had resigned and asked the principal to keep the news quiet. She had applied for and been awarded a teaching position back at the school in Frankfurt where they had met. She had even changed her vehicle insurance coverage on the Trivoli. It was waiting for her at her sister's home in Luzerne. She had thought of everything. Everything that is, except how to keep Rich's heart from breaking into a million tiny pieces.

Rich wondered if she had thought that telling the kids would be easier than telling him. "They have their own lives," she had insisted. Wouldn't they be happy for her eventually? It had not gone well. Their beautiful, well-adjusted children had been as stunned as he had been.

Both Scott and Sandi had wept and begged their mother to re-consider; but Sally was firm and unyielding in her decision to leave their family.

"Rich, please try to understand. This is painful for me as well. I've just had longer to live with the inevitability of it all. I knew I could never go back to living with you as your wife. I've known it for a long time."

The kids had looked decidedly uncomfortable with that statement, and Rich had quickly left the room for a long walk around the lake.

That had been a long and difficult year ago. Now here he was sitting at this house on the lake, a newly-divorced man of 58 years, with a hard won peace in his heart that he would not have thought possible last year at this time.

He had returned to their apartment in Mons to find her personal items removed—something else she had arranged without his knowledge—and divorce papers waiting for him in the mail. The speed of it all still left him dazed. But school had begun, there was a play to cast, rehearsals to plan, papers to grade…and so the rhythm of his life resumed, minus part of his heart.

Telling his family about the break-up had been one of the most difficult things he had ever done. He had sworn the kids to secrecy until he could get his bearings and decide what to tell his folks, as well as his brother and two sisters. In the end he had sent all of them a letter trying to explain what was still so new and hurtful to him. He asked them not to blame Sally entirely.

Surely he should have seen this coming and done something to prevent it—he just wasn't sure what it was he should have done. The reaction from his family had been swift and entirely one-sided. They did blame Sally, and they were not about to hear any reasonable explanations. He was reminded of something an old girlfriend used to say, "My mind is made up. Don't confuse me with the facts." The facts were that she was gone from his life, safely and seemingly happily encamped in her old life in Frankfurt.

As the year had moved along, buoyed by schedules and rehearsals and grades to record, Rich kept in touch with his siblings and his parents at least once a month. Their lives moved on as well and he was pleased to hear that his sister Beth's two teenage children, Charlotte and Jason, both had parts in the musical at their high school. Sister Barb reported that his nephew Tyler had won a starting position on the football team and his niece Gabby would be a junior varsity cheerleader. His brother Jeremy, that late-in-life child with an equally late-in-life marriage, was still dealing with tricycles and bicycles. He and his wife JoAnne juggled busy careers and a set of triplets. All in all, his busy family did not have much time left over to worry about their oldest brother, who had had his life ripped apart so suddenly.

It wasn't until his Christmas vacation last year that he had even had a chance to think about what his future might be. Should he stay at SHAPE? Try something new? Return to Hong Kong where he had taught before he and Sally had moved to Belgium? He had felt at totally loose ends. He had almost decided to begin a job search through his many international connections when he received a letter from his sister, Barb. He remembered how his heart had seemed to tear again as he had read her carefully-composed letter.

Dearest Bro,

It's been awhile since I have put actual pen to paper when corresponding with you. What did we do before e-mail—oh yes, I remember, we let Uncle Sam work for us. I thought I would write a letter instead of e-mailing or calling so that you could have some time to think over a crazy idea that I've gotten into my head.

So, what's the crazy idea, my brother is asking himself about now...and here it is: I think you should move back home. I know you've lived in far-flung places for more years than you ever lived in the U.S., but I think it is time for you to come home. And I'm not just saying this because of what that awful former sister-in-law (twice removed for being a jerk) has done to you; although that is certainly the catalyst that sprung this idea from my head.

Rich, Mom and Dad are just not doing real well. She hasn't wanted me to bother you with any of this because she is so concerned with your situation, but Dad has been slowing down a lot, and the doctors think it may be time for them to move into town from the farm. We all live so far away now, and I think the time will soon be upon us that some difficult decisions will have to be made. I know we would all feel so much better if you were in the area to kind of assess things for us.

Now, this isn't entirely a lame brain idea. I do actually have an idea of what you might do for a job. Do you remember Mr. Jenkins, the English teacher at BGM? Well, he's been the head of the English Department forever, and he just announced that he is retiring. I read about it in the Marshtown Journal the last time I visited Mom and Dad. So...do you see where I'm going with all this? If you wanted a complete change of pace, you could apply for his job...and did I mention that the principal at BGM is Craig Seeley—Class of '69 Craig Seeley? I know you guys weren't best friends or anything, but I know he's followed your career, and he asks about you whenever we happen to run into each other on my visits home. So, what do you think? Is there any way that an international superstar of your caliber could find happiness back in his hometown? If happiness seems too much to reach for right now, then how about contentment? I can speak highly of the emotion.

Lots to think about I know, Rich. Please do give this some thought. We can talk or e-mail about your decision.

Much Love,

Barb

He had laid down the letter and wondered, "How dense could he possibly be?" It had not even occurred to him that he might be needed at home. Mom and Dad had always been his rocks. When had they gotten old? How old were they now? He always lost track. Let's see, he was 58. Mom and Dad had been high school sweethearts and had married after Dad got back from his tour of duty in Germany. He had been born less than a year later in September of 1951, so that made them what, 80ish? Really? 80? That was old! No wonder they were beginning to experience some health problems. His own arthritis could predict the weather about as well as any weatherman on the television.

Living back in the States though, that was a tough idea to get his head around. He had just finished his two-year term as president of the International Drama Society, and he always looked forward to the board meetings scheduled in various locations around the globe. Wait a minute. Drama societies couldn't compete with his folks needing him. He should at least give Craig a call and talk to him. What could it hurt? As he reached for his cell phone to place the international call, he realized that somewhere deep in the recesses of his memory, he still remembered the phone number to his high school. So much for early Alzheimer's for him!

The phone rang in the far distance of southeast Iowa, and he realized that with the time difference the office should be just about ready to close for the day. He was relieved to hear a kind and melodious voice answer after only a couple of rings, "BGM High School, this is Mrs. Lucas, how may I help you?"

"Mrs. Lucas," he began with his best mind your manners voice in full swing. "My name is Richard Knight, and I was wondering if I could speak with Craig Seeley about the upcoming vacancy in the English Department?"

"Not until you tell me what you've been up to all these years!" came her laughing reply. His silence told her that she had caught him off guard so she was quick to explain. "Rich, this is Linda Alexander, I was a year behind you at BGM!"

"Linda Alexander! What a great surprise! I remember we had a blast working on "The Fantastiks" together. I thought I heard you were living in California? You married David Lucas; didn't you?

"Yes to all questions" she replied. "We moved back here about ten years ago. Dave's mom and dad wanted to retire, so he took over the farming operation. That has always been his first love—and thankfully I'm a close second!" We've done all right—fortunately the land was free and clear when Dave took it over—but farming isn't what it once was around here. I've been working as Craig's secretary ever since we moved back. Heaven knows, someone has to keep track of him. With four boys of my own, I'm well-schooled in guy speak!

"I'm sure that's a very handy language to know!" Rich agreed. "Is Craig available?"

"He is," she replied, "I'll put you right through."

That had been six months, a few dozen e-mail messages, and an incredibly long online application ago. He and Craig had conducted his interview via instant messages on his computer in late April, and by early May he had a contract in hand to become the head of the English Department at BGM High School for the next academic year. In addition to being head of the department, he would be teaching two senior English courses, a junior composition course, and a freshman advanced placement English Literature course. He had been blessedly spared any lunchroom or study hall duty, but he knew that his supervision of the three other teachers in the English Department would take up any spare moments he found in his day.

This was especially true since one of the teachers would be brand new. Craig had been surprised to find himself needing a new Freshman English teacher after last year's new hire had announced she was engaged to a man in Middleswarth, Pennsylvania. She would be moving there over the summer to be married and teach out there. Rich wondered if Craig would hire someone fresh out of college or look for a more seasoned teacher. Unfortunately, seasoned teachers were not often attracted to rural schools with their lack of social life and substantially reduced salaries. Speaking of which, he hoped that he would not have to take too much of a salary cut in order to return to his hometown. Clearly it would be a cut in salary, but surely the cost of living would be less in small town Iowa than it was in Mons, Belgium. He already knew that the cost for his apartment would be approximately half what it was each month in Mons. He had been astounded when Craig told him that his old elementary school in Bentley had been converted into apartments. Depending on the one he chose, the rent would be between $400 and $600 a month including utilities! He had acted quickly and had rented the two-bedroom unit sight unseen.

Of course he could have moved back into his old bedroom at his folks' farm, but that would have seemed just a bit too much like taking a step back in time. Besides, he needed some privacy—even if it was only to sit in the dark and wonder how his life had gotten off track so quickly. No, he promised himself that he would not do that. He had great kids, good health, and now a new job. What was past was past. The more interesting question was what would be in his future?

Chapter Six

Oscar and Verna Lee Swenson

She was not used to such chaos. Her big farm kitchen was usually pristine clean, but this morning as she looked around her there were far more things out of place than in place. She sighed; it had seemed such a good idea in theory. Selling most of their belongings and moving into one of Scott's new apartments in the old Bentley Schoolhouse made sense in so many ways. She and Oscar were still in relatively good health, but they just didn't want to continue to keep up a big yard and an even bigger house. They would be able to travel whenever they wanted, and when the winds blew hard in a harsh Iowa winter, it would not be Oscar out there plowing the long driveway to the road.

But the sheer volume of STUFF was almost more than she could bear. How had they accumulated so many objects in fifty-five years of marriage? She blamed it on this big house. When they had first been married, they had lived in an eight hundred square foot house. She had had the philosophy that if she hadn't used it or worn it in a year, out it went. Of course, that philosophy had been pre-children, so it had been easier to enforce in her mind.

Now, there were the remnants of four children, grown and gone their own ways but with surprisingly large amounts of their lives left behind in Mom and Dad's upstairs. As she looked around her kitchen, she realized that not all of this clutter could be blamed on the kids; she needed to take full responsibility for two cupboards full of butter tubs and Tupperware containers.

She had uttered an edict at the Christmas table. "Kids, you all know that Dad and I have decided to move into one of Scott Samuel's apartments that he is renovating in Bentley. I'm here to tell you that if there is anything that you want from your bedrooms upstairs, you have the next six months to move it out." They had chuckled at the comment, but she had not been kidding. When June rolled around she began to call auction houses in the area and had settled on the first Saturday in August. At the Fourth of July barbeque she had told each child that they had until August 1st to remove anything they wanted from their rooms. They had at least looked interested in the concept. Still, here it was the end of July and not one box or piece of furniture had disappeared from their rooms.

Well, she couldn't worry about that now. She had plenty of her own junk to sort through. "How many salt shakers do I need to keep?" she wondered aloud.

"One!" came the answer from the doorway as she looked up to see Oscar, the love of her life, enter from the mudroom.

She laughed, "You're absolutely right, my dear—we won't be having holiday dinners anymore, so one set should do us!"

"How's it going?" he asked as he took her in his still muscular arms.

"I'm making some progress, but not enough" she informed him. "I've decided to just start packing what I want to take and leave everything else in the cupboards. I'll let the auction house deal with the rest."

"That's pretty much my philosophy out in the garage and barn," he agreed. "Of course, it helps that I've let the grandkids sell off my antique tools on e-Bay for the past couple of years. The kids who have kept up with it have a pretty nice nest egg built up for college."

He snagged a few cookies from the always full cookie jar and poured himself a cup of coffee and settled in for a mid-morning snack "It's still kind of hard to believe that this time next month we'll be settled into Scott's apartment," he admitted.

"Our apartment," she corrected him. "Yes, it's pretty hard for me to imagine too. But remember, we've always said we would know when it was time to pack it in. Neither of us wants to end up the way your folks did--carted off to the nursing home straight from the hospital, never seeing their home again."

He brushed the crumbs off his lap and rose to head back to his own packing and sorting. "I'm sure you're right, dear. You always are." He kissed the top of her gray hair and she swatted him on the behind as he turned to leave.

"Always have been, always will be," she agreed as he headed out the door.

Chapter Seven

Moving Day

The second Saturday in August dawned bright and clear. The humidity had been near 90% for a week, but today it was gratefully in the 60's. That made the 80 degree temperature at 7:00 in the morning actually tolerable. Five trucks of various types and sizes began their slow and measured way to Bentley, Iowa, from Des Moines, Cedar Falls and rural Van Buren County. Inside the trucks moved the lives of six people of divergent ages and backgrounds. Yet they had one thing in common, they would all soon call the old schoolhouse in Bentley, Iowa home.

Andrea looked around at the boxes and furniture that she had gleaned from her large home and realized once again how grateful she was to have Will home this weekend to manage this move. "I know you hated those two years that you earned your living moving other people's lives on your back, but your experience has saved me a lot of headaches!" she told her son.

"I'm just grateful that you're not a pack rat like some people I moved. I'll never forget the day I packed someone's doodles!" he reminded himself as well as his mom. "I think you're taking the right amount of stuff – your couch and chair from the sunroom, the bedroom set from Aunt Holly, a kitchen table and chairs, your desk, and SEVENTEEN BOXES OF BOOKS!!!"

"William Roger Hogan, you are exaggerating. I am absolutely sure there are no more than fifteen boxes of books!" She smiled as her son stooped to give her a peck on the cheek as he moved one of those fifteen— or seventeen—boxes of books into the U-Haul she had rented.

She looked around the spacious living room that had been the destination of so many groups over the years. Book club, bridge club, women's Bible study, and family gatherings galore had taken place in this room through the twenty-five years she had lived here. She once again realized how grateful she was to have had the foresight to purchase this large home when her marriage ended all those years ago. It had seemed to be a folly at the time, but she had fallen in love with the big old Victorian, and she had known that no amount of common sense would keep her from buying it and creating a home for herself and Will.

Now it was time to leave this home behind for the time being and create another home in a small town at the edge of her beloved Iowa. She shook her head and wondered what new adventures awaited. She also wondered if she was a little nuts, and decided that she probably was—but she was up for the adventure—wasn't she?

Trish took one look at the two football players she had hired to load her furniture into her rented U-Haul and knew that she had made the right choice. Coach Samuels had given her their names and numbers and advised her to hire them to help her move the contents of her tiny apartment. They towered over her, but she could immediately tell that they were gentle giants.

"Ms. Wilkins, I'm Tony, and this is Matt," said the shorter of the two giants. Matt grinned and immediately she knew this move would be a piece of cake. They proceeded to make short order of her little Cedar Falls apartment that she had called home for two years. She had carefully packed all of her boxes and even emptied the contents of her dresser to avoid asking the two young men to see anything that might make them—or her—blush. Her couch, dresser, kitchen table, and desk were all the "big pieces" she owned. In less than fifteen minutes she was staring at bare walls and a carpet that was badly in need of vacuuming.

Rich Knight backed the U-Haul up to Oscar and Verna Lee's Swenson's back door and hopped out. It was early on the second Saturday in August but the kitchen was already bustling with activity. "Richard, can I fix you up some bacon and eggs?" Verna Lee asked as Rich walked in through the mud room.

"No thanks, Mrs. Swenson," Rich replied, "got to watch my weight."

She laughed as he sat down at the big kitchen table and poured himself a cup of coffee from the white carafe that was always kept refilled in the Swenson's kitchen. "Boy am I glad I decided to come to your auction last week!" Rich told Verna Lee. "I bought everything I'll need to set up housekeeping at my new apartment."

Verna Lee turned from the kitchen sink to look at him and laughingly asked, "What does that say about me, since I still have plenty left over after the auction to set up housekeeping for Oscar and me? Somehow I think I'll learn to live without eight sets of Tupperware containers—and the fourteen lids that didn't fit anything!"

Rich downed the last of his coffee and swung into action. "Guess I'd better start loading the small stuff. Hopefully by the time I'm finished, that boy of mine will be here to help me with the furniture."

"I can't wait to see him—he must have grown a foot since he spent the summer with your folks in '01." Verna said.

"He's a good-sized boy all right" he agreed. "Now let's just see if he can lift!" As he finished the sentence, he saw his 1998 Chevy Blazer pull into the farmyard and his son, Scott, jump out and hurry over to where Rich and Verna Lee were standing. He clapped Rich on the back but scooped up Verna Lee in a bear hug. "Mrs. Swenson! Wow, good to see you! Do you still make those great chocolate chip oatmeal cookies?"

"Of course, I do, young man. I think if you head in through that door you'll find a cookie jar filled with them!" she assured him.

"I'm on my way!" He turned to his dad. 'That was one of the best things about staying with Grandma and Grandpa while you and Mom were in India that summer—Mrs. Swenson's chocolate chip oatmeal cookies!"

"Oh, I've eaten my share through the years," Rich informed his son. "Just be glad you can still enjoy them without worrying about your cholesterol!" He watched fondly as his boy swooped down on the cookie jar and came back to the mud porch fortified for the work ahead of him.

"Well, Mrs. Swenson, we'll get started here and try to get out of your way before your crew shows up to move you and Oscar."

"They're not due here for another hour," she replied. "And Richard, you're going to have to get used to calling us Verna Lee and Oscar now that we're going to be neighbors."

"I promise to try, but it's a long established habit that may take time to break. Now, I'd better get busy and get these boxes loaded up. It sure was nice of you to let me leave all this stuff here after the auction last week. I promise you, they'll be gone in a jiffy."

It certainly didn't take long for Rich and Scott to load the boxes of dishes, cups, glasses, pots, pans, and yes, one set of Tupperware into the U-Haul. Next came the 1930's – era bedroom set from one of the upstairs bedrooms and the set of twin beds from another bedroom somewhere in the old farm house. These and the couch, table, chairs and end tables were safely tucked away in the old weathered barn across the farmyard. When Rich had decided to attend the Swenson's auction last Saturday, he had hoped to find a bed for himself and maybe a table to sit at while he drank his morning coffee. He figured he could pick up the rest of the furniture that he needed in the coming months. But he had fallen in love with the rich dark wood of the bedroom set, and the round oak table with six chairs seemed to be forcing his hand in the air as the bidding progressed. When all was said and done, he had more than enough furniture to make his life comfortable and to establish a home base for his two kids.

As he and Scott pulled their respective vehicles out of the farmyard he saw the Swenson's kids descend upon the home place. Verna Lee had told him that the kids had insisted on doing all of the moving of her carefully packed boxes and were even going so far as to put everything away. In fact, Verna Lee and Oscar were set to host a BBQ for the new residents that very evening. He wondered if there would be bratwurst.

Verna Lee watched Richard and Scott pull away just as her own crew pulled into the farmyard. "Excellent timing," she thought as she turned to go back into her kitchen. They had been living on takeout meals and TV dinners since she had packed up the last of her dishes. She had watched as the auction house folks hauled everything else out to the long tables set up in the side yard, the front yard, and even around to the other side of the house. She had not cried one tear when she saw the accumulation of several decades of living head out the door. Now it was beginning to catch up with her just a little. They would be making quite a change in their lives once that U-Haul was loaded. They would spend their first night in only the third home that she and Oscar had ever shared together. "No sense worrying about that now!" she declared to herself as she walked through the back door to greet her brood. "God will know we've moved, and that's all that matters," she told herself as the horns of four pickup trucks, three SUV's, and a U-Haul truck sounded the warning: "Its moving day!"

The U-Haul that Scott had rented in Marshtown yesterday listed slightly to the left as it sat in the yard at his folks' farmhouse, but it looked as if it would hang together long enough to get his few possessions moved.

"Mom!" he called as he opened the back door of the century-old farmhouse, "Where's Dad?"

"He's out in the barn, as usual," his mother assured him. "Why don't you sit down and have a cup of coffee and a piece of toast before you begin all this moving business. Not that I understand why you want to move when you have a perfectly good room right upstairs."

He sat at the round kitchen table and for what seemed like the hundredth time reassured his mother about his upcoming move. "Mom, you know I've loved living with you and Dad these past few years, but it's high time I'm out on my own again." He accepted the coffee she poured and smiled as she put four pieces of toast in the ever present oversized toaster. He'd take a few minutes to talk to her and reassure her once again that this move would be the right move for him.

"You know you love what I've done with the old schoolhouse, so please stop fussing and start thinking about what you're going to do with my room. It will be cleared out about half an hour from now!" he laughingly scolded his mother.

"Well, I can tell you that I certainly intend to paint it and refinish those hardwood floors before I decide anything. All those years of posters, baseball cleats, and wet uniforms have taken a toll on that old room of yours," she admonished. "Actually, I'm thinking about making that my very own sitting room. I've always liked the way the early morning light comes in through those two big front windows. I could put in a small couch that would fold out if one of the grandkids wanted to spend the night…and an antique desk…I've always wanted one that folds down with glass shelves on the side."

"Sounds like Dad will be plenty busy before the harvest gets underway!" he joked with the little lady that had been his rock for all of his thirty-some years. He remembered how hers had been the first face he had seen when he woke up from surgery and the many hours she had spent helping him rehab his busted knee. The knee that would not support him to run down the football field, but was plenty good enough to stand on the sideline and coach some of the best young kids you'd ever hope to find.

He finished his toast, drained the last drops of coffee, and turned to face his mom with one last thought. "Mom, you know that the second apartment upstairs can be available for you and dad with just a few months' notice to the new tenant," he reminded her once again. "I designed it with the idea that you and Dad might join me there one of these days."

"I know you did, Scott, and I appreciate that," she in turn assured him. "We're just not ready to give up the homestead yet."

"Oscar and Verna Lee Swenson are younger than you and Dad," " he said. "They're moving in today!"

"Well, that's all fine and good for the Swenson's, but it's not right for us, not yet, anyway." she insisted.

"OK, Mom. I'll stop bugging you about it—for a while anyway, but this conversation is not over. Now, I'd better line up that old man of mine unless you want to help me carry a walnut bedroom set down the steps and out to the U-Haul."

"I'll pass. But I'm sure your father can't wait," she replied, with a soft smile for her boy.

"What can't I wait to do?" Scott's father John asked. He had walked in the back door just as they were finishing their conversation.

"Help me move my bedroom set out to the U-Haul!" Scott explained.

"Oh, I think I can restrain my enthusiasm long enough to have a cup of coffee and a couple pieces of toast," he assured them. Scott's mom put in four more pieces of toast, and Scott poured himself another cup of coffee. What were a few more minutes when he had years of living in his new home ahead of him?

Trish arrived at the old schoolhouse in Bentley ten minutes after her U-Haul arrived. The boys she had hired to help with the move were driving the truck, and they had passed her shortly after they left the edge of Cedar Falls. She had only made one quick pit stop, but was never able to catch up to them in her trusty Ford Focus. The guys were taking a break under the beautiful old oak tree that had graced the front of the Bentley School since Hoover had been President. She had the keys to her apartment in her pocket, so there hadn't been much that they could do until she arrived—except slug down Mountain Dews and Ho Ho's as a mid-morning snack.

"Looks like we're the first to arrive," she told the boys. "Good thing Scott gave me a key to the front door!" She unlocked the heavy front doors and the boys found a couple of bungee cords in the U-Haul to hold them wide open. Trish moved quickly to Apartment Number 1 and unlocked the deadbolt. The door swung open and she was once again struck by the way the sun flooded into the room. A smile spread across her face. She turned and found the guys right behind her.

"Wow, this place is so cool!" they both exclaimed at once.

"I agree," she said, "and I can't wait to get my stuff inside. Let's go, boys!"

Just as it had not taken long for Tony and Matt to load up her apartment, they also made quick work of the boxes and the furniture. Before she knew it, she was unpacking her good china—her four-piece stoneware set that she used when she had company—as opposed to the old Melmac plates that she regularly dined on. When the boys had brought in the last of her boxes and set up her bed in the only spot that made sense, she pulled a fistful of twenties from her billfold. She paid them the amount agreed upon—and added a twenty for each of them. Their grins showed their heartfelt appreciation.

No sooner had the boys pulled out of the driveway to return the U-Haul to Cedar Falls than in pulled another one. This time Andrea's son Will jumped down from the driver's seat and greeted her warmly. "Hey Trish, you beat us here!" Will declared.

"Not only that, I'm half moved in!" she teased him.

"We won't be far behind you," he explained. "Mom barely scratched the surface at our house with the stuff she brought with her. She's going to be living a lean and mean existence here in Bentleyville."

"I take it you don't think much of the metropolis of Bentley, Iowa?" she questioned, easily catching the sarcasm in his use of "Bentleyville."

"Well, you've got to admit, it's a little different from Austin—or even Des Moines!" he defended himself.

"Ah, but it's not that different from Lancaster, Pennsylvania," she countered.

"I'll have to take your word for that!" he agreed. "Now, I'd better start unloading. Mom can't be far behind me, although she has been known to take significant detours when she sees Garage Sale Signs!

As if on cue Andrea's RAV pulled in behind the U-Haul, and she joined Will and Trish on the lawn. "What, no good garage sales on the way?" Will teased his mom.

"Very funny, young man," Andrea countered, "but for the record, there *weren't* any good garage sales along the way!"

"Trish, where's your truck?" Andrea inquired. "Are you still waiting for the big burly college kids to show up with it?"

"They've been here and gone!" Trish crowed. "I'm half moved in already. I'm available to help you guys get your stuff in as well."

"We won't turn down the free help," Will said, with a sigh of relief in his voice. "I was wondering how I was going to get the foldout couch up the stairs with only my weakling mom to assist me!"

"Between the two of us we should be able to handle one end," Trish assured him.

Since the couch had been the last thing loaded, it was front and center for them to tackle as Will opened the doors to the big U-Haul. Will maneuvered the cumbersome piece of furniture to the edge of the truck bed while Trish and Andrea each took a leg and began to walk the couch off the back of the truck. When it was just about to tumble off the truck, Will jumped down and positioned himself to receive the other end of the couch as it made its way off the truck. As soon as it was safely on the ground, they all turned so Will would be going backwards up the outside steps and then up the seven steps that led them to the Main Floor. They were just making their way through the outside doors and about to tackle the remaining seven steps when Andrea heard a truck door slam and a deep voice call out, "Hey, wait up! I'll help with that beast!"

Andrea did not know who had uttered those blessed words, but she was very grateful to hear them. Even half of the back end of the couch was very heavy, and she would be more than willing to give up her burden to whoever was running up behind her.

Her thanks were on the tip of her tongue as she and Trish gratefully released their load into the arms of the man who had come to save them from aching backs. "I can't tell you how glad I am that you chose this moment to arrive!" she began as she moved aside so that he could take the couch from her. Just as she released her grip, she looked into the man's face. She was flabbergasted to see that the man relieving her of her furniture burden was Richard Daniel Knight, the man that she had lived with during her senior year of college.

"Andi!" Rich exclaimed. "What in the world?" he asked as he struggled to get the beast of a couch into his grip without taking his eyes off of her.

"Richard!" Andi cried and backed away to let the two men maneuver the couch up the stairs that led to her apartment.

When they disappeared through the door, Trish touched Andrea on the arm which broke her momentary paralysis.

"I take it you know that man?" Trish quizzed as she studied the perplexed look on her friend's face.

"Oh, you might say that." Andrea managed. "Richard, or I should say Rich, since that is what everyone but me calls him, and I have a long history."

"What what, what?" Trish was brimming over with curiosity.

"It is way too long of a story to tell you right now. Just suffice it to say that this isn't the first apartment building Richard and I have moved into together. But, not a word around Will; he doesn't know a thing about my past, and I'd just as soon leave it that way."

"Oh, you so owe me, Andrea Hogan! I will get the whole story out of you before your head hits the pillow tonight!" she teased. Her friend just smiled. Was that the beginning of a blush moving up Andrea's cheeks? She couldn't quite tell as Andrea hurried through the doors to catch up with the guys before they managed to set the heavy couch in the wrong place.

As she entered her apartment, she found Will and Richard introducing themselves. Blessedly the couch was right where she had wanted it. Will turned as his mom entered the apartment. "Hey Mom, I'd like you to meet Rich Knight. He's your upstairs neighbor." Will was astounded as he saw his new moving buddy sweep his mother into his arms, in what could only be described as a full body contact hug.

Rich Knight was hugging his mother, and he wasn't letting go! Trish entered the room in time to hear this bear of a man ask in a choked voice, "Andi, how many years has it been?"

Andrea quickly decided that she had better be the one to come up with an explanation for this man's surprising behavior if she wanted to be the one to control how much information about her past was revealed in the next few minutes.

Andrea managed to extract herself from Richard who seemed in no hurry to let her go. She saw the deer in the headlights look on her son's face and the look of absolute amusement on Trish's face, and plunged into her explanation.

"Trish, I'd like you to meet Richard Knight—Rich, I mean. I'm the only one who has ever called him Richard, even his mother didn't call him Richard, so really I shouldn't either. I mean if everybody calls Rich 'Rich' then I should call him Rich, and I will call him Rich. Trish, this is Rich Knight, Richard – I mean Rich, this is Trish Wilkins. It looks like we'll all be calling this place home!"

Trish and Richard, Rich, that is, shook hands and everybody turned to look at Andrea, waiting for further explanation.

"Richard and I went to college together," she explained. "UNI, the first time around, that is. We, uh, had several classes together." She trailed off as the inadequacy of the explanation struck her as not worthy of that engulfing hug she had recently experienced.

"Don't forget about that play we were both in during our senior year," Rich added. "Didn't you play Aunt Sadie or some such character?"

"Yes, my claim to fame: Aunt Sadie in "Gentlemen Prefer Blondes!" She began to laugh.

"Of course there was the famous gray hair scene that you will never live down!" Rich joined her in laughter and then quickly sobered up as he noticed the two young people looking curiously at both of them now.

"That's a story for another time," Andrea insisted. "Now we'd better get a move on this move or I'll be sleeping in that U-Haul tonight."

"Why don't I help you guys get things inside while I wait for my reinforcements to show up? My boy Scott stopped over at his grandmother's to pick up a few boxes I had shipped there from Belgium," Richard explained.

"You have a boy?" Andrea asked.

"And a girl!" Rich explained.

"Boy, do we need to catch up!" was all Andrea could think to reply.

They moved boxes and furniture with the usual chitchat among friends accomplishing an unpleasant task. The heat of the day, the blessed coolness of the marble hallways and the fact that Rich would need to climb an additional set of stairs soon occupied their conversations.

Trish kept giving Andrea inquiring looks and at one point whispered, "Tonight, you spill your story, or I'll start making one up on my own... and I have a wonderful imagination!"

True to their word, the children of Oscar and Verna Lee Swenson handled the entire move for their parents. The boys took care of packing the tools and miscellaneous items Oscar had decided to take with him and the girls hauled boxes until all that remained in the house were the pieces of furniture that they had decided to take with them to the new apartment.

Oscar was surprised to find that even a pared-down number of tools still took up the better part of a pickup bed. His eldest, Larry, looked at the size of the load and remarked, "Good thing Coach Samuels gave you a corner of the storage room in the basement of the schoolhouse! I can just imagine the look on Mom's face if you tried to bring that skill saw into her brand new kitchen!"

"I knew this move wouldn't work unless I had a spot to tinker—Coach knew that, too. That's why he offered me the storage room. He knew I wouldn't budge without my tools."

"Well, I think you'll be just fine at the new apartment," Larry assured his dad. "And just think no more snow to plow or grass to mow."

"Truth be told, that's just what I'm going to miss," Oscar said quietly. He gave his head a good shake and declared, "Now, let's get this show on the road! Verna Lee is determined to have this move over and done with by this afternoon. I have been instructed to set up the charcoal grill as soon as we arrive so we'll be ready for a big cookout she's planning for all of you, and the other new tenants to boot!"

Chapter Eight

The Barbeque

True to their word, Verna Lee and Oscar's kids and grandkids let their folks lift nary a teaspoon as they precisely orchestrated their move. By 2:00 in the afternoon the last glass was washed and stowed away, and the last tool had found a home in Oscar's new basement workshop.

No sooner had that last teaspoon and tool been put away than plans began in earnest for the barbeque that the Swenson's had planned to celebrate the occasion. Oscar had ordered up thirty half-pound hamburger patties and three dozen brats, and a couple dozen hot dogs to boot. Meat was not going to be a problem.

Oscar was tightening the last of the bolts on his mega-sized gas grill. His eldest boy, Dan, was helping him get everything in place before turning on the gas. Would it light or blow up? Either scenario was an option. When the button was pushed, amazingly, it lit!

"Okay, Dan Boy, let's get this operation organized," Oscar announced. "Why don't you head down to the schoolhouse basement and bring up about six of those 8' tables we saw when we were unloading my tools. We'll use a couple for serving, one here by the grill, and the rest for seating. I guess you'd better bring up about 30 chairs as well."

"Sounds like I'd better recruit some help from the younger Swenson boys," Dan decided, and went off in search of his sons and nephews.

Meanwhile, Barb and Lindsey, the middle daughters, had thought ahead and distributed potato salad, macaroni, salad, Snicker salad, three bean salad, watermelons and the makings for homemade ice cream among the refrigerators of the tenants in the five apartments. Everything would appear at a moment's notice, ice cold and safe from any dreaded salmonella. As they distributed the salads and other goodies they introduced themselves to their folks' new neighbors—or re-acquainted themselves in some cases. They extracted promises from each of the new tenants to come outside for the barbeque, beginning at 4:00. Since everyone had skipped lunch, this early time for the meal was very appealing.

By 3:30 the mouthwatering smells of roasted beast began to drift into the open apartment windows, and it wasn't long before new tenants, old friends, and a dozen relatives of Oscar and Verna Lee were gathering around the grill, downing a cold beverage of their choice.

Scott was amazed to see the elaborate setup that the Swenson ladies had rigged up in a very short amount of time. The younger Swenson boys had dragged the heavy eight foot tables up from the basement and the girls had washed them down. They found their mom's plastic tablecloths in one of the boxes they had moved from the farm. Held down by bricks found scattered around the grounds, the tablecloths were just waiting to be covered by bowls, plates, glasses and most importantly, food. The old wood and metal chairs were not the most comfortable-looking contraptions, but they were sturdy. Their occupants wouldn't have to risk winding up on the ground if they leaned a tad too far to one side or the other.

At a few minutes before 4:00, Dan Swenson climbed up on one of those sturdy chairs and declared that it was time to eat, but first, everyone had to go to their apartments and bring out the cold food. Before he dismissed the group, he offered a heartfelt blessing. "Lord, we come before you on this beautiful summer day that you have created, and we thank you for bringing us all safely together to this place where old and new friends unite. Now, bless this food that we are about to eat and may it nourish our bodies so that we may continue to do your work on this earth." He went on to add, "And the congregation all said…" to which the crowd roared, "AMEN!" He called out, "Let's eat!" Dozens of folks scurried to the various apartments and returned with enough food to feed an army.

As soon as the food was assembled, Oscar invited folks to choose their meat from the dozens of items he and Dan had grilled in the last hour. He encouraged the young men in the group to take one of each variety and smiled broadly as he noticed the enormous paper plates the girls had brought, half-filled with good old Iowa meat.

The long tables were soon filled with folks enjoying one of the great treats of living in Iowa, a picnic *extraordinaire*.

Before the last of the folks were even through the line, Dan had set up the ice cream freezers and the sound of rich cream, sugar, and vanilla flavor churning could be heard in the background. The guests filled up on the delicious food, leaving just enough room for a little homemade ice cream.

Chapter Nine

Andrea Hogan

When the last dribbles of ice cream had been licked away, the guests at the barbeque began to drift away. The first to leave were Oscar and Verna Lee's grandchildren, all with more interesting places to be on a Saturday night.

As Rich's son made his departure and Andrea's son Will headed up to his mom's new apartment, the tenants and their landlord found themselves sitting around the last of the sturdy tables that had been put up for the event. Scott was the first to speak. "Looks like it's just us," he said, stating the obvious.

Trish put into words what they all were feeling. "Scott, I just can't tell you how happy I am, all of us are, to be living here! Thank you so much for saving this schoolhouse so that it could become our homes." Murmurs of assent could be heard around the table.

Scott ducked his head, embarrassed by the heartfelt admission from the young woman. "Well, I'm just glad you all agreed to be my tenants!" he countered. "I was all for saving this old school from being used as a warehouse or torn down completely—but I'm sure not in a position to restore it as a museum to my childhood!"

At that he jumped to his feet, and he and Rich folded up the table while Oscar and the ladies carried the chairs downstairs to the storage area. They all stopped to admire Oscar's new workroom. It was filled with boxes of tools and small pieces of useful equipment. Scott was relieved to see that not only would any "fix-it" projects have the right tool for the job, but most likely Oscar's advice would be readily available.

At last they all climbed the stairs to their own apartments. Even though it was only 8:00 in the evening, they all seemed ready to call it a night. Well, not quite everyone. As Andrea headed toward her apartment, Trish reached out for her hand and whispered into her ear, "You owe me a story before your head hits the pillow tonight. Meet me in the library at 9:00!" Andrea smiled and nodded her agreement.

With a couple of wine glasses and a bottle of blush in her hand, she made her way to the library just before 9:00. Will was happy to see her head out the door as he struggled with the television and all of the electronic gadgets that it would take to keep his mother connected to the outside world.

Trish was equally punctual as she carried a small cooler with what looked like several ice cold bottles of beer peeking out through the ice. Andrea had to laugh as Trish walked through the door with her cooler. "Looks like you're ready for a long story, but trust me! I don't think it will last longer than one, or at most two beers!"

"Those Boy Scouts have the right idea when it comes to being prepared," Trish assured her. "So, no lollygagging, tell me the story of Andrea and Rich, or I guess you would say Andi and Richard!"

"First of all, I wouldn't call it anything much, and certainly not the stuff that novels are made of," she corrected her friend. "So, here's the whole 'sordid' story for your amusement," she began. "Richard and I had a class together our junior year of college. I think it was International Government, or finance, something international as I recall. My roommate Janet was also in the class, as was Richard's roommate Jim. We were teamed up to do a presentation on banana farming in Costa Rica, and we all seemed to get along pretty well. As it turned out, Janet and Jim got along a little better than that. They started dating toward the end of the semester, and one thing led to another and pretty soon they were inseparable. This was all fine and good, and I didn't think that much about it as I headed off to Des Moines for my internship at the Legislative Service Bureau. Janet and I had signed a lease for our senior year before we left for summer vacation, and like a dummy, I figured she would hold up her end of the bargain. At the last minute, the two lovebirds both got summer jobs at a girls' camp in Maine. They went off in a hurry to meet up with the camp bus in New York City. I'd heard that Richard had planned to stay in Cedar Falls over the summer so he just kept the apartment that he and Jim had shared."

"I was more than a little surprised when the phone at my folks' house rang one Friday night and it was Richard, Rich, on the other end of the line," she continued. "He told me that he had just gotten a letter from Jim and asked if I had one from Janet. I told him that all I'd heard from the lovebirds was one postcard with Camp Lackawanda in the photo. I was very curious, of course, and pressed him for details from his letter. It seems that Jim and Janet had decided to skip their senior year of college and go backpacking across Europe instead. I was stunned. I knew Janet could be a little flighty and headstrong, but to just up and go like that, well, it was beyond me. But obviously not beyond the two of them!"

"I was pretty much in a state of shock when I read the letter," Richard explained. "The first thing I thought was, 'How in the world am I going to pay the rent?' I told him that I had been thinking pretty much the same thing as he gave me their news. He went on to tell me that Janet and Jim had also thought about that problem and had suggested that perhaps he and I, Richard and me, could be roommates. My silence was deafening. Richard was quick to assure me that it was meant as purely platonic, and that Jim's room was the larger of the two in the apartment, and wouldn't I think about it for a while rather than say "No" right away? I agreed to think about it and took his phone number. I promised I would let him know within the week.

"Hey," Trish interjected. "Wasn't this the era of *Hair* and Haight Ashbury, and free love?"

"Not in my parents' house!" Andrea assured her.

"What did you do?" Trish asked curiously.

Andrea went on to explain that this left her in quite a pickle as well since she couldn't afford her apartment alone. Since she was in Des Moines for the summer, it didn't give her time to advertise and find a new roommate, not that she particularly wanted to live with someone she didn't know.

"I decided to call my landlord to see what ideas he might come up with," Andrea went on to explain. "When I did, he said he happened to have a couple with a two-year-old child looking for a two-bedroom apartment standing in his office right then. He told me I could get out of my lease and he would send me a check for my share of the deposit. I gave him my address and Janet's address and just like that, my apartment was gone!"

"So, there I was, fifteen minutes after Richard's call, and I was homeless!"

"Yikes!" Trish exclaimed. "What did you tell your folks?"

"Absolutely nothing," Andrea replied. "Remember I told you I was an 'oops' baby, my dad was 51 and in the hospital with his first heart attack when I was born, and my mom was 39. So, these were not real "with it" people. My sister was already married when I was just a little girl, so I was really raised more as an only child, and a pretty protected one at that. It had been hard enough on my parents to send me away to college."

"So I take it they didn't do the whole 'Taking my daughter to school!' bit like other parents that I would see at UNI?" Trish asked.

"No," Andrea replied. "I had my own car and just packed it up each year, and off I went."

"Didn't they visit you at school?" Trish asked.

"Those were the days when you didn't just jump in your car and head off for an afternoon visit. My dad was always tentative about driving on the highway, and Mom barely tooled around Des Moines. When I left for college my dad bought me a 1966 Chevy Catalina. I had always just driven myself back and forth. In those days you could also store furniture in the basement of the dorm where you lived. Since Janet and I had planned to move from our dorm room to an apartment, most of my stuff was still in the basement of Campbell."

"Could you have moved back into the dorm?" Trish asked.

"Once again, another age and time," Andrea explained. "Housing was so tight that once you gave up your dorm room, it was snapped up by a freshman desperately seeking shelter."

"So, Richard's apartment is starting to look pretty good about now?" Trish inquired.

"Indeed!" Andrea assured her. "I was pretty much stuck. Of course, I didn't dare tell my folks, but I decided to call Richard back and take him up on his offer."

"So, how did you plan on making this work?" Trish inquired.

"Well," Andrea replied, "Not only did I *plan* to make it work, I actually *did* make it work. My folks never knew that I lived with Richard my senior year of college."

"You're kidding!" Trish exclaimed. "How did you pull it off?"

"I figured all I really needed to do was to keep Richard from answering the phone since my folks weren't the kind to surprise me on a Saturday morning or something like that. So, I arranged to have a separate phone line put in my bedroom. Again, no cell phones back then, but it was no problem to have a second line installed in the apartment, and that's what I did."

"But, wait a minute!" Trish interrupted. "If this was all so platonic, why didn't you just eventually tell them the whole story so you didn't have to live in fear of getting caught?"

"As Paul Harvey likes to say, that is the rest of the story!" Andrea admitted.

"Oh boy, this is getting interesting! Wait a minute, I need another beer," Trish made her pause while she refueled. When she was settled back in the big leather chair again, she demanded, "On with the story!"

Andrea continued, "So everything was working out just fine. When I called Richard to tell him I would share the apartment with him, I explained to him that my parents would not be keen on this plan. I told him about the separate phone line, and the general keeping mum attitude that I would be adopting for this plan. He was fine with that and was just grateful I was willing to share the rent, which by the way worked out to be $50 less a month than it would have been in the other apartment with Janet.

So, we arranged to meet on the Saturday before classes started, and he would help me move my stuff out of the basement of Campbell Hall and just generally help me get moved in." Andrea paused as she came to a natural break in her story.

"OK," Trish pressed her, "Get to the good stuff!"

Andrea laughed and continued her story. "We turned out to be pretty agreeable roommates. He was much neater than Janet ever was, and we both liked to cook as it turned out. Since we no longer had dorm food to fill us, we started cooking each evening at the apartment. Neither of us was dating anyone so we just kind of settled in and enjoyed each other's company. We started shopping together and even started trying some inexpensive wines, at least something a step up from Boone's Farm."

"Boone's what?" Trish asked.

"You are so young, my dear!" Andrea laughed as she explained. "It was a brand of horrible wine with a screw top, but it was cheap. As I said, we branched out from there and tried some wines with real corks in them!"

"As I recall," Andrea said, "it was the night that we discovered Blue Nun wine that everything changed. Richard had made a chicken fettuccini dish, and we both discovered that Blue Nun was a very enjoyable little wine. So much so that we were working our way through a second bottle while I was doing the dishes. That was the deal: if you cooked, you didn't have to clean up. Richard put a Ray Charles album on the stereo. It was the first part of December, and it just happened to be snowing outside when Ray starts singing, "Baby, its Cold Outside." I'm in the tiny kitchen doing dishes and swaying to the music when Richard brings in more dirty dishes, and he's singing along. Suddenly I'm not doing dishes anymore, and we're dancing through the kitchen door into the living room. Ray keeps on singing when that song is finished, but Richard and I stand in the middle of the living room with candlelight playing off the snowy window panes. He took my face in his hands and leaned down and kissed me, and I found myself kissing him back."

"And then..." Trish prompted.

Andrea's face was becoming more and more color-coordinated with the blush wine that she had been sipping, and decided that Trish had heard quite enough details for one night. "Let's just say that after that night, we had a guest bedroom in our two bedroom apartment!"

"Oh, phooey!" Trish exclaimed. "You're just getting to the good part, and you cut me off! What happened? Why aren't you happily married and celebrating your thirty-something wedding anniversary?"

"That was so long ago," Andrea explained. "I'm not really sure I can tell you exactly what happened. We had a few great months playing house, going out to movies, inviting other couples to the apartment for impromptu dinner parties. But, life changes when you least expect it. Richard had always planned to go to graduate school in Boston, and I was offered a position in the Legislative Service Bureau beginning in September. We lived in the apartment throughout the summer and both of us worked at the Campus Book Store. Suddenly it was the end of August. It was time for Richard to move to Boston and for me to move back to my folks' house until I could find a place to live in Des Moines. We talked about my possibly going out to visit in the spring, but I don't think either one of us quite knew what to make of the whole situation."

"Didn't you write letters or call or do something to keep the relationship going?" inquired Trish.

"We wrote back and forth for a while. We were both just incredibly busy, and neither of us had one of those fancy answering machines—so we just gradually seemed to cool off.

I met Will's dad when I was working, during the next General Assembly of the Iowa Legislature. I fell head-over-heels in love with him, and Richard just kind of got lost in the fever that was Bill Hogan." Andrea explained.

Trish laughed, "Sounds like a story for another night and another cooler of beer. I'm beat! I think I'd better hit the hay while I can still find my bed."

"You're right," Andrea agreed. "That is indeed a story for another time!"

Just then the door to the newly-christened library opened, and Will Hogan walked into the room, followed by none other than the subject of Andrea's story, Richard Knight.

"Look who I found at our front door!" Will announced as he gestured toward the older man who followed him into the room.

Trish was on her feet before Andrea could even register the presence of the two men in the room. Trish addressed Will with far more energy than she had been able to muster just moments before. "Hey, Will, I need to stretch my legs before I head for bed. What do you say we polish off these two beers and take a quick walk around town?"

As Trish was propelling Will through the door with two beers in her hand, he had little choice but to venture out into the quiet sounds of small town Iowa.

As the pair headed out into the August night, Rich turned to Andrea and asked if he could join her. "I get the distinct impression we are being left alone."

As Andrea handed him a wine glass and the bottle of wine, she had to agree. "Well, you see, I just told Trish the story of us."

Chapter Ten

Richard Knight

Rich accepted the glass and the bottle of wine Andrea handed him and sat down with a sigh, "Ah, I see you're still drinking white zinfandel." Andrea laughed, "Some habits die hard." she admitted.

"I believe we tried white zinfandel right after we discovered Blue Nun," Rich recalled.

"I'm afraid I stopped experimenting with wine soon after you left for Boston, and I've enjoyed good old Beringer's white zinfandel ever since," Andrea admitted.

"Well," Rich mused, "I've had some of the finest wines in all of Europe, and most nights I'd still prefer a glass of white zin, or even Blue Nun! I guess it's true. 'You can take the boy out of the country, but you can't take the country out of the boy!'"

Andrea laughed, "I know what you mean. I remember being in a swanky bar in Hell's Kitchen and ordering a glass of white zin, only to have the bartender look down his very long nose at me and inform me that his bar did not carry such a common wine."

Rich joined in her laughter as he poured a glass of the pale pink wine and raised his glass in a toast, "To old friends!"

"To old friends!" Andrea agreed.

"So what was the giant rush out the door as Will and I arrived?" Rich asked. "I get the distinct feeling that we were being left alone together on purpose."

"Not too subtle, is she?" Andrea admitted

Rich settled back in the leather arm chair and asked the obvious. "So, what have you been up to for the past thirty-some years?"

Andrea laughed. "I'll give you the Cliff Notes version for now, and we can get into the details later."

"Fair enough," agreed Rich.

"After we left Cedar Falls, I moved back to Des Moines. I lived with my folks for a couple of months and spent every weekend looking at apartments until finally I found one that wasn't too depressing. I started at the Legislative Service Bureau in September, and on Valentine's Day the next year, I met Will's dad. He was an intern for a State Senator, and was delivering a bill request."

"That's a pretty romantic beginning," Rich interjected.

"Yes, I suppose it was. It was pretty much a whirlwind courtship as we ended up getting married the following October," Andrea conceded.

"So, love at first sight, but not everlasting love?" Rich asked.

"Wow!" Andrea admitted. "That sums up the relationship pretty well. Actually, most times I explain the collapse of my marriage by quoting a line from e.e. cummings. It says, 'I love your body and I love it well, does it not also stand to reason that I shall also come to love your mind?'"

Rich looked at her, waiting for an answer.

"Ah, not so much…" she added. "But we were married for 17 years, and some of them were happy. And I have the light of my life, William Roger Hogan II, so all in all, not a terrible experience. How about you—the Cliff Notes version, please!

"Well," Rich began, "I think I can be equally as brief. After grad school I was able to get a job at the American School in Frankfurt. It was a great mix of kids from a wide variety of backgrounds, and I fell in love with teaching—and directing plays. I was involved with one of the other teachers for a couple of years, but just knew in my heart that she was not 'the love of my life.'"

"Those are pretty hard to find," Andrea interjected.

"So true," Rich agreed. "I was completely alone for about five years and then I was introduced to my ex-wife, Sally by a friend of mine from school, David Olson. She was an English/Drama person at another school in Frankfurt, and we really did hit it off right from the beginning. We were married in 1985 and because her biological clock was ticking, we had two children in three years. You met Scott today, and my daughter's name is Sandy. Two summers ago our family rented a house on Lake Redfern for the summer. Almost exactly one year ago to the day, Sally let me know that she would not be returning to her teaching job in Mons, that's in Belgium, where she and I had been teaching for the past few years. Turns out she's decided she was no longer in love with me and wanted to return to her old teaching position in Frankfurt."

"Oh goodness, what a shock—and you didn't see any of this coming?"

"I'm sure I should have, but I was really very happy. A home, family, fulfilling work, what more could a person ask for?" he pondered. "I think Sally pointed out that there was no passion. Frankly, I think passion is overrated, but don't get me started. This is the Cliff Notes version, and that about wraps it up. My sisters convinced me to move back here to be nearer our folks since they're having some health issues. I think the change will be good for me."

"I think you may be right. This seems to be the place for new beginnings, you, me, Trish, this old schoolhouse, starting a new adventure!" Andrea agreed.

"So how long have you been teaching?" Rich asked. "I thought you were into government or politics or something bureaucratic."

"Well," Andrea replied, "counting the three months that I was student teaching, about…three months!"

"Wait a minute; are you the new 9th grade teacher? Craig Seeley told me about you," Rich said.

"I am," Andrea admitted.

"Man oh man, what a small world this is!" He sounded as astonished as he looked.

Chapter Eleven

Scott Samuels

He lay back in the freshly made bed and stared up at the stars that were so clearly visible from his bedroom perch in the sky. He let out a long and well deserved yawn and thought about how the day had gone. He could hardly believe that this dream of his had finally come true. Six months ago this building still had boards in place of new windows and studs where walls should be. Now it was home to six new people, five new friends really. The Barbeque organized by Verna Lee and Oscar had been a wonderful ending to a long and back-breaking day. It was just the sort of thing that he had envisioned when he started this hair-brained scheme. He remembered how he had been determined to out-bid old man Schearer to keep the school building he loved from becoming a warehouse for air conditioners and furnaces.

In truth it had not been too hard to out-bid him. There were plenty of empty storefronts in Bentley that the Plumbing and Heating mogul of southeastern Iowa could obtain for next to nothing—he had just seen a good deal when it came around to him. Mr. Schearer would have sold off the tin from the garage roofs, the copper from the plumbing, and the oak flooring from the gymnasium and made a tidy profit and still had a place to store the inventory of his trade. Scott could have done that, too. But that was not what he had had in mind when he hatched his plot a little over a year ago. He wanted this old school house to breathe with life again. He wanted to open the doors to the townspeople and have this old brick building welcome a new generation of Bentley kids, as well as their parents, and grandparents. He wanted this to be so much more than just an apartment building. He could see pot lucks, coffee klatches, rummage sales, maybe even art and craft classes, all taking place in that beautiful gymnasium. He could see it all happening…if someone would just step up and make it all happen. Who would that be? Certainly not himself, he could barely manage to eat supper during football season, and the rest of the school year wasn't much better as he also served as the assistant basketball and softball coach.

His eyes grew heavier and his mind slowed and just before he drifted off to his first night's sleep in his new home, he felt himself smile and he thought of all those folks closing their eyes around him. For the first time in a very long time, he felt no worries. He was on his way to fulfilling his dreams. The people and plans would materialize. For once, he was not in this adventure alone.

Chapter Twelve

Andrea Michelle Hogan

Sunday morning found Andrea cooking Will's favorite breakfast—Cinnamon French Toast with lots of crispy bacon so that she could send her boy off for the long drive back to Austin. Fortunately, she had brought the basics of housekeeping along with her so that she could make the good strong coffee that he liked so well and the double dipped French Toast that had been a staple of his diet since he could walk and talk.

As she finished mixing the batter and taking the last of the bacon out of the frying pan, sure enough a bleary-eyed Will Roger Hogan appeared around the doorway of the world's smallest bedroom and pulled her into an awkward embrace as she stood over the new stove, bread ready for dipping.

"Mother of mine, you are truly a gem among women!" Will announced as he smelled the bacon, coffee and cinnamon wafting toward his handsome nose.

Andrea couldn't help smiling as she placed the first of many pieces of French toast into the heated skillet. "You didn't think I was about to send my boy off on a long journey without adequate nourishment; did you?"

"And there wouldn't happen to be the makings of three or four roast beef and provolone sandwiches lurking in your new refrigerator?" Will asked.

Andrea smiled and admitted that those items might just be sitting in the refrigerator waiting to become his favorite sandwiches. She could have also told him that there was a big bag of Fritos and a bag of Pistachio's ready for his trip as well—but he would find that out by the time he hit the Missouri border.

"So, how far will you try to get today?" she asked cautiously. She never got used to the long distance driving her son was capable of. Ever since he had moved for Adamantine Spine Moving for a couple of years, he seemed to be able to drive anywhere at any time of day or night.

"I hope to make it to OK City before I take a quick cat nap and then motor on home," he informed her. "I don't have to work until 5:00 tomorrow night, but I'd like a few hours of shut eye in my own bed."

She smiled and placed three pieces of French Toast on his plate that already held six pieces of bacon. She handed him the warm syrup and softened butter, and he began to pack away a breakfast that should last him well into his trip. Just as she was putting her own French toast into the skillet, she heard a tentative knock at her brand new "old" door. She realized it was the first knock in her new home, and she couldn't help but smile. As she called, "Come in!" the door swung open, and there was a bleary-eyed Trish moving haltingly toward the table in the bright living/dining/kitchen space.

"OK, I was literally awakened by the delicious aroma of bacon frying and coffee brewing, you owe me compensation in the form of black coffee and at least two pieces of bacon." she informed the room.

"I can do better than that" Andrea informed her, "How about some French toast to go along with that coffee and bacon?"

"That should make it worth getting out of bed—even with a slight hangover—how many beers did I consume during your story last night?" she asked Andrea.

As Andrea was giving Trish a furious head shake, Will asked, "What story?"

Trish was quicker than Andrea. "Oh nothing, Will—she was just telling me about what a difficult baby you were.

"I resemble that remark," Will laughingly replied.

Andrea quickly changed the subject and brought the conversation around to their plans for today.

"So, are you going to the Lutherans with me or the Methodists with your grandmother?" Andrea quickly asked Trish.

"I promised to show up at Bethany Methodist for the 10:00 service, so I'm heading for the shower as soon as I finish this wonderful breakfast," Trish informed her. "But I promise to go with you to Trinity Lutheran sometime soon. I know how hard it is to walk into a new congregation where you don't know a soul."

"It will be different for me," Andrea admitted, "I've been a member at St. John's in Des Moines all my life—baptized, confirmed, married, and probably buried there as well."

"Not for a long, long time, Mother," Will interjected. "I intend to have you around well into your dotage!"

"I'll try my best to get old and senile before I leave this world behind," Andrea assured her constantly worrying son.

"Now, both of you had better hit the showers, err, separately, of course!"

"Yes, Ma'am!" the two young people cried in unison.

Chapter Thirteen

Richard Knight

Richard rolled over in bed, saw the bright sun streaming through his ten foot high bedroom windows and promptly pulled the pillow over his head and fell asleep again. When he awoke two hours later, he was surprised by the absolute quiet that surrounded him. Having lived the past nine years on a busy street in Mons, Belgium, this quiet was definitely noticeable. When he hauled himself out of bed and looked out into the parking lot of the Bentley School House Apartments, he saw one of the reasons for the absolute quiet: he was the only tenant home. Clearly a church going group, he thought to himself. Well, that was fine. Better that than a bunch of late night party types with beer cans in the hallways. He was getting used to solitude since the divorce, and he found that he didn't mind his own company too much.

He managed to find the coffee pot, coffee, and filters in his box-filled kitchen, and before long the aroma of Ethiopian blend coffee filled the room. A little more rummaging and he found the homemade strawberry jam that his mother had just given him and the loaf of bread that she so thoughtfully had brought to him yesterday during the midst of the move. He smiled at the memory of his little mother hopping out of her ancient Toyota Corolla with a bag of necessities as she came to see her boy's new home.

As he sat at the Swenson's old mud room table and looked around this new home that was really quite suddenly his, he marveled a little at the speed this change of his life course had taken. This new home of his would take some getting used to. He felt suspended in the trees up here on the second floor. The living room/dining room/kitchen was one open space with the two bedrooms and one bath down the hallway. His bedroom was slightly bigger than the first bedroom, and it contained a walk-in closet and a small, but perfectly adequate, master bath.

He smiled at the thought of the last apartment that he and Sally had shared with the kids in Mons. That bathroom with the miniscule shower, the kitchen that was no bigger than his current walk-in closet; still, he remembered more laughter than complaints. But, come to think of it, one of the reasons it had worked was because they were rarely all home together. Scott had already gone off to college, and Sandy and Sally were constantly involved in evening activities. Often it was just himself and the cat after he got home from late afternoon play practice. Had Sally stayed away on purpose? He'd never know the answer to that one. The time for asking had long since passed.

He gave his head a hard shake and brought his thoughts back to the present. This was his home now, and he better make the best of it. He looked forward to Sunday dinner at his mom and dad's house. He could count on two hands the number of times he had enjoyed that treat in the past thirty years. No doubt it would be fried chicken with mashed potatoes and gravy. That was his favorite Sunday dinner. Healthy eating could wait until tomorrow.

His toast was finished, and he'd polished off one cup of coffee on his way to finishing off the pot. He decided that his game plan would include a long shower and then an hour of wrestling with 'do-it yourself" book shelves so that he could begin to unpack the twelve boxes of books that currently lined his living room wall. Then it would be off to his folks' for lunch that he knew would be on the table promptly at noon.

As he stood under the blessedly strong flow of water from the shower in his master bathroom, he found himself thinking of Andi. What a strange and small world this had turned out to be. It had been over thirty years since he had seen her—and yet he would have known her if he had passed her on a crowded sidewalk in New York City. She even smelled the same! Now he was going to be her boss! He found himself looking forward to that. He had always known she was a talented person, he knew that she would make a great teacher, even if she was coming to this field just a little late in her life.

Andi Hughes? No, Andi Something-else. She still used her married name because whatever it was, he remembered it was the same as her son Will's. That reminded him that it was another new school year, and he always looked forward to the excitement, the potential, the kids. He had to smile. He was certainly in the right profession. How awful it would be to be in a job that was just a job.

He jumped out of the shower and into a pair of shorts and a T-Shirt from one of the many musicals he had directed through the years. He'd better get to building bookshelves. He could practically smell his mother's fried chicken already!

Chapter Fourteen

Oscar and Verna Lee Swenson

The commotion reminded her of little kids stopping by to see if Oscar could come out and play! Shortly after he had finished breakfast and headed to his new basement workshop on this bright and sunny Monday morning, the little brass door knocker on Apartment 2 had been very active. Each time there would be one of Oscar's old buddies standing there looking around her for Oscar. With each one that she sent downstairs, she calculated how much coffee would be left in the Carafe that she had sent downstairs with Oscar at 7:30 this morning. Good thing she had sent down a half dozen cups as well! Even those would be gone before too long so she decided to dig out her avocado green 30 cupper and head downstairs to set up a real coffee corner in Oscar's new workshop.

She was welcomed into the workshop with good natured laughter and received half a dozen whistles when she sat down a plate of Banana Bread straight from the oven.

She filled the coffee pot from the sink that was designed for mop buckets and in a few moments the smell of freshly brewed coffee filled the small room.

She looked around and smiled. Seated in a semi-circle facing Oscar's new work bench were Harold Bartels, Roger Kolander, Ben Slocum, Bill Padget, and Vernon Olmstead. Not an ounce of hair color left among them. Not much hair for that matter. They were on their favorite topic, "What's to become of our town?" She knew she had better skedaddle before they asked her opinion.

Around noon she heard Oscar lumbering up the stairs from the basement and was grateful to see that she would only be feeding her husband lunch. "Where did that gaggle of geese disperse to?" she asked her companion of over fifty years.

"Well, we drained the 30 cupper and polished off the Banana Bread so they all thought they might mosey on down the road to find some lunch—either at home or over at the beer joint." he informed her. He smiled as he told her, "I just kept straightening my work bench and they just kept talking."

"Talking is what those old blowhards do best, if you ask me." She replied. But she was smiling when she said it. "Now, you'd better sit down and help me polish off some of these leftovers from Saturday's picnic. I swear we'll be eating brats till Labor Day if I don't figure out a way to use these up."

"What do you say we invite the Coffee Group to lunch tomorrow? It shouldn't take long to polish off the brats and potato salad if you spread it out among those old coots." Oscar offered.

"And just where do you propose they sit here in my mini kitchen? I suppose I could put two on the countertop, but that gas stove might get a little uncomfortable." She teased.

"Problem solved" he assured her. "I'll throw up one of those 8' tables that Scott has in the storage room, and we'll be all set."

Verna Lee looked around at their compact little home and wondered where in the world he would put an 8' table

Oscar saw her bewildered look and assured her, "Not here—down in the gymnasium".

Verna Lee looked relieved but not yet convinced. "Don't worry, I'll ask Scott's permission when I see him tonight." He proposed.

"Well, I suppose—just this once" she relented. "But I'm here to tell you that I do not intend to cook and clean up after a bunch of old coots on any kind of a regular basis."

"That's not a problem either, my darling wife" he said. "I found an entire cupboard of cafeteria trays, glasses, and even silverware. I promise if you cook, we'll clean up."

"Oh my" Verna Lee exclaimed "What have I gotten myself into?"

Since most of the leftovers were being stored in the old cafeteria's giant refrigerator, Verna decided to just warm everything up in the cafeteria kitchen. She found things in surprisingly good order. A little dust here and there, but nothing a quick wipe and some Mr. Clean wouldn't take care of. She unearthed one of a half dozen electric roasters that she saw stored in a large cabinet and started to warm up the brats and onions slowly. The rest of the meal came together quickly and truly wasn't much more than opening up containers and setting out the contents. She cubed the rest of the watermelon for dessert and called it good. It felt nice cooking in a big, well equipped kitchen. She found herself moving from counters to refrigerators and the stove like she owned the place. When it came time to set out the spread, she rolled up the metal partition that separated the kitchen from the cafeteria and was surprised to find that the half dozen retired guys that had shown up yesterday had grown to an even dozen. Oscar was in the process of setting up another 8' table, and she grabbed a few more trays and pieces of silverware.

"Oscar Swenson—where did all of these guys come from?"

"Well" Oscar admitted, "I might have made a couple of phone calls this morning".

Verna Lee shooed him away with her dishtowel and thanked the good Lord that there was plenty of food to go around—even if the crowd had doubled.

True to his word, Verna Lee did not have to lift a finger once the lunch was served. She fixed a plate for herself, took it upstairs to her sunny kitchen, and wondered why she hadn't invited some of her friends to share the lunch as well?

At about 3:00 Oscar arrived in the apartment with a grin settled into his lined face. "Now that was fun!" he exclaimed, as he wrapped his strong arms around his lifelong companion.

"Well, I have to admit it wasn't too much work on my part—but goodness, what would have happened if any more men had shown up?—I'm betting you polished off all of those leftovers in short order."

"Actually there was a little of everything left after we all had seconds, so a few of the guys bit the bullet and went back for thirds. We cleaned up the dishes—including all of the serving bowls and returned all of the trays and silverware to the right places. I think we'd pass a state inspection, or a Verna Lee inspection even.

Verna Lee smiled at the insinuation and admitted, "You know, it was kind of nice to see you guys all eating together, and it made me wish I had invited some of my lady friends as well."

Oscar was eager to pursue the idea, "You know when I talked to Scott last night about using the tables and the cafeteria for this get together, he was very excited. He told me that this was just the kind of thing that he was hoping would happen here."

"But how would we finance something like this? We're comfortable financially, but we couldn't continually provide the funds to cook for a dozen, or maybe even two dozen people," she worried.

"Can you provide a good meal for $5 a person?" Oscar asked

"Of course I can Oscar Swenson, I'm a good Iowa cook, anyone can feed people for $5 a person!"

"Those fellows downstairs insisted on paying you for your trouble, and every one of them put $5 in the pot without even a suggestion from me." With that he handed her $60 in fives and ten's.

"What if we just started off slow and did this once a week?" Oscar inquired?

"Oh my, Oscar, I'm not sure I want to get into something like this so quickly after we've moved."

"How about if you call your friends Gertie and Gladys and ask them to help?"

Verna Lee brightened immediately. "Oh, what a good idea, Oscar— Gertie used to cook right here at this school—she'll know what to do."

Oscar smiled quietly as his bride began to make lists while reaching for the telephone to call Gertie. The Bentley School Community Meal Program had been born.

Chapter Fifteen

Andrea Hogan

She held the big gold key in her hand and noticed that it was trembling just a little. This was her first classroom. After years of wishing and dreaming and a couple tough years of working hard to achieve her lifelong dream, here she was; ready or not, she had arrived. The heavy door swung open with an appropriately friendly creak—almost the exact sound her knees made on a rainy day! She smiled as she studied her new home away from home—Room 105 at the Bentley/Grimball/Marshtown consolidated High School—BGM for short. She knew she would spend more waking hours here than any place else for the next nine months, and she loved the thought of it.

The classroom itself wasn't anything special. It was about 20' x 30' with twenty five desks in five neat rows and a wall of windows that looked out on the perennial garden. Thank goodness it didn't look out onto the playground or the student parking lot. She could just imagine how much of a distraction that would have been to young and wandering minds. But it did have a good solid wooden desk where she could keep her books and her pens and it was her very own, well, hers and the BGM School District. She felt immediately at home and began to busy herself with unpacking her box of items to personalize the room. She laughed when she looked into the box and saw one picture of Will and about seventeen peace symbols. "Gee" she wondered, "Do you think they'll get the idea that I'm into 'peace'?" She found places for her peace symbols, her peace plaques, and even her teddy bear holding a peace symbol. Her picture of Will found a home on the corner of her desk where he could smile over her on good and bad days.

When she looked around the room she realized what this room needed, cried out for even, plants! Big ones! She wondered if she could get anything at the Pamida in Marshtown? That would help make the room warm and welcoming. She wanted her classroom to be a place where students felt comfortable to just "hang out". She remembered Mr. Carnes' room at East High in Des Moines. Kids would gather before and after school to talk about issues and politics. She wanted her room to be that kind of refuge. She wanted kids who would talk and not tweet. Kids who would dream of changing the world. In short, she wanted a younger version of herself. She wanted to be the teacher who would nourish those young minds, just as hers had been nourished all those years before. Oh, yes, and she wanted to teach them the meaning of a declarative sentence. She almost forgot that, she was also there to teach Freshmen English and Composition.

As she smiled and started to re-arrange the books in the bookcase, clearly castoffs from students long since gone, Craig Seeley stuck his head in the room and asked, "Getting settled are we?" Startled from her revelry, she nearly jumped out of her skin as she assured Craig that indeed she was getting settled in.

He grinned as he looked around her room with her peace symbols clearly displayed. "Let me guess," he inquired. "You voted for McGovern, didn't you?"

"Worse," she confessed,. "I caucused for Muskey!"

They both laughed as he confessed to having voted for McGovern as well. "These kids today, they have no concept of what it was like in America, in Iowa in the 60's," he lamented.

"Tell me about it," Andrea joined in, "Trish wasn't born until 1984! She didn't even get the reference when I asked her how Big Brother was doing. She thought I meant some reality show on television."

Craig laughed but quickly turned serious. "You know, Andrea, I'm not sure I'd have the nerve to do what you're doing."

Andrea was immediately worried at his comment, "What do you mean, Craig?"

"Well, I've been teaching and serving as a principal for well over thirty years now, and I know we're the same age. I'm just not sure I'd have the nerve to start out as a brand new teacher at our age."

"You know, I wasn't sure I wanted to try and fulfill this dream until I read a very little book called *The Last Lecture of Randy Pausch*. Somehow reading that book, I just had an epiphany, and I knew I had to try."

"Well, more power to you my friend." He smiled as he moved his lanky frame from the door. "Remember, my door is always open to you if you run across anything you'd like to talk about, and depend on that new department head of yours. Rich Knight has been teaching English for forever. There isn't much about teaching and kids that he doesn't know."

"Thanks, Craig" she replied. "I appreciate the offer. I'm sure I'll take you up on it—but I hope not the first day! Now, tell me where I can buy some plants to liven this place up"

"I was just at Pamida, and they've got a bunch of really big plants on clearance, they may need some TLC to get them back to life, but if you want to try, I think you'll find plenty there."

"I've saved a few plants in my life. I'll give it a try." She gathered her books, keys and purse together and headed for the door. Craig watched as she carefully locked her room and tucked the key into her pocket.

"I can barely recall my first classroom" he remarked. "But I do recall how it felt to walk into my very own classroom for the first time. Congratulations, Andrea, and if I haven't said it before, welcome."

"Thank you Craig" she answered. "I do feel welcome. Now, let's see if I can save a schefflera or two along the way."

His eyes lit up at the sound of the word schefflera. "Did you know," he inquired, "that your schefflera either has mites or is thinking about having mites?"

Andrea laughed, "Actually, I did know that. I read it in some plant magazine once."

Craig laughed too, "I think I read the same article!"

They parted at the parking lot, and Andrea congratulated herself once more on her decision to move here. This was going to be a good place to live.

Chapter Sixteen

Richard Knight

The rain was beating with late summer ferocity against Rich's apartment windows, and the cracks of thunder were all too frequent when his cell phone began ringing. He was surprised to find that the phone showed that Craig Seeley was calling, at what, 9:30 at night?—that seemed a little late for a social call.

He opened his phone and greeted his new boss with a slight trepidation. "Hey, Craig, what's up?"

Craig was blunt and to the point. "Rich, I think you'd better meet me over at the high school as soon as you can. I just got a call from the Highway Patrol, and they said the big oak tree on the north side of the building just got hit by lightning and it crashed into the roof of the auditorium. Bring Scott with you. This could be bad." He hung up before Rich could ask any more questions.

Rich moved quickly across the golden oak boards of the second floor hallway and knocked firmly on Scott's door. A startled Scott opened the door quickly and was surprised to see his new neighbor standing there in a bathrobe and flip flops. Rich quickly told him what Craig had said, and they both parted to pull on blue jeans and rain gear. Meeting again in the hallway, they both had ponchos on and flashlights at the ready as they quickly decided to take Rich's Blazer to navigate the eight miles to Marshtown.

The sight that awaited them at the high school was not a pretty one. Volunteer fire departments from Grimball and Bentley joined the

Marshtown crew to illuminate the huge oak tree that was seemingly permanently implanted in the roof of BGM High School.

Both men hurried to the cluster of firemen standing around Craig Seeley. The rain had mercifully let up, but the sky continued to crackle with lightning and distant rumbles of thunder. Craig saw them coming and stepped aside to apprise them of the situation. "Quite a way to start a new school year," he grumbled as he led them toward the fallen tree. "I haven't been inside yet, but I'm pretty sure we're going to find the ceiling of the auditorium on the stage and the rain soaking through the upholstery on the auditorium seats"

"That's going to be a mess." Rich added, "Those seats were shot when we sat in them forty years ago."

"Yeah, you're right," Craig agreed He waved his hand to indicate the whole rainy mess and then added, "And have you thought where you're going to have your fall play?"

That shut Rich up. But it was Scott who was instantly alive with a great idea. "Let's have it in the cafeteria at my apartment house. There's still a small stage at one end, and, man, do I have folding chairs!"

Both Rich and Craig looked at him in amusement. Craig was the first to respond, "Well, Scott, we might just have to take you up on that offer. But right now I see Virgil Coonrod pulling up with the Mega Crane so I think we'd better see if he can lift that old tree off what used to be our auditorium."

Chapter Seventeen

Scott Samuels

The morning light did not bring many surprises when Scott and Rich returned to the high school the morning after the storm. Sure enough, when the crane lifted the 100 year old tree off the roof of the auditorium, there was precious little to save inside. The main support beams had crashed through the stage floor, and the seats that were not covered by branches were soaked through with rain. Behind the stage could be seen hundreds of costumes soaked with rain and mud from what used to be the Props Room. He could tell this would be a complete tear down and re-build. He was just glad the insurance company would pay for this remodel. He'd have to remember to tell his brother about this though—it would be a great project for his small construction company.

Scott turned to Rich who was kicking at the bricks that scattered the ground around what had been the space that he would have held rehearsals for the fall play. "Well, Scott" Rich began, does your offer still hold for the use of the cafeteria at the Bentley School House for the fall play?"

"You bet it does" Scott reassured his new friend.

"I think we're going to have to take you up on it," Rich informed him. "I'll cast the play next week, and we'll start rehearsals right after Labor Day."

"What play are you doing?" Scott asked.

"It's a melodrama that a friend of mine wrote a few years ago—in fact, I'm hoping he can make it to one of the performances—he lives up in Cedar Rapids."

"Cool, then we can shout 'Author, Author'" Scott mused.

"Right," Rich agreed somewhat dubiously. "So can we start rehearsing right after school?"

"You bet," Scott assured him. "I'll let Verna Lee and Oscar know what's going on. They talked to me yesterday about doing a community lunch once a week, but they'd be done by mid-afternoon."

"A community lunch—what a great idea—my folks would love to do that." Rich exclaimed.

"Have them call Verna Lee. I think they're forming a committee and all that good stuff. It's really just what I wanted when I started this project almost two years ago. I've always dreamed of apartments on the top two floors and kind of a community center in the old cafeteria area. I really lucked out when the place came with all the equipment including tables, folding chairs and plastic lunch trays."

"We'll certainly put the folding chairs to good use and bring more from the high school if we need to," Rich assured him. "How many do you think we can fit in there?"

"The Fire Department has already figured that out for us. There's a sign at the entrance that says the capacity is 356."

"Then that's how many tickets we'll sell," Rich joked. "It will be the social event of the season".

"In a small town like Bentley, you won't be far from the truth with that statement," Scott agreed.

Chapter Eighteen

Oscar and Verna Lee Swenson

There was a knock at the door of their apartment right during Wheel of Fortune.

"Who could that be?" wondered Verna Lee, "Certainly not one of the kids, they know better than to interrupt their dad during Wheel of Fortune!" She opened the door to find, Rich Knight, standing before her.

"Evening Verna Lee" he began, "I hope you've finished supper."

"Oh my yes, Rich," Verna Lee explained, "We're still 5:00'ers for supper. Meal's finished and the dishes are done, Oscar washes and I dry, oh, but if you're hungry, I can always warm up some leftovers in the microwave."

"No, no, I'm fine. I was really hoping to talk to you and Oscar for a few minutes." With that Oscar hit the "mute" button and waved Rich into the living room which was actually just the left side of the big sunny room that served as living room, dining room and kitchen for the old lovebirds.

"What's on your mind, Rich?" Oscar inquired as he directed him to a seat on the far end of the comfortable old couch.

"I've been trying to figure out how we're going to have a Fall Play now that the auditorium is out of commission."

"Quite a storm last night," Oscar agreed. "I couldn't believe the damage that one tree could do!"

"Yes, it did a number on the whole roof and the back wall of the auditorium. I'm sure it's a complete tear down and start over," Rich explained.

"Good thing the district has good insurance," Verna Lee added.

"I don't envy Craig and all the paperwork this will involve," Rich replied. "But from the Drama Department's point of view, it will be a godsend in the long run. It will mean new lights, sound equipment, and finally decent seats! Right now though, we have to figure out how to put on a play in the old cafeteria/gymnasium of this magnificent building."

"Here?" Verna Lee asked excitedly.

"Scott offered as soon as he saw the damage," Rich explained

"What a way for you to start out your new job," Oscar shook his head in disbelief.

He couldn't help but think what fun it was going to be to have the young people practicing in the cafeteria while he was working in his new workshop just to the right of the stage.

"What can we do to help, dear?" Verna Lee asked as she patted his knee.

Rich laughed and told them, "I'm so glad you asked. Here's kind of what I have been thinking, just first blush, mind you, so nothing is cast in concrete. I was hoping that, Oscar, you would take charge of helping the props crew build some very simple sets. Scott tells me you have your workshop pretty well complete down there in the basement."

"Rich, don't worry about a thing. I've got plenty of scrap lumber back at the farm. Just give me a couple of young people to heft and tote, and we'll build New York City if we need to."

"A few simple sets will do us, Oscar, but I have no doubt that you could re-create New York City if you put your mind to it," Rich laughed as he turned to Verna Lee.

"And I'm looking for a favor from you and your friends as well."

Verna Lee's eyes lit up as she sat up straighter and turned to see how she could be of assistance in this grand adventure. He explained, "All of our costumes are ruined beyond repair. Beyond the fact that the tree limbs shredded most of them, and the rain and mud soaked the rest, there's no safe way to get to them to even try to rescue the few that might be salvaged. We have to start from scratch, and I was hoping that you and a few of your friends might be able to outfit this show. There are only seven characters, and no one changes costumes, so one outfit each will do it."

Verna Lee's eyes lit up as she immediately began to plan the attack on the costume issue. "Well, I sold my sewing machine to Gladys Millen, but

I'll just make her bring it back and her old portable as well. We'll set up shop in the cafeteria, go through all our old stash of material, and I'm sure we'll come up with whatever you need."

"That's great, Verna Lee, I knew I could count on you!" Rich exclaimed. "I have patterns from other schools where I've worked so as soon as I cast the play and we know sizes, you ladies can get started. These will be turn of the century costumes so you'll need a fair amount of material; I can probably scrounge up $100 if that would help."

"Well, we'll just see what we can find amongst the community," Verna Lee assured him. "I'll let you know if we run into any problems. Now, we're going to want to be sewing the same time you're rehearsing so we can do fittings and such, will that be problem?"

"I can't think of a better background noise than the soft whirring of your wonderful machines," Rich assured her.

Rich thought of one more thing to ask these two lively senior citizens. "Scott tells me that you're going to do a community lunch once a week. My folks would love to do something like that."

Verna Lee laughed as she explained, "Well, it started out as once a week, but already we've expanded to Monday, Wednesday and Friday. We ladies have decided that if these old coots are willing to pay $5 for lunch, we're willing to make it three days a week."

"That sounds like quite an undertaking" Rich suggested.

"Oh, no, dear, we have it all worked out with teams to cook and serve—and, of course, the men do the dishes while we play cards. It's the perfect arrangement. You just tell your folks to give me a call; we'll get them all signed up for a team, and we'd love to have them join us."

"I'll do that, Verna Lee," Rich assured her. "I'm so grateful to be back in this part of the country where neighbors are like family and they'll do anything for you."

Verna Lee patted his knee again and assured him, "We're glad you're here too dear."

Oscar unmuted the TV and encouraged the young man on the screen to "buy a vowel, dummy!"

Yes, it was good to be home

Chapter Nineteen

Andrea Hogan

This was her very first staff meeting as a certified teacher, and she couldn't be more thrilled. She looked around the room at the forty some teachers who comprised the high school faculty at BGM High School and marveled that she was among them. After thirty years in a tedious state government job, her reward for long suffering and early retirement was before her, she was a teacher. Craig Seeley hushed the buzz not with a gavel, but a high-pitched whistle between the fingers of his right hand. The meeting had begun.

"Good morning, all," he greeted them. "Well, this is certainly not the way I wanted to start a school year!" Murmuring and groaning prevailed as he went on to explain the latest from the storm damage incident of last week.

"Here's what we know for sure," be began. "The oak tree on the south side of the school was uprooted and crashed into the auditorium— probably from straight line winds that ranged from 85-90 miles per hour." Appropriate whistles and murmurs of alarm could be heard around the room.

"The insurance adjustors were here the next day, and the auditorium has been declared a complete loss. As some of you may know, the auditorium is an addition to the school, as in it was new in 1956. That still makes it 53 years old, but when you compare it to the Main Building, it's practically brand new!" Hoots of laughter accompanied his odd comparison.

"I've asked Rich Knight and Jan DeWoody to head up a committee to work with the architect to design a new addition," he continued. "I figured Rich knows what we need for the theater stuff, and Jan with her artistic background can pick out colors that don't remind me of a funeral parlor. If we're lucky, it will be complete in time for next year's Fall Play, but anything you had planned to use the auditorium for will need to be moved to the Cafeteria, or in the case of the fall play, to Scott's house!" The staff laughed as they all got the inside joke of "Scott's house" being the old Bentley Elementary School. Almost all of them had toured the apartments at some point during their reconstruction.

Andrea smiled and leaned back in her chair to survey the room as Craig Seeley went on to discuss the need for a coordinated lunch schedule so that the cafeteria could be cleared in time for orchestra rehearsal beginning with fifth period. Ah, the fine points of keeping a school running complicated enough without the loss of entire section of the building.

Eventually Craig got around to the actual agenda for the meeting which included introducing the new teachers. He pointed first to Trish and asked her to introduce herself. Even though she knew Trish's story, it was good to hear her confident young friend let the rest of the group know how sure she was of herself and her abilities. Richard was next, and he kept his story short and to the point. No mention of his divorce, or his parent's health. Of course, the last name was familiar to many of the teachers who knew his folks. Finally it was Andrea's turn.

Andrea took a deep breath and began. "I'm probably the oldest newbie teacher in the history of BGM," she confessed. "But please know that this is what I want to do and that I have worked very hard for the past two years to learn to be a good teacher. I spent thirty years in government and knew all those years that what I really wanted to do was teach in a school just like BGM. Now I'm here, and I can hardly believe it. I know I'll have to deal with my share of bureaucracy and paper work, but please just know that every day that I get to stand in front of a classroom and teach is a day that my dreams have been fulfilled." She stopped abruptly when she realized how idealistic she sounded. There was a silence for a brief moment, and then the applause began. She felt her cheeks grow bright red and sat down quickly while the teachers around her smiled and continued to applaud.

Craig was smiling as well when he finally brought the room back to order. "Thanks Andrea," he said. "Every once in a while we need a reminder of how lucky we are to be here. Now, we'd better get back to the agenda, or we'll be stuck in here through lunch."

Chapter Twenty

Trish Wilkins

Trish smiled at her grandmother over the miniature dining table that lived in one corner of her "deluxe" suite at the Marshtown Retirement Community.

"Nana Sue, you've made your little apartment so homey, I almost feel like I'm back in your kitchen on the farm."

"Well, the surroundings may be small, but that doesn't stop me from making a mean pot roast with all the trimmings," her diminutive grandmother replied. "Now tell me all about your first week of school as an honest to goodness teacher!"

"Oh, I loved it Nana," Trish assured her. "I have a wonderful sunny classroom on the backside of the building. I can look out my windows and see miles and miles of corn and soy beans ripening in the late August sun. That's the plus side, the minus side is that I'm on the third floor and until I got the janitor to unstick the windows, it was as hot as Hades up there. Once I got the windows open though, it was very pleasant. The school provides big fans to circulate the air. Craig Seeley says that unlike those city schools, BGM never has to let out early because of high temperatures. We always get a good breeze up on our little hill. Of course, that is probably also why we got hit by lightening the other night and those winds tore up that tree and crashed it into the auditorium. Of course it's bad that we've lost the use of our auditorium for nearly a year, but it needed updating anyway, and now the insurance will pay for it," Trish stopped abruptly. "Oh my goodness, listen to me. It's not like me to go on and on, but I'm just so excited."

"Well, of course, you are my dear. Here, have some potatoes and tell me about the kids you have in your classes," her grandmother urged.

"Oh, that's the best part, Nana; they're all really nice. Of course, a few of the boys tested me the first couple of days. I actually used one of the techniques I learned in school and it worked! Whenever they started acting up, I'd just gravitate over toward their desks and continue the lesson from a very close proximity to their chairs. Sure enough, they shut up and listened, I think, just to keep me from breathing down their necks, but it worked! When I student taught in Des Moines, the kids just seemed so much meaner. Of course, there were lots of nice kids, too, but the atmosphere was just completely different than it is here."

Her grandmother thought for a moments and then replied, "I've never lived anywhere but here in Van Buren County, but I do think there is something about this area that just breeds good people."

Trish laughed, "I completely agree with you, Nana. Now, since I've cleaned my plate, don't you think we'd better cut into that apple pie sitting on that counter not two feet from my nose?"

Nana Sue laughed, too, "Well it might take you a few more steps to reach the ice cream in the freezer, but that is the advantage of small quarters!"

Chapter Twenty-one

The Old Bentley Schoolhouse

It was 3:45 p.m. on a Thursday afternoon in early September and the Old Bentley Schoolhouse, was buzzing with activity. The hum of the sewing machines was drowned out by the voices of the old coots who were arguing over the drawings they had spread out before them. Even a simple three act melodrama required half a dozen different scene changes complete with revolving backgrounds that covered all scenes from indoors to outdoors. The actors were going over the blocking with Mr. Knight while Mrs. Hogan furiously scribbled notes to help Mr. Knight remember where he was placing everyone for each scene. Andrea Hogan had been a little surprised to find that she would be expected to be the assistant director for the Fall Play, but she chalked it up to "Other duties as Assigned" and dove into the production with relish. She had acted a little in her church productions, but had never directed so was eager for the new knowledge this assignment would give her. Fortunately Mr. Knight's rehearsals were always complete by 5:30 pm so her day wasn't any longer than it had ever been when she worked at the State Capitol. Back then she had had a twenty minute commute home. Thanks to the destruction of the auditorium, her commute was about sixty seconds from stage to her door.

On the kitchen side of the old gymnasium/cafeteria Sue Olmstead and Joan Rust were whipping up some oatmeal chocolate chip cookies to go with the milk that was already sitting in ice on the counter. As they pulled the first industrial sized tray out of the oven the smell of hot yummy cookies was overwhelming and Mr. Knight had to call a five minute cookie break, which he called while he was getting a good long head start to the front of the line.

All in all the old school was humming. Andrea looked around at all of the activity and felt something that had been missing from her work life for a good long time, contentment, no actual happiness. She loved what she was doing and someone was actually paying her AND giving her health care benefits. Life was good.

Chapter Twenty-two

Andrea Hogan

Andrea and Trish checked to be sure they had everything they needed for their shopping expedition to Fareway's in Marshtown. They had their grocery list, coupons and cans to return for redemption. Cloth grocery bags...nope! "I'll run into my apartment and get some," Trish offered. Andrea smiled remembering that if Will forgot his reusable shopping bags, he punished himself by not using any plastic bags from the grocery store. More than once he and Andrea had juggled too many groceries too far of a distance.

Just as Trish arrived on the scene with the bags, Rich and Scott arrived on their way to Marshtown as well. "Hey ladies," Rich greeted them. "What's on your agenda today?" Trish was quick to tell of their adventure, "We're on the way to Marshtown to buy the ingredients for lasagna."

Rich's eyes lit up as he asked in wonderment, "You mean, you still make Birthday Lasagna? I thought that delicious concoction would have been outlawed by the food police long ago!"

Andrea laughed and explained to her two bewildered friends, "My lasagna is kind of famous, people used to ask for it as birthday presents, well, Valentine's Day, Memorial Day and Chanukah presents too."

Scott was quick to pick up on the possibility of a free meal and asked, "So when shall we be at your place?"

Andrea was equally quick to respond, "7:00 sharp, and you guys are responsible for the wine." They all left the big comfortable building laughing and headed for their vehicles for some serious shopping.

Trish asked as they got into Andrea's Rav, "since we invited the guys for supper tonight, don't you think we should try and squeeze Oscar and Verna Lee in as well?'

Andrea explained, "I already invited them for tonight, but Verna Lee explained that this is their Square Dancing night and if they didn't show up, there would be an odd couple!"

Ten hours later the four old/new friends were finishing up the third bottle of wine after stuffing themselves with lasagna, salad, garlic bread, and to top it all off: homemade cannoli's. When the sweets had been devoured, they moved to the comfort of the Library/Principal's office to finish their wine and evaluate their first month of living, and working, at the Bentley School House Apartments.

Scott looked particularly happy as he stretched out his long legs onto the coffee table that flanked the two leather couches he had purchased for this room "Well, folks," he began, "do you like living here?"

Trish was the first to answer with an enthusiastic "Yes!"

Andrea went on to speak for the entire group when she explained, "Scott, you have created a wonderful space for living, working, and playing here. I can't believe how comfortable my apartment is. The windows let in so much light—and I love how they open wide to let in the evening breezes. We're just up high enough that we don't have to worry about prying eyes and with all the trees surrounding the building; I haven't really used the air conditioning much at all. Not to mention the wonderful hardwood floors and my efficient kitchen. I came from a 2000 square foot house, but I still have plenty of room here."

Rich was the next to weigh in on his new digs. "Compared to our flat in Mons, I feel like I'm living in a palace! Those Europeans are willing to put up with the tiniest spaces just to be near the center of town. We had amazing views but a bathroom the size of a broom closet."

Scott seemed pleased with their answers. "I can't believe how quickly this place is turning into the community center I had hoped it would become."

Andrea interrupted him to let him know of one more activity that he may not have heard about. "Did you know that Verna Lee has organized a bridge group that's going to meet every Sunday night? Rich and I will be playing with them for the first time Sunday night. It's a real cut throat group, a whole dollar to play. The winner will make enough to go out to lunch—if it's Dutch treat."

Scott raised his glass of Merlot. "To the Bentley School House Apartments…long may they provide us with a home."

The entire group agreed, "Here. Here."

Chapter Twenty-three

Verna Lee and Oscar Swenson

Verna Lee swore under her breath, well what she called swearing anyway. "Fiddle sticks!" she exclaimed. "These button holes will be the death of me yet." She and her friend Sue Olmstead were busy with the turn of the century creations that would clothe the actors and actresses in the upcoming production of *She Was Only A Ferry Man's Daughter, But She Nearly Sank His Heart,* the melodrama that would be presented in just two short weeks. Sue reached for Verna Lee's garment and handed her a pair of knickers she was hemming. "Let's switch. After these knickers are hemmed, they need a new zipper, and I know you will do that better than I will." Verna Lee smiled. It was good to have friends who knew you so well.

Soon the young people would fill the old gymnasium with their wonderful youthful enthusiasm. The play was beginning to come together. Rehearsals were held every week day except Friday, and there would soon be Saturday and Sunday rehearsals thrown in for good measure. She marveled at how quickly the young people learned their lines. This was a particularly fun play, complete with villains and big signs that told the audience when to "Boo" the bad guys.

Oscar's crew was equally busy at the other end of the old gym. They had designed and constructed six different sets that rotated on wheels that Oscar had found in a box that he had moved from the farm. He was particularly tickled that the wheels had been used. He had bought them for $1 at a farm sale and just knew they would come in handy one day. He had been right. He'd have to remember to tell Verna Lee. But first he'd better get busy with a paint brush so that the parlor scene would look different than the railroad station. He looked around to see 86 year old Don Buss high up on a ladder painting leaves on a tree. "Hey, Don," he offered, "how about if I paint the leaves and you tackle the grass and rocks?" His old friend seemed happy to make the switch.

Oscar was still amazed at how much activity was happening at the old school house, even without the play being staged there. The Community Meal had quickly grown from once a week to five days a week. The ladies cooked, and the men cleaned. After lunch there would be cards and quilting and scene building and sewing. No hands were idle, and the old friends enjoyed the late summer days together. They would often move their work out underneath the big oak trees that lined the front yard of the venerable old building. When the young people arrived for play practice at about 3:00, there were cookies and milk and peanut butter and jelly sandwiches to nourish and refresh them. Oscar noticed that the fellows often found their way to the lunch counter for a late afternoon snack. When the clock started to crawl toward 5:00, the ladies packed their materials away, and the old men put away the saws and tools. Soon they would head home to simple suppers with wives or pet dogs, and sometimes both.

Chapter Twenty-four

Richard Knight

Rich smiled as the young people in front of him began to really get into their characters. The villain had perfected his snarly laugh, and the heroine had her fainting gesture down pat. He loved it when a play started to come together. These melodramas had proven popular with the audiences in Europe, and he hoped the fun and silliness would be enjoyed by his home town folks as well. Just then one of the students brought by one of the audience reaction cards for his approval. A giant "BOO" was drawn in calligraphy ready for a pretty young maid to encourage participation in the play. Along with the free popcorn that would be provided for the audience to throw at the villain, it would make for a fun and rowdy evening.

Rich noticed Andi across the gymnasium in some deep discussion with one of the volunteer seamstresses. She seemed to be emphasizing that the necklines in the turn of the century outfits would need to be high-collared. She was right, of course—no scoop necklines back then. He was glad to have her help. He was glad to have her back in his life. Well, not really back in his life, perhaps around his life was a more appropriate term. He admired the way she had with people. Always seeking compromise, always with a smile on her face, she knew how to live life well.

He tried to remember how he had let her slip from his life. Their time together had been so brief, and his life at graduate school had been so difficult. Hadn't they planned to have her visit during spring break? What had become of their feelings for each other? Had they really tried to keep those feelings alive? He simply could not remember.

But here she was again. He wondered if she had ever thought of him over the past thirty some years. He'd have to ask her sometime. For now, the male lead just zigged when he should have zagged and stepped on the female lead's toes. There was much chaos to straighten out. But then when wasn't there in his life?

"Let's take that from the top of page seven," he shouted to his young charges. "And, John, turn left instead of right when you come in through that imaginary door."

Chapter Twenty-five

Andrea Hogan

Andrea smiled as she heard Richard, no Rich, she had to remember that, instruct young John Hanson to turn right instead of left. John had a hard time with left and right to begin with, and he was just now learning the helpful trick she had taught him, your left hand makes an "L" when the thumb and first finger are raised. That little trick had helped her many a time.

She saw that the ladies were packing up their sewing machines and putting on sweaters to ward off the nip in the air that had just recently descended upon them. Autumn was her favorite time of the year, and this first year in her new home town was not disappointing her. The trees had begun to ripen into the colors she loved best, burnt orange, creamy yellow and there was even a touch of crimson here and there.

She saw that rehearsal was beginning to wind down, and she glanced at her watch to see that it was almost 6:00 p.m. later than Richard, Rich, usually ran the rehearsals. He liked to have everything finished up and the kids heading for the Activity Bus just a little after 5:30 each evening. He figured two and a half hours was plenty of time to take away from chores, jobs, and studying. Besides, he said it got him home at a decent hour, even more so when his commute was up two flights of stairs instead of 45 minutes on a commuter train to the city center of Mons, Belgium.

She gathered her papers that she had been grading between costume fittings and headed toward the door just as Rich said good-bye to the last young person. He saw her walking in his direction and offered a kind smile and some nice words of encouragement.

"Andi," he began, "I can't thank you enough for all the work you've put into the costumes and the props. It's really starting to come together don't you think?"

"I thought the same thing today as I was listening to the rehearsal," she agreed.

"Now if we can just get young John Hansen to remember his right from his left, we'll be in business."

Rich laughed and clicked his fingers, "You taught him the left hand making an "L" trick didn't you? You taught me that thirty five years ago, and I can't tell you how many times I've passed it on to kids and adults alike. Funny, I hadn't remembered that you were the one that taught me that until just now."

"I resemble that remark," she admitted.

Rich laughed again. "So you're the one who taught me that, too! I even have a framed "Zits" cartoon with that line. I couldn't remember how I ever started saying it, but now I remember, it's your line, and you learned it from some guy you went to high school with, Chuck Taylor, right?"

Andrea was impressed. "How did you remember that? I can barely remember the name of my high school, let alone some guy who taught me to say, 'I resemble that remark', and by the way, I have that same cartoon framed."

They laughed together as they headed up the steps to their respective apartments. As Rich turned to head up the steps to his third floor abode, Andrea had a sudden thought, "Hey Richard, would you like to share left over lasagna with me? There's plenty for two."

"Why, don't mind if I do Ms. Andi. Let me drop off my stuff, and I'll be right down. What a treat, Birthday Lasagna leftover, even better than the first time!"

She noticed that she had called him Richard and he had called her Andi.

Thirty minutes later he had been persuaded to finish off the last dab of Birthday Lasagna, and she ran water in the old stoneware baking dish to give it a chance to soak before she tackled the dishes. They were still sitting at the table when she heard footsteps cross the hallway and then a quick knock on her door. She called out "Come in!" glad that she didn't have to lock her door every moment of the day and night here in Bentley, Iowa.

Moments later Trish popped into the room and stopped dead in her tracks when she saw Rich Knight sitting at Andrea's kitchen table. "Oh, hey, I'm sorry, I didn't know you had company," she stammered as she backed toward the door.

Andrea smiled and told her, "I persuaded Richard to finish off the Birthday Lasagna so you and I would not be tempted to pick at it for the rest of the week! I was just going to offer him some 'light ice cream' for dessert. Want to join us?"

"Well, maybe a small bowl. I actually ate Birthday Lasagna for supper, too, since you sent a dish home with me Saturday night."

"So, how about it Richard, can you be tempted?" she asked as she smiled at her old friend.

His reply of "I resemble that remark" was lost on Trish but made Andi honor him with one of her biggest smiles.

Chapter Twenty-six

Trish Wilkins

Trish scanned the faces at the BGM High School weekly staff meeting. Of the forty some people who sat in the Library and listened as Craig Seeley explained why the computer system had failed to record attendance for the past three days, she suddenly realized that she was not only the youngest teacher there, but she was the youngest by at least a decade! Probably the next in age to her was her landlord Scott Samuels. Even he seemed old. "Let's see," she thought, "he said he graduated from here in 1995...using my amazing math skills I calculate him to be approximately...32 years old. Yikes!" What had she gotten herself into? These people were all very nice. They had bent over backwards to make her feel welcome and part of the team...but she couldn't help but think that this team was more into Metamucil than Gatorade.

She smiled as her eyes met those of her dear friend Andrea Hogan. Andrea was like a second mom to her. They ate supper together several nights a week and always managed to find time to chat about their days— often while enjoying a glass of wine or a bottle of beer in the "Principal's Office" as they had taken to calling the space that Scott had created in the corner of the old school building. She absolutely loved her apartment with the huge windows and the beautiful hard wood floors. She even liked her tiny shower with the huge shower head. What she did not love was the fact that she had not been on a date since she arrived here. What she did not love was the fact that she had not been salsa dancing in months. What she did not love was that she needed a haircut and she had not found a decent stylist within fifty miles. She was stolen away from her inner thoughts by the slight vibration from her blackberry that told her she had a text message. She smiled when she glanced down at her phone to see that the text was from Will Hogan. Ever since he had returned to Austin they had kept in touch via text messaging and a few late night phone calls. He was such a nice guy. He was very handsome. He was very far away. She nonchalantly moved her phone from the table to her leg and looked down to see what Will had sent. She had to stifle a laugh as she read. "R U stuk w the old fts?" She was so good at texting that no one even noticed as she replied. "Ys—wh R U?" His reply let her know he was having a lot more fun than she was because according to his text message he was,"@lk, hving a cld 1" She let him know she was jealous when she texted back: " Drk 1 4 me!" She jerked back to attention as she heard Principal Seeley call out her name on a fairly long list of people who were clearly expected to do something, she just wasn't sure what. She found out quickly though when he asked if any of them would not be able to work the football game this Friday night. No hands were raised. Why not work the football game? It was the height of the social season in this small town. She looked over at Andrea and smiled. It may be a little dull here…but you couldn't beat the people who helped make it dull.

Chapter Twenty-seven

Scott Samuels

Scott looked across the library and caught Trish sending a text. No one else seemed to notice since her fingers barely moved and she kept her eyes on Craig Seeley most of the time. She sure was pretty. He compared her to the other female teachers in the room and realized that she was at least ten years younger than any of them. So that made her about ten years younger than him, he surmised. Was that too much of an age difference? He heard Craig dismiss the meeting, and he found himself walking out the door with Rich.

Rich looked at him curiously, "What's on your mind coach? Your forehead looks like a dirt road I once traveled in Costa Rica?."

"I guess I was pretty deep in thought. Unusual for me, I know. I was just wondering if I should ask Trish out when football season ends. I've got a few weeks before basketball practice begins, and it would be nice to have some female companionship for a change, not that I haven't enjoyed our racket ball games! What do you think?"

Rich laughed. "Man, I am so not the right person to ask! After the way my wife dissected my heart, I have completely sworn off all thoughts of women for the foreseeable future!"

"Really?" Scott asked. "I thought you and Andrea would make a nice couple."

"Been there, done that," Rich quipped.

"Huh?" Scott responded

"Oh, I forgot you weren't around the day we all moved into the apartments."

Rich replied. "Andi and I knew each other in college. Well, actually we sort of lived together for a year."

"How do you 'sort of' live together?" Scott asked.

"It's a really long story, but suffice it to say, we started out as platonic roommates thrown together by two roommates who abandoned us and ended up as something quite different," Rich hedged.

"Wow, that's weird," Scott responded. "But I still think you and Andrea would make a nice couple."

"If I ever find my heart again, I'll take your advice under advisement. So, are you going to ask Trish out?" Rich asked.

"Nah, I don't think so," Scott replied, "I think I'll just call Diane who teaches over at Keo High and see if she's still single. She's my age and is probably a better choice for dating material. Besides, I guess it could get pretty awkward since I'm Trish's landlord and all."

"That's probably a wise decision," Rich advised as they reached their respective vehicles.

"You, on the other hand, should ask Andrea out." Scott laughed.

"Well, maybe, but I can't think about anything except the melodrama right now, and you have a football championship to win, so no women for either of us for now!"

"You're right about that!" Scott shouted and jumped into his truck.

Chapter Twenty-eight

Verna Lee and Oscar

Verna Lee surveyed the chaos around her and smiled. She marveled at what a different life she was living than just a few short months ago. When they had lived on the farm, her life had revolved around her home and farm and her husband's needs; now she rarely set foot in her new home from early morning until time to prepare a quick supper for herself and Oscar. She also knew she hadn't been as happy since the kids had flown the coop. She had always believed in the Shaker motto: "Heart to God, Hands to Work." Idleness did not become her. She certainly did not suffer from any idle moments these days.

The once a week lunches she and the ladies cooked for the men had quickly grown to five days a week. It really had not proven to be too difficult though. There were five teams of three ladies each. They planned their menus on Friday mornings and then headed to Marshtown for shopping after lunch. If they felt guilty about the $5 per meal they were charging the men, it was quickly extinguished when they thought about how lucky the men were to have such good companionship and great food besides. Many of these men had been fending for themselves by opening cans of soup and eating deep fried anything at the tavern.

A large portion of the cafeteria had been transformed into workspace for the construction and painting of backdrops for the melodrama. The sewing machines that had occupied one corner of the cafeteria had been packed up and returned to sewing rooms or closets in the ladies' home. The costumes for the melodrama had been completed and hung neatly on a rack provided by Gladys Millen. Each day as the ladies sewed and fussed over the young people, they could hear the dialogue becoming surer and fewer mistakes made as the actors moved around the stage. By the time the costumes were completed all of the ladies knew most of the lines in the play almost as well as the actors.

Verna Lee realized that she would certainly miss this entire hubbub when the melodrama was finished. She wondered to herself, "Why can't we form a Community Theater group?" Between the small towns in the county, she was sure there would be enough interested actors. Didn't Carl Wells once say that he had directed some community theater productions when he had lived in Texas? She would have to talk to him about that. She reminded herself to mention it to him at the Sunday afternoon bridge tournament that had also become a staple of the community. Now she'd heard talk of a duplicate bridge group meeting on Friday afternoons. This was becoming a busy place indeed.

She saw her sweetheart across the room, carefully painting an interior scene for the melodrama. Next to him, painting just as carefully, was his grandson Benjamin. Two generations of Swenson's working together, enough to warm any grandmother's heart. Oscar was every bit as busy as she was these days. Thank goodness Scott had insisted that he take over the large janitor's workroom just off the cafeteria. It was now his very well-organized workshop that had been the hub of activity since they had moved in two months ago. Scott had even insisted that Oscar keep track of any little repairs or improvements that he made around the building and before this month's rent had been due, they found a note in their mailbox reducing it by $50. It had been a nice surprise for any couple on a fixed income. Oscar had grouched a bit about the amount claiming that the four hours he had spent on fixing the leak in Trish's apartment and installing the garbage disposal that Andrea had purchased was not worth $12 an hour, but Verna Lee had told him to hush, and to just tell Scott he had worked fewer hours than he actually had the next time. That solution seemed to make Oscar happy.

She looked at her watch and realized that she had better carve out some time today to keep reading, *Water for Elephants* which was the first book in the newly inaugurated **Bentley Reading Bee Book Discussion Group**. She wasn't sure why it was named *Water for Elephants* since so far it was about an old guy in a nursing home, but, oh well, she figured it would make sense eventually.

As she moved toward the door to the cafeteria, she chuckled to herself. This was indeed quite the life she and Oscar were living, and she wouldn't change a minute of it.

Chapter Twenty-nine

Richard Knight

John Hanson had finally learned his left foot from his right, and all of the students knew their lines and their characters. All in all he was very pleased with his first production in his old elementary school. Rich looked around the big old cafeteria/gymnasium and had to smile. He had stood on that very stage and won the 6th grade spelling bee. He also remembered that he had gone out in the third round of the county wide spelling bee, so much for a trip to Washington D.C. for the nationals. They weren't even telecast back then. Now it was time for this group of young people to shine on this old school house stage. This melodrama was such a hoot. It had been written by his friend Darrin Crow and performed at Ushers Ferry Historic Village back in the 90's, and he had looked for a chance to stage the production ever since. He laughed whenever he thought of the long and meaningful title: *She Was Only A Ferry Man's Daughter, But She Nearly Sunk His Heart.*

There would be plenty of villainous activity along with damsels in distress and more than one romance to whet the appetite of the audience.

He had to remember to put the popcorn machine in the Blazer and to arrange with Craig for a custodian to be assigned to clean up the old gymnasium every night after the performance. He certainly didn't want any extra work for Scott, or more likely Oscar and Verna Lee who would clean up any mess they found before Scott even woke up. No, there would be no mess for anyone to clean up. He was so grateful for the use of the space; he would be sure it was spotless even if he had to clean it himself. Which, if he didn't remember to talk to Craig would be exactly what he would be doing; he'd better do it right now!

Chapter Thirty

Andrea Hogan

Andrea felt like she was being pulled in seventeen directions at once. Her small apartment which had been commandeered for the girls to change into their costumes and put on makeup was overflowing with teenagers and senior citizens trying to help those teenagers transform into turn of the century maidens. It didn't help that parents kept stopping by to check on things. Trish leaned over to Andrea and whispered, "I don't think they're checking up on the kids as much as they're checking out your apartment to see what Scott has created out of this old building."

Andrea nodded her agreement, "Hey, if they can see anything under all these costumes and bottles of makeup, let them snoop!"

The hairspray was wafting through the small space, and everyone seemed to need something from Andrea at the same time. When Jenean Griffin, the heroine, appeared before her with tears in her eyes, she knew she was in trouble. "Mrs. Hogan," Jenean wailed, "I can't find my brooch for my costume. It was here last night at dress rehearsal, and now it's gone!"

Andrea though quickly, "Trish, would you please go into my bedroom and look on top of my dresser for a jewelry box. Inside you will find the ugliest brooch you have ever seen. Bring it here and pin it on Jenean."

"How will I know I have the right one?" Trish asked in a panic.

"Don't worry. You can't miss it. Besides, I only own one brooch." Andrea reassured her.

She was back in less than thirty seconds; it was after all a very small apartment. "You were right, it is the ugliest brooch I've ever seen, but it will work great for this play." Trish pinned the brooch onto a very much relieved heroine, and Jenean went on to have her long black hair braided in the style of the turn of the century.

Andrea and Trish looked at each other and smiled. "Crisis averted," they both said at once, and laughed.

Chapter Thirty-one

Richard Knight

The old school house literally buzzed. The girls were dressing in Andi's apartment, and the boys were trekking two flights up to his bachelor accommodations.

He already knew it was a sell out as they had sold every ticket available and had even added a performance on Sunday afternoon, that was already three quarters full. He smiled when he remembered how his students at SHAPE in Mons had been thrilled to get all of their family and a few teachers and students to attend their performances. What a difference it made living back in a small town. The school play was a highlight of the social season in the BGM district, and he knew they would play to appreciative audiences all weekend.

He checked his watch and discovered that it was high time to round up the cast and get them ready to launch his first production at BGM High School. Soon the audience would be booing and hissing with delight as they got into the action of *She Was Only a Ferryman's Daughter, But She Almost Sunk His Heart*.

With all of the actors in place, Rich stepped on to the little stage at the old Bentley School House and addressed the audience which had spilled out from the folding chairs so that the youngsters were parked on the floor in front of the first row. He noticed they had saved plenty of popcorn for peppering the villains as had been suggested in the program. This was going to be a fun night.

He put up his hand to quell the surprisingly brisk applause at just his appearance on stage. "First of all," he began, "let me thank all of you for coming out tonight to support our actors and your school. We all know that this production would not be happening at all if it weren't for the generosity of Scott Samuels who has graciously turned his "rec room" back into the community facility that it had been for many years. In fact, this grand old building has been transformed, not just for tonight's use, but for the community of Bentley and the surrounding area. Thanks to Scott and Oscar and Verna Lee Swenson, this place has become a 'hot bed' of community activities. The sets and costumes for this production were created right here while the actors practiced. Each afternoon we all enjoyed the cookies, sandwiches, and beverages provided by our adopted grandparents, and I think we would all like to acknowledge their hard work and great support by asking them to stand and accept our thanks and appreciation." With those words he motioned for Verna Lee and Oscar to stand and to mounting applause all of the other "helpers" in attendance rose to accept the accolades of the audience and cast members who stuck their heads around the partitions designed to hide them from the crowd to cheer with great abandon.

After the applause died down, Rich continued with his instructions to the audience; "Now folks, I'm not sure if you have ever attended a melodrama before, but I'm here to tell you that it's a little different from attending a regular play. During this evening's performance we will be having one of our fair young damsels walk across the stage with various cards indicating an emotion or a word or two of dialogue that we would like the audience to add. For instance, you may see the card indicating… with this a young lady strode across the stage with a large card that instructed BOO HISS…and if you see this card, you will naturally…" and with those words the audience gave a rip roaring 'BOO HISS'. "Ah, I think you've got the idea! So, with those instructions, I will high tail it off this stage just as soon as I tell you that we have one final treat in store tonight. The author of this play is in the audience tonight, and you will have a chance to meet him after the performance." Appreciative applause broke out before the play had even begun.

"And now, without further adieu, I bring to you the Van Buren County premier of *She Was Only a Ferryman's Daughter, But She Nearly Sank His Heart.*" With that he stepped off stage, and Kristin Turnquist and Emily Bartels stepped on stage to begin the opening dialogue.

The laughs started almost immediately, and the popcorn flew as soon as the villain appeared on stage. The audience cooperated with their BOO's and HISS's, and the evening took on the magical air of people having fun and enjoying each other's company every bit as much as what was occurring on stage.

As he heard his actors utter the final words of dialogue:

Goodman: Aleda, I love you, and I don't care one bit for the dictates of fashion and etiquette. All I know is that if you'll marry me, I'll be the happiest man in the world.

Aleda: Oh yes, yes, Goodman. I love you, too.

Goodman: When I thought I had lost you, my heart nearly sank in despair.

Aleda: But now that you have won the ferryman's daughter, we will float down the river of life together.

Goodman: Come rocks, or rapids, or sandbars.

Both: My one love!

He knew he had a hit on his hands.

The appreciative crowd rose to its feet and kept right on applauding as Rich came back onstage to invite Darrin Crow, the author of the play, to join him on stage to say a few words. Darrin was as pleased with the audience reaction as Rich, and he took the opportunity to thank his old friend for producing his little creation.

As Darrin took his seat again to appreciative applause, Rich once again raised his hand to gain the attention of the audience. "Finally this evening, I would like to thank an old friend and new colleague for all of her work to make this evening a huge success. Would Mrs. Hogan please come on stage and accept our thanks?"

Andrea had been applauding with the rest of the audience so she was surprised to be called on stage, but she scampered up the steps happily to applause meant for her. One of the cast members handed Richard a beautiful bouquet of yellow roses which he in turn handed to her and gave her a small peck on the cheek. As he leaned in close, he whispered in her ear, "I seem to recall that yellow roses are your favorite." Her radiant smile told him he had remembered correctly.

Chapter Thirty-two

The Principals Office

All of the popcorn had been swept up and the folding chairs straightened back into rows, and four new friends were relaxing in front of a gentle fire in The Principal's Office, all with their adult beverage of choice firmly clenched in their weary hands.

"What a night!" Rich exclaimed. "I've had many an opening night in my career, but this one takes the cake. The audience was so warm and friendly, a far cry from European audiences I can tell you that!"

Scott, Andrea, and Trish each added their assessment of the evening, and it turned out to be unanimously positive. Andrea's yellow roses were displayed in a large vase on the fireplace mantel. She smiled as she asked Richard, "How in the world did you remember that yellow roses are my favorite flower?"

"Honestly", he replied, "I have no idea. When I ordered the flowers, the florist asked what color and 'Yellow' came out of my mouth. As I thought more about it, I remembered one time when…" He noticed that Scott and Trish were listening eagerly so he left the sentence unfinished and just said, "I'm glad you liked them. I really could not have pulled this show off without you."

"Well, it's nice to be appreciated," Andrea concluded and quickly changed the topic to plans for the rest of the weekend. "So, we'll have the cast party at John Hansen's house tomorrow night and then strike the set on Sunday afternoon."

Richard was about to agree with the time frame of the weekend when Verna Lee's grandmotherly curls popped into the room quickly followed by her diminutive body. "Hello, you hard working people. I'm glad to see you've got your feet up, you deserve a little rest after this wonderful evening."

Scott was quick to voice what they were all thinking, "Won't you come in and visit awhile? You and Oscar worked every bit as hard as we did!" The others all chorused their agreement.

"No, No, Oscar's already in bed, and I'm not far behind him. I just wanted to talk to all of you about a couple of things, and I figured I would find you here 'dissecting' the evening. Now, I've been meaning to bring this up for weeks and after tonight, I just think it makes even more sense."

The four teachers looked questioningly at her so she continued, "I'm just amazed at the talent those young people displayed tonight, and I figure the apple doesn't fall too far from the tree." The teachers did not look any more enlightened. "What I'm saying," Verna Lee explained, "is that if there's this much talent in the children of our county, surely we can find equal or greater talent in their parents, and grandparents for that matter!" Only slightly less baffled looks greeted her. "We need to start a community theater right here in the old Bentley School Building." The lights began to dawn. And with those lights, the ideas and possibilities began to form as well. Even as tired as they all were, it seemed a tremendous idea.

Rich was the first to respond, "Why, Verna Lee, that's a great idea. I'm surprised there hasn't been a community theater troop here before this, it's high time."

"Now I wouldn't expect it all to fall on your shoulders to organize it Rich, but we would like your advice about how to get a project like that off the ground. The first thing I think we should do is get a hold of Carl Wells, the Bank Manager at Marshtown Savings and Loan—I understand he was an actor and a director when he lived in Arlington, Texas, in the 90's."

"That sounds like the place to start,." Rich agreed.

"Good, I'll drive over there on Monday and see what he has to say and from there we'll form an organizing committee,." Verna Lee assured them.

They all smiled at her as she hesitated in the doorway. "Well, there is one more thing I wanted to talk to all of you about,." she began. "I don't want to seem like I'm assuming that you don't all have perfectly lovely places to go for Thanksgiving, but I also want to be sure that you all know that you are invited to the Community Thanksgiving that we are planning in the cafeteria".

Simultaneously the four teachers felt their mouths begin to water as they thought of roast turkey, mashed potatoes, and green bean casserole.

Verna Lee went on to explain, "We've just all gotten so good at cooking for a crowd that we thought we'd just combine several families' celebrations and invite anyone who isn't invited somewhere else and before you knew it, we were organizing a full-fledged banquet for a hundred or so people."

"Of course, we checked with Scott before we started organizing this extravaganza so I know he and his folks will be joining us, but I want to be sure that the rest of you know that you are invited as well."

Rich was the first to speak, "It sounds like a great idea to me. Mom has already said it would just be the three of us this year as the other kids are going to their in-laws for the holiday."

Andrea was next in accepting the invitation. "I was planning on cooking for Will, Trish and her grandmother—and the thought of pulling a full-fledged dinner out of my miniscule kitchen was a little daunting. But I insist you let me make something to contribute."

Trish was also eager to accept the invitation. "I'm in," she agreed, "I'm going wherever Andrea is going!"

Verna Lee was very pleased, and her broad smile showed it. "Don't worry; we'll tell all of you what to bring, or we'll hit the guys up for a few bucks to help purchase turkeys. This is going to be quite a party!"

She waved good-bye as she headed for her own apartment.

"Well, this is turning out to be quite the hopping place," Scott remarked. "I had hoped it would become kind of a gathering place for the town, but this place is becoming a full-fledged community center—and I couldn't be happier."

With that the four friends finished their drinks and headed off to their respective homes, each realizing that this place had truly become a home and not just a roof over their head.

Chapter Thirty-three

Andrea Hogan

As the autumn leaves around the Old Bentley School House began to fall from their heavenly perches, life fell into a comfortable routine for Andrea. She absolutely loved all of her classes, even though teaching Freshmen English and Composition had seemed overwhelming at first. As she had introduced a lesson plan on book reports, she had gotten the usual groans and complaints, until she told the class that graphic novels would count as well. Will had actually introduced her to this alien form of fiction several years ago. Never much of a reader due to his attention deficit disorder, he could polish off a graphic novel in a matter of hours. The drawings and the simplified dialogue worked wonders to keep his attention, and his collection had grown to impressive numbers before he decided to liquidate when he moved to Texas. She had actually purchased some of his "tamer" novels and had kept them during her two years at UNI and now had established a bit of a library in the back of her classroom.

Not all of the students had chosen a graphic novel to write their book report on, but a goodly share of the boys had gone in that direction. She even offered five extra points for some original art work at the end of the report that related to the story line, whether it was based on a regular book or a graphic novel. A surprising number of the students added some art work, and she quickly made a collage to proudly hang in her classroom. As she was hanging it, she suddenly felt like a real teacher, not just an actor playing one on T.V. She laughed at herself and was surprised to find that she was not alone in her room.

She was startled to hear Richard's kind voice, "If you're laughing at your own jokes, they must be good enough to share."

She turned and returned his smile. "I'm just laughing at myself; I just thought to myself that I finally feel like a real teacher, not just an actor who plays one on T.V."

"Oh, you're a real teacher all right. I can see it in the eyes of your students as they leave your classroom. They always look like they've been fed when they leave here. They're talking, and it's even occasionally about what they've been learning. Remember, I've been doing this for a lot of years. You're a teacher all right. You may even be a great teacher, but I'm saving those thoughts for your evaluation at the end of the year."

Andrea didn't know what to say so chose to say nothing. She gathered her bags and walked out with Richard toward the parking lot. As October moved into November the days grew shorter, and she was grateful for the thought of her warm and cozy home waiting to welcome her. She knew that there was a giant pot of bean soup waiting for her to warm up and serve with some corn bread she would whip up. Trish often ate supper with her, but she had recently started taking a stained glass class at the Community College in Marshtown so she had been eating with her grandmother on Tuesdays and Thursdays and going directly to class from there. On impulse she turned to Richard and asked, "Any interest in sharing bean soup and corn bread tonight?"

"That sounds great," he quickly replied. "I was contemplating having either a Banquet TV Dinner or a Healthy Choice TV Dinner; both can stay in the freezer for another night!"

"OK," she replied. "Supper at 6:30. Be there on time or Wheel of Fortune starts without you."

He was prompt and arrived at her door with a pint of Haagen Das Ice Cream to share for dessert. "I'm bringing dessert, but not enough to satisfy or kill us," he announced as she opened the door when he knocked.

"I'll put it in the freezer for safe keeping. Grab the remote; Vanna's about to start turning letters!" He did as he was instructed, and they settled at her kitchen/dining room table to enjoy hearty bean soup and hot from the oven corn bread. Before she could say it, he beat her to the punch with her standard line, "Taste's good if I do say so myself!"

She punched him on the arm and warned him to keep quiet and eat or Pat Sajak would have to tell him to 'Shush!' They ate while playing Wheel of Fortune and almost always were able to complete the puzzle before the contestants.

At the end of the half hour game show, their bowls were empty, Richard's for the second time, and they had polished off the last of the cornbread. Andrea switched the television to digital music on the oldies channel, divided up the pint of Butter Pecan ice cream between them, and they discussed the students and how different they were from the Europeans that Richard had taught throughout his career. As they finished their dessert, Richard began to gather up the dirty dishes and tossing a dish towel toward Andi, he declared, "I'll wash. You dry."

Andi laughed and decided not to argue with him. She suddenly remembered that he had always washed while she dried during the year that they had lived together in Cedar Falls. She wondered if he was remembering the same thing. Her thoughts were distracted when Richard suddenly began singing "My Girl" along with the Temptations. She had forgotten what a wonderful voice he had, she really should try to get him to join the choir at Trinity. She was thinking about the sparse choir at her new church home when suddenly the dish cloth she was holding disappeared from her hands and she found herself being danced around her miniscule kitchen. She had also forgotten what a good dancer he was. She laughed and followed his lead around the table until the last of the voices faded into the soundtrack of the oldies station. They stopped dancing, and Andi found herself looking up into Richard's eyes. Then he was kissing her.

"Oh my!" her thoughts raced as he lingered, and she found herself kissing him back and enjoying it more than she could have imagined.

Richard pulled back and looked at her with surprise on his rugged face. "Whoa! I'm surprised I did that!"

Andi smiled at him, "Could have pushed me over with a feather."

Richard tried to explain, "It was just so nice to be here, good friend, good meal, Wheel of Fortune, dishes...I'm sorry, Andi, I just don't know if I'm ready to pursue that kiss any further. I'm still so messed up emotionally." He looked like a lost puppy at that moment, and Andi was quick to re-assure him, "Don't think anything about it; it was just the moment, I'm not looking to make you crazy."

"Thanks, Andi, I appreciate that. One of these days I'll be ready to move on, but I know I'm just not there yet. Now, we'd better get these dishes done and both head to our respective lesson plans. I'm teaching *The Metamorphosis*, and I can't wait to try and convince these kids that the main character wakes up one morning as a giant insect."

Andi was quick to agree, "Yes, dishes first, dangling participles and run-on sentences next." She smiled at Richard, patted him on the cheek, and continued to dry dishes steering the conversation to the safe topic of the upcoming Community Theater Formation meeting.

Chapter Thirty-four

Trish Wilkins

Her Blackberry buzzed during 9th grade Algebra class, but she couldn't look at it. She forbid her students from using electronic devices during class so she couldn't very well dig through her purse to find out who was texting her. She figured it was Will; he had called last night and told her he would let her know when he was leaving St. Louis. He had made the trek from Austin to a friend's house in St. Louis yesterday and would complete the trip to Bentley today.

As soon as the bell rang, she made a beeline for her purse and was just a little surprised when her heart skipped a beat when she found that the text message was indeed from Will. She read, 'Lving St. L. B ther B4 dk.' It took her half a tick, but she was easily able to translate, "Leaving St. Louis, Be there before dark." She wondered if she was excited to see him simply because she had not seen any friends her age since August, or if all those texts and phone calls over the last few months had caused a little seed of interest to sprout. She figured she'd find out soon enough. The plan was to have dinner at Andrea's house that night and then head to Marshtown to see if they could scare up any place to dance.

She heard the dull roar of students heading down the hallway for the next class and just as she was about to put her phone back in her purse, it buzzed again, and she read a text hot off the fingers of Will Hogan. She read, 'Ht ic ot St.L. 4 Dr.fld. Crping at 20 Pry 4me'

She quickly translated, 'Hit ice outside of St. Louis, Four Wheel Drive failed, creeping at 20 miles per hour. Pray for me.' She quickly texted back: 'Praying!' And so she did.

When she checked again after class, she found another message that read, 'Tks. Pr wkd, ic nw rn C aftr sch' She was relieved to learn that her prayers had worked, that the ice had turned to rain and that he would be seeing her soon.

She found herself nervously wandering around her apartment after she got home from school, dusting here and there while keeping one eye on the parking lot that stood just below her living room windows. When she heard tires crunch on gravel, she flew to the window and with great relief saw William Roger Hogan step out of his battered old Blazer that had once again gotten him from Texas to Iowa. She backed away quickly from the window, but she thought she saw him glance up to her apartment before he headed to the big double doors that would lead him to his mother's apartment and where she would join them in a little over an hour. Suddenly she could not stop smiling.

She decided to take a shower, as much to pass the time as to wash the day of classroom dust off her body. At exactly 6:00 p.m. she knocked on Andrea's door and was enveloped in a hug by Will as soon as he opened the door. She noticed from her perch about ten inches off the ground that Andrea's face belied a certain curiosity. As far as she knew, her son was hugging someone he had met once on a weekend in mid-August.

The conversation flowed freely as Will, Andrea and Trish all caught each other up with their lives since the grand move in August. Will was full of information about his new radio show on WKMT from Austin, Texas. Both Andrea and Trish had been following the new show on their computers and had spent several Saturday nights ensconced in The Principal's Office with adult beverages and popcorn enjoying Will's eclectic choice of modern and classic folk music. Will Elliott Whitmore had become a fan favorite and since he hailed from nearby Keosauqua, Iowa, a bunch of the BGM teachers had gone to see him live at Pzazz in Burlington. It had been a late night, and Andrea had been happy to let Trish drive them both home on the dark and curvy highways of southeastern Iowa.

Now they laughed as they listened to Will's story of eccentric music lovers in Austin. He had had requests for everything from Zydeco to The Kingston Trio, and thanks to his huge music library he was able to play each request.

They polished off Andrea's delicious Walnut Chicken and cleaned up the dishes in record time with three willing pairs of hands at the ready. As they were relaxing in the tiny living room, Will broke the news to his mother that he and Trish planned to head to Marshtown to see if they could scare up any dancing, and she took the news with her usual calm grace.

"What a good idea," she replied. "Trish has been living an all too quiet life here in the booming metropolis of Bentley, Iowa. Dancing will do her a world of good. Just be careful on the roads, they may be slick as the weather gets colder this evening."

"We should be fine," Will assured her. "My 4-Wheel Drive is working again, and Trish is spending the night with her grandmother so she can drive her back here tomorrow for the big Turkey Day Celebration."

Andrea looked alarmed. "When was your four wheel drive not working?"

Will tried to put her mind at ease, "Its okay, Mom; it's just a little glitch occasionally. Most of the time it works great."

Andrea was not convinced. "Well, I still think we should have it looked at before you leave on Sunday. I've found a really good mechanic in Marshtown, and they can probably squeeze you in on Friday. I'll call first thing Friday."

"If that makes you happy, then that's what we'll do," Will assured her. "For now, Trish and I are going to see if we can find some music to dance to. I hear this young lady's joints are about to become brittle for lack of dancing." He reached out his hand to pull Trish from the couch, and she realized that this was the first time he had ever touched her hand. She hoped it would not be the last.

The weather had indeed grown chillier as the sun had set on this late November day. Still, bundled up and warm with the anticipation of an evening out with this handsome man, Trish relished in Will's courtesy as he opened the passenger door for her and made sure she was safely tucked inside his rugged old Blazer.

They chatted easily as they made their way to the county seat of Van Buren County. Marshtown was close to 8,000 in population so it could boast an ancient K-Mart, Pamida, and even a Mickey D's, out on the highway, of course. It also had its fair share of bars, and that's where Trish and Will headed to try and scare up some music to dance to. Trish noticed that the grocery store parking lots were packed in anticipation of the day of feasting the next day.

Trish had already scoped out the bar scene, from her car, so she could suggest a likely candidate for music and dancing. The place she chose was at the far end of Main Street, and she was hopeful when she saw a number of cars in the parking lot with a neon sign flashing "Liv music" Close enough.

Once again Will jumped out of the Blazer to open her door and provide a hand to steady her descent to the ground. Oh, she liked this boy! As they made their way into the "Corner Place Saloon," they heard the distinct rhythm of country music spilling from the tiny stage at the rear of the saloon. Trish turned to Will, "I know you're a folk music fan, but how do you feel about country music?" Will laughed. "Living in Texas has certainly broadened my musical tolerances, and it just so happens that I tolerate country music quite well."

Trish laughed, "Good, because I get the feeling that this is as good as it's going to get when it comes to "live music"—or even "liv music". They settled themselves at a table near the stage and ordered two Leinenkugels from the young waitress who stopped by quickly to take their order.

The three members of the band, "The Van Buren Ramblers," made up for in enthusiasm what they lacked in talent. The music flowed around them, and they soon found themselves tapping their toes and enjoying the music in spite of themselves. They agreed that the salsa dancing they both knew how to do wouldn't quite fit with the country down beat. Just as they were giving up hope of dancing though, another young couple got on the floor and started to do a pretty credible two step to the beat of the band. Trish and Will looked at each other and, as if rehearsed, said, "I can do that!"

So it was onto the dance floor they went. After a somewhat shaky start, they soon got the hang of the steps and what they lacked in talent, they also made up for in enthusiasm. When the band took a break, Trish and Will found their way back to their table, quickly polished off their Leinies, and ordered two more. Will was quick to explain, "That's my last beer for the night. I tend to be super cautious these days after a friend of mine got arrested for OWI last year. He only tested at .086, but the laws in Iowa and Texas are the same, and anything over .08 takes a gigantic bite out of your life. So, I just don't take any chances." Trish was actually relieved to hear Will be so careful about alcohol. She had always worried that she would find herself in a situation where she wouldn't be sure if her date was sober enough to drive.

The evening slipped by quickly as the pair danced and drank their Diet Cokes. Finally the band announced that this would be their last song as they all had to get up early tomorrow morning, too. They played a cover of Garth's Brooks song, *The Dance*, and Will took Trish in his arms and gently swayed to the music as she rested her head against his broad chest.

Will left the waitress a generous tip since the price of their four beers and multiple cokes did not equal the amount of money they would have spent if they had just been drinking alcohol all evening. She smiled broadly at them as they put on their coats and headed back out into the cold November evening.

Andrea had been right—the roads were a little slick as they headed toward Trish's grandmother's retirement complex. The Blazer had just warmed up as they reached the complex and neither Trish nor Will seemed ready to head back out into the cold. They spoke quietly for a few minutes until Trish conceded that she had probably better head inside. She had her own key to the complex so she would not need to wake up her Nana, but she still didn't want to be too late, just in case she was still awake. This time she knew better than to reach for the door handle as she waited for Will to round the front of the truck before he opened her door. "Step carefully, or we'll both end up on our rear ends!" He held onto her tightly as they walked carefully toward the tiny porch that led to Nana's retirement digs. It seemed very natural for Will's arms to wrap around her as they stood in front of the apartment door. Trish could tell by the flashes of color coming through the curtains that Nana was either still awake and watching TV, or asleep in her chair. She was not eager to slip inside though as she felt warm and content in Will's arms. With little hesitation he drew her even closer to him and pressed his lips to hers. They kissed for a wonderfully long time until they both began to realize that it really was November in Iowa and even though their kisses were warm, their feet were cold. They broke away from each other with broad grins on their faces. "Okay, well, then, guess I'd better go in," Trish felt as flustered as she had ever felt.

Will reluctantly agreed, but gave her one last hug before he turned, walked down the step and promptly fell on his butt. They both began to laugh as he quickly picked himself up from the sidewalk and "skated" to the Blazer. Trish stayed on the porch until Will reached the truck and waved as he carefully pulled the trusty vehicle into the quiet street in front of Trish's grandmother's retirement community.

Trish opened the front door to Nana's apartment with her key and was not surprised to find her grandmother snoring slightly in her favorite chair with a late night TV show host keeping her company as she slumbered. She woke as Trish moved into the apartment and asked with genuine interest, "Did you have a nice time with your young man?"

Trish was still smiling broadly when she declared to her grandmother, "Nana, I have just kissed the man I am going to marry."

Chapter Thirty-five

William Roger Hogan

Will woke to the smell of a turkey roasting, and he realized he was smiling. What was that dream he had just been snatched from? Oh yes, he had been kissing Trish. His smile widened when he remembered that it hadn't been just a dream. He had kissed Trish, and it had been very nice, very nice indeed. He found himself thinking about the entire evening. She was so easy to talk to. She was so pretty. She tasted divine. He could not remember when he had been so smitten with a girl. He had dated so many girls through the years and for one reason or another it had always ended badly. He had found himself a little gun shy in Texas, and he had not dated anyone since he moved down there a year ago. He certainly hadn't planned to date someone who was a friend of his mother! Of course, his mother had always been an excellent judge of character, with the possible exception of his own father, and he really wasn't too surprised that he had been attracted to someone who also liked his mother.

His reveries were interrupted by the clatter of pots and pans on a hard wood floor, and he jumped out of bed and threw on some sweatpants and a T-Shirt to see what in the world was going on in his mother's kitchen.

As he emerged from his mini bedroom, his mom looked up from her perch on the floor in front of an overflowing cupboard. "Oh, Will," she cried, "I'm so sorry I woke you up. I thought I could find my pie pans without the entire cupboard erupting, but as you can clearly see, I was wrong!"

As Will helped his mom to her feet, he assured her that he would have been getting up soon anyway. "I promised Trish I'd help her bake two pumpkin pies first thing this morning so they would cool by the time we eat at 2:00."

"I didn't know Trish was coming back with you last night, I thought she was staying with her grandmother overnight," Andrea queried her son.

"She's just planning on coming back first thing this morning with her grandmother in tow," Will explained.

"Oh, dear," Andrea said worriedly. "The roads are still pretty slick this morning. It's supposed to get warmer pretty quickly, but they aren't advising driving until after 10:00 this morning."

Will turned to head to the bedroom and his ever present cell phone, "I'll call her right now and tell her to stay put—pumpkin pies aren't worth getting into an accident."

He was very relieved when she answered on the first ring, but the words that followed sent waves of fear through his stomach. "Oh, Will, I was just reaching for my phone to call you. Nana and I just went into the ditch. We were going so slowly, but suddenly the car just started spinning, and I couldn't get it back under control, and we just kind of floated into the ditch, but we are totally stuck, the doors..." and the line went dead. Will quickly dialed her number again, but the call went directly to voice mail, and Will knew that meant that Trish's phone had run out of battery.

All through this brief conversation Andrea stood stalk still waiting for news of her dear young friend. Will threw her a quick glance as he raced toward his bedroom to put on warm clothes, "Mom, call 911 while I get changed. She didn't have time to tell me where she was, but I'm betting she's not very far out of Marshtown on County Road V51, it's the only way I know to get from here to there so I'm betting it's the way she knows, too."

Will was only gone for a few minutes, but in that time Andrea had reached the dispatcher at the Sheriff's department, only to find out that the two deputies on duty were tied up with accidents and that it would be hours before a tow truck would be able to get to her, if they knew where she was.

When Will heard this news, he was more determined than ever to find this young woman who had so recently stolen his heart. He grabbed his keys from the hook by the front door and turned to let his mother know what his plan was. "If Trish calls, let her know I am on my way and not to get out of the car unless absolutely necessary. Try to find out for sure where she is and give me a call on my cell phone"

Andrea couldn't help asking, "What about your four wheel drive, are you sure it's working?"

Will paused as he headed out the door. "I tell you what; you're in charge of praying that the four wheel drive kicks in."

Andrea smiled as she headed for the bedroom and some time on her knees asking not only for the four wheel drive to work, but for safe passage for her beloved son and Trish and Nana as well.

Will nearly ended up on the seat of his pants as he hurriedly made his way to the parking lot next to the big old schoolhouse. The sidewalks and his Blazer were covered in a thin sheet of ice that he attacked with the super scraper his mom always insisted he carry. Before he did that though he tried his key in the lock and was so grateful to find that the lock had not frozen; he jumped in and started the motor to give the old girl a chance to warm up completely before he tried to engage the four wheel drive. He did a little praying of his own while he scraped the windows and the rear window. He knew that he would need every bit of visibility that he could muster to make this rescue mission a success. Finally, the windows were clear of ice and as he jumped into the Blazer, he was glad to note that warm air had begun to blow from the heater vents. He said one final prayer, backed up, turned toward the driveway and punched the four wheel drive button. He heard the clunky old gears grind into place and immediately felt the grip on the driveway tighten. The four wheel drive was working, and he knew the old girl would take him anywhere he asked her to go. He affectionately patted the dashboard and told his trusty old vehicle, "Let's go get that girl of mine."

The going was indeed slow, even with four wheel drive. He was the only vehicle on the road as far as he could tell. He drove slowly through the little town of Bentley and turned onto V51 that would lead to Marshtown, some eight miles to the west.

Will wondered to himself how far Trish has gotten on these slippery roads. Not far, he thought, especially if her grandmother's car was one of those "boats" that the elderly seemed to think would keep them safe from all harm.

The miles slowly crept by as he cautiously maneuvered his way on the old blacktop county road. The road was definitely covered in ice, but his four wheel drive gripped the road and kept him chugging along with few problems. As he tried to accelerate though, he felt the back end begin to fish tail, and he quickly backed off the accelerator. He chuckled to himself as his mother's old saying leapt to his mind, "Rather get there late than have them ask, 'Don't she look natural?'" He figured it worked for him, too! He knew, too, that Trish and her grandmother had to be very uncomfortable, wondering what to do and not knowing when help would arrive.

He checked his odometer and noted that he had gone six of the eight miles to Marshtown. He began to doubt his assumption that she would have taken V51, maybe her grandmother had sent her on some short cut that neither of them knew about. Just as he felt the panic rise in his throat, he spotted a giant blue car two hundred feet ahead in the left hand ditch. It sat there perched on the two banks of the ditch as if it were suspended by a giant magnet. He blasted on his horn and began to slowly crawl to a stop. It wouldn't help a thing if he went into the ditch himself. As he slowly approached the vehicle, he needed to decide where the safest place was for him to park. He surveyed the road and decided to just pull off the side of the road opposite the stranded pair and maneuver from there. It was unlikely that anyone would be joining them in the next few minutes. As he stepped from his vehicle and headed toward Trish and Trish's grandmother, the sun suddenly came out from behind a cloud, and he could feel the feeble warmth on his cheek. He found himself addressing the sun as he headed across the highway, "What took you so long?" He just hoped that Trish wasn't thinking the same thing about him.

He could tell that she had been crying, but the look that filled her face at the moment was pure relief. After he safely crossed the road, he carefully began to climb down the bank of the ditch that led to the giant vehicle that held his new love and her beloved Nana. As he approached he could see that Trish was rolling down the window to talk to him. Instead of talking, she burst into tears, mumbling something about being sorry to have gotten into this mess. He quickly hushed her with a quick kiss and told her that he was just glad they were both okay. She assured him that they were. He leaned in and smiled at the little lady next to Trish in the big old car. "Well, Mrs. Stewart, I've been looking forward to meeting you, but I just thought we might find a better time and place." His smile reassured both of the women, and they smiled back at him.

"Now, let's get the two of you out of here!" he declared.

"That may be easier said than done," Trish informed him. "The doors are all stuck shut."

"Well, Nana Stewart," Will asked, "how spry are you feeling? Could you climb out through the window?"

Nana studied the window with interest and decided, "Yes, I wouldn't want to make a habit out of it, but I think I can get out with a little help."

"Trish and I will be right here to navigate," Will assured her.

Trish handed him their purses and a bag of groceries before she pushed the seat all the way back to give her more maneuvering room, and headed out the window into Will's waiting arms. She found her footing on the slippery bank and turned to face Will with a grin on her face. "One door and one to go," she assured him.

Nana Stewart decided that she'd be able to maneuver better without her long black coat on so she wiggled out of that and sent it through the window first. Fortunately, she was wearing black wool slacks and a thick sweater so she would be protected from the cold. She made her way over to the window from the passenger seat. "Well, there's no good way to do this, so here goes." She put her head through the window and with Will and Trish steadying her every move, she managed to slide herself out and right into Will's strong arms. Will set her down gently on the slope and still keeping their arms around her slipped her coat on and buttoned her up. Will stepped in front and made sure that each step was sure. Trish brought up the rear and in a matter of moments they found themselves safely on the blacktop, just a few feet from the safety of Will's trusty Blazer. Will opened the back down and helped Nana into the back seat and got the seat belt around her. He then helped Trish to climb up into the driver's seat and over to the passenger seat. Will made one more trip across the now thawing highway to retrieve the purses and groceries before they all piled into the Blazer ready for the trip back to the safety and comfort of their homes in the schoolhouse.

Before he even turned the truck around, he called his mother to let her know that her prayers had been answered and they were on their way home. He held Trish's hand all the time that he spoke to his mother and was reluctant to let it go when he turned to the task of driving them all safely back home. As he glanced in the rear view mirror to be sure Nana Stewart was still fine, he noticed that bag of groceries sitting next to her.

He turned to Trish and asked, "What's with the groceries?"

She looked at him like he was nuts and replied, "Well, I still have to make my pies for the meal today!"

He smiled broadly and decided that this plucky girl was indeed the one for him.

Chapter Thirty-six

Andrea Hogan

Andrea peeled apples and looked anxiously out of the apartment's windows waiting for Will to return with his precious cargo. The sun was now fully shining around the fluffy clouds that dotted the November landscape. The trees were dripping as if a sudden rain shower had come up, but it was only the ice melting hurriedly as the sun rose higher in the sky. For such a dangerously slippery start to the day, it was going to end up being a beautiful Thanksgiving Day, warm enough for a walk after lunch.

She was more than a little relieved when she saw the old Blazer pull into the parking lot. Will wasn't taking any chances with any lingering ice on the sidewalks as he pulled up to the edge of the walk and jumped out to help Nana Stewart out of his back seat. Before she could blink she saw Trish by his side ready to steady the spry 80+ Nana as she exited the Blazer and headed to the front door. She was glad to see that Nana gratefully accepted the help and arrived safely at the school house door. She lost sight of them at that point, but knew that the small crisis was now past and the day could proceed with only a little delay for an icy rescue.

Will arrived back in her apartment a few minutes later carrying an old pair of tennis shoes that he had dug out of the back of the Blazer. He greeted her with a kiss and let her know that he was going to head for the shower.

Before he could disappear into the bathroom for what she knew would be a long shower, he was her son after all, she couldn't help but ask, "Will, what's up with you and Trish?"

His grin spread over his face, and then his eyes got very serious. "Mom, I think she is terrific. I actually thought that when we went for that long walk last August while you and Rich got reacquainted. These past few months we have been texting, talking and emailing. Our evening last night just solidified my feelings; she's everything I want in a girlfriend. I don't know where this is heading yet, but I've got to tell you, it feels serious."

Andrea was more than a little surprised to hear all this from her darling boy. "Will, wow, that's a lot for your mother to take in!" she confessed. "I know I love Trish like she was my own daughter. I also know you haven't had the most success in your past relationships. I'm not prepared to risk losing Trish's friendship if you get back to Austin and suddenly fall head over heels for some Dallas Cowboy Cheerleader."

Will looked taken aback. "Ouch, Mom," he cried. "Actually, I guess I deserved that remark. I haven't had the best track record with women. In fact I've begun to worry that I might have the same failure to commit issues that Dad has always had, but this past year in Austin I've really spent some time re-examining my heart."

Andrea interrupted him, "Oh, honey, I didn't mean to make you feel bad."

Will was quick to reassure her, "No, Mom, its okay. I really do want you to know that I'm serious about Trish, and I promise I will go slowly with this relationship and try not to break any hearts, especially my own."

Andrea gave her sweet boy a big hug and as she pulled back from him found herself asking, "How is your father? Is he still with what's her name, Bethany?"

Will gave a wry laugh. "No, that was two girlfriends ago. His new lady friend's name is Marilyn. She's very nice, and I really think he's going to marry this one. She doesn't have any kids so she can afford to spoil Dad, which is of course just fine with him."

Andrea shook her head and gave Will a quick hug. "Go. Shower. I'll put your boots by the heat vent and hopefully they will have dried out by the time you need to head out again."

Chapter Thirty-seven

Thanksgiving Dinner
The Bentley Community Center

Even though the dinner wasn't scheduled to start until 2:00, folks began arriving shortly after noon. These were the committee folks. Each three or four person group had a task to perform so that everything would be ready to serve right at 2:00. At that Verna Lee felt sure that the old coots that were used to eating at noon would be a starving pack of wolves by 2:00, but they would survive she knew. Speaking of the old coots, she noticed that they arrived promptly at noon to begin to set up the tables and chairs that would need to serve the 105 people who were scheduled to attend the holiday event. Besides inviting their families, the core group of women also called the weekly newspaper in Marshtown and a nice young reporter had come by to take their picture and written a nice article about the event. The calls had poured in and most everyone who called had wanted to contribute something to the event. The ladies had held a meeting and organized committees that had done their work, and now the big day was upon them.

Verna Lee stepped inside the kitchen area of the cafeteria and quickly checked to see how the three turkeys that she was roasting were doing. The carving committee would arrive any minute now so the meat could be taken off the bones and placed in electric roasters for serving. In addition to these three birds, she knew that there were three more roasting in Andrea's, Scott's and Rich's apartment. Scott had been the most nervous of the bunch in getting the assignment to cook a turkey. He had never had a close relationship with his kitchen, and roasting the Thanksgiving

Turkey seemed a dangerous place to start. Verna Lee had assured him that she would show him just what to do. When she had stopped by his place at 10:00 this morning, the bird was in the oven and browning nicely. Scott would survive his first encounter with a fowl of a different color. She remembered that she had seen a fairly large package in the corner of his living room. Tied up neatly with brown paper and string she thought that it seemed just a bit odd in a bachelor's apartment. What was he doing? Collecting art work? It hardly seemed likely. Her curiosity about the package was overcome by her concern for Scott's bird, and she didn't give it another thought as she checked his temperature gauge and assured him that the bird would be done in plenty of time. She instructed him to bring the pan down to the cafeteria by 12:30 for carving and was off to Rich's apartment in a flurry of tennis shoes and apron strings.

She couldn't help but say a big prayer of thanks for the weather that had turned from icy to wet, and now she noticed as she glanced out of the window at Rich's apartment, the pavement was completely dry in some places. What a disaster it would have been if they had been forced to cancel! There was food coming from every part of the county!

As she entered the cafeteria, she was glad to see that the ladies from Trinity Methodist were busy decorating the tables with golden plastic table clothes, brown napkins and the silverware she had rounded up from the cafeteria kitchen. She also noticed that one table was laden with various china patterns. She had contributed twelve plates and various friends and committee members had come up with the rest. It just seemed too tacky in the extreme to eat a Thanksgiving Dinner off of paper plates. Plastic glasses and decorated paper coffee cups were barely acceptable. The committee had decided to scatter the various patterns throughout the tables to give the setting a more eclectic look. She needed to remember to take a photo from the stage when all of the place settings were arranged.

For now she was convinced that all was running smoothly, and she headed to her apartment to check on the massive green bean casserole that she had volunteered to make. She ran over the menu in her mind. Turkey, of course. The Knights were bringing two huge hams from hogs they had butchered last week. She knew those would be delicious done on Richard Senior's smoker. What else? Let's see, Gladys, Emeline, and Gertie were bringing Party Potatoes. They were using a commercial product that Gertie was able to get for the mashed potatoes and gravy. She thought there were about a dozen green bean casseroles coming and at least that many salads and side dishes. The Home Science Department at the high school had made twelve dozen deviled eggs using her recipe that called for a dash of sugar and a teaspoon of balsamic vinegar for each recipe. Heavens, it must have been a learning experience for the students just to figure out the right proportions for twelve dozen eggs. Anyway, they looked beautiful with the paprika garnish. Then there were the relish trays. Scott's mother and his Aunt Betty had made up fourteen relish trays complete with watermelon pickles, pickled beets, sweet pickles, celery, carrots, and Betty's special dill dip. Each table would have a tray to munch on while they waited their turn to go through the buffet line.

While she was musing about the menu, she noticed that the ladies had completed the placing of the china plates on the tables. What an array of colors and patterns there was to behold. She quickly climbed the steps to the stage so she could get a panoramic photo of the whole cafeteria. It had been magically transformed from a tired old room to a banquet hall filled with fall colors and decorations. Now all they needed were the people. She glanced at her watch and realized that those people would be arriving in less than an hour. She saw the "old coots" assembling in the kitchen to begin the carving process. She felt a slight panic setting in, knowing how much they tended to talk while they worked. She decided to get the ball rolling as she called from the stage, "Ok, boys, enough chit chat. Let's get those birds carved. I'm heading up to Rich's, Andrea's and Scott's to tell them to bring theirs down in fifteen minutes. Start carving please!" They had all been good husbands, and some still were, so they jumped into the task and soon enough turkey legs and breasts were fast filling the five roasters that Verna Lee had placed around the kitchen. Now she just hoped that none of the electrical outlets would blow.

As the meat piled, the guests began to arrive and the serving tables filled with covered dishes. When the men finished their carving, Gertie enlisted some of them to stir the mashed potatoes and still others to stir the gravy. More and more folks flowed through the door and found places to sit among family and friends. At just before 2:00, Scott found himself behind a microphone asking for the group to find their seats. Verna Lee noticed that the mysterious package had been brought from his apartment, and she was more curious than ever to find out what lay behind the brown paper wrapping. As it turned out, she was the first to know the contents of the package.

When Scott had everyone's attention he welcomed everyone to this very special Thanksgiving meal. "Before I ask Reverend Knudson to say our grace, I would like to ask Oscar and Verna Lee Swenson to come to the stage." The two old lovebirds looked at each other in surprise, but headed for the stage nonetheless. When they arrived, Scott continued with his comments. "You know, folks, when I bought this old school house nearly two years ago now, I had a vision of this old cafeteria filled with people laughing and having a good time." Laughter ensued. "So, clearly that vision has been fulfilled." He laughed right along with them. "But more than that," he continued, "I wanted to breathe new life into this old building."

Calls of "You rock!" came from several corners of the room.

"Well, I may have restored this building to a usable home for half a dozen people, but it is these two dear friends who have breathed that life into this building. From practically the moment they arrived, they have organized and sponsored events that have turned this room from a dusty construction storage facility to the gleaming and functional space it is today. Oh, I know they have not acted alone. There are many of you here today who have contributed to the revitalization of this building and this room in particular. I know Rich Knight was eternally grateful when many of you helped him put on the fall play just a few weeks ago. So, to honor the work of all of you, I would like to ask Oscar and Verna Lee to unwrap this package, and then I'll be asking some of you fellas to deal with it tomorrow."

Verna Lee and Oscar looked at each other curiously, but began to quickly unwrap the package. Inside was a beautifully lettered sign that proudly stated: BENTLEY COMMUNITY CENTER. Verna Lee and Oscar's smiles were at least a mile wide. Scott asked Verna Lee to say a few words, and they were few indeed. Her entire speech consisted of, "Oh my goodness, Scott, what a lovely surprise. Now, the potatoes are getting cold, let's eat!"

Scott quickly moved the proceedings along and asked Rev. Knudson to come to the microphone to say grace. Members of the committee dismissed the assembled group table by table, and everyone was devouring the Thanksgiving feast within twenty minutes. The cacophony of voices and children laughing was music enough, but just in case Scott had set up his MP3 player with Christmas music piped through the High School's portable speaker system. Scott stood for a moment more on the stage surveying this wonderful gathering, but then he noticed that his folks had joined the line toward the banquet tables so he scurried to take his place. He hoped there would be a slice of Andrea's apple pie left when he got to the dessert table. The smell of it as he carried it from her apartment had made his mouth water, and he had been hard pressed to place it among the other desserts and not hide it in Oscar's work room! But he had been a good boy and his reward would be a slice when he got through the main banquet tables which were also laden with wonderful delights. Of course, he'd have to try Trish's pumpkin pie as well—he couldn't play favorites! Then there was Gladys Millen's banana cream with real meringue...and, of course, his mother's fudge...and his Aunt Dorothy's cherry cobbler....

Chapter Thirty-eight

Richard Knight

The weather had taken a nasty turn in the days following the Community Thanksgiving Dinner. Rich remembered wistfully the mild weather that he had enjoyed in Malaysia. Of course, it got plenty cold in Belgium and Germany during their years in those European countries. Still, it was the four distinct seasons that Rich loved about Iowa so he figured he'd have to take the good with the bad.

He was just sitting down to an early supper of soup and a couple of crusty rolls that Andrea had shared with him when his cell phone began playing Pachabel's Canon which was the tone he had designated for his folks' land line at the farm. He flipped the phone open and before he could give a greeting, he heard his mother's worried voice asked a very odd question, "Richard, is your father at your place?"

"Mom, what are you talking about? Dad's never comes here without you. Why would he start now?" He could hear the fear in his mother's voice as she explained, "I thought he was just out in the barn futzing around, and now I just noticed that the garage door is open and his truck is gone"

Richard felt a jolt in his heart, but he tried to remain calm as he questioned his mother. "Couldn't he have just decided to run to town and didn't bother telling you?"

"Well, I suppose that is possible, but Richard I've been meaning to talk to you about Dad. He's been having some pretty strange reactions lately. He's been quite irritable and has even accused me of plotting against him," she admitted.

"Mom, that's completely not like Dad; you should have told me what's going on." He couldn't help letting the anger fill his voice.

His mom was crying softly as she admitted that she should have told him about these personality changes. Rich was immediately contrite. "No, Mom, I'm sorry. I should have been paying more attention. I've been pretty wrapped up in my own life and after all that's why..." He caught himself before he admitted that his siblings' concern about their parents was one of the reasons he had moved back home. "Mom, just to be sure I'm going to round up my friends here at the schoolhouse, and we'll check a few of his likely destinations."

His mother's reply was soft and clearly frightened, "Thank you, Richard, I'd appreciate that."

Rich was putting on his boots and grabbing his coat even as he assured his mother that everything would be all right. Fortunately, Scott, Trish, and Andrea were all home and quickly jumped into outer wear as Scott and Rich decided on the best strategy to search. Their movements alerted Verna Lee and Oscar, and they opened their door to see what the commotion was. When they were filled in, Oscar insisted that he and Verna Lee would look around Bentley and suggested that the others pair up as well so that one set of eyes could watch for the truck and one set could watch the road. It was decided that Rich and Andrea would head to Marshtown and Scott and Trish would check out Grimball. If Trish and Scott finished checking out Grimball before they located Rich's dad, they would head to Marshtown to help Rich and Andrea cover the much larger county seat town. Verna Lee grabbed their rarely used but always charged cell phone and her list of her fellow tenants' phone numbers that she blessed the Lord for always keeping handy. She knew the others had each other's numbers programmed into their cell phones, but her handwritten list would work. Her fingers could still dial a telephone for heaven's sake!

Rich gave them one last set of instructions as they went their separate ways, "I don't really know where to tell you to look, but you might start with the hardware stores, I think he's more likely to be there than the beer joints, but I'm not really sure about anything at this point. Just please call me first; whether it's good news—or bad."

Verna Lee and Oscar didn't have far to go to begin their search. They began by driving up and down the two blocks that constituted the Main

Street of their new home town. They drove down the alleys behind each of the mostly abandoned buildings on either side of Main Street. No sign of Richard Senior's Silver Ford Pickup. They traversed every block in Bentley before they decided that Rich's Dad, wherever he was, was not in Bentley. They headed back to their little home in the old school house to wait for news.

Rich's phone rang as they were half way to Marshtown, and he fervently hoped it was his mother saying that his dad had returned home with some bolt he couldn't live without. It was his mother, but her words only added to his worries. His father did not have his wallet with him; she had found it on his bedside table. Richard hated to speak the next sentence, but he felt he had to. "Mom, I'm going to call the Sheriff's Office. Will you call Mrs. Bartels and ask her to come over and sit with you until we find dad, or he shows up at home?" he was quick to add.

"Yes, Richard, I think it's time we make both calls." The resignation in his mother's voice devastated Rich. Rich turned to Andi who was driving so he could be on the lookout, "Andi, I'm really scared." Andrea reached over and squeezed his hand, and Rich did not let go. "I'm praying and driving, Rich, I've done both many times. We'll find him." He reluctantly let go of her hand and reached for his cell phone to call the Sheriff's office.

The dispatcher at the Sheriff's office turned out to be the daughter of his sister's best friend. "Lord, love a small town," he thought. She was quick to assure Rich that she would put out the description of Richard Senior's truck immediately. She also assured him that it wouldn't be just the two Van Buren County deputies looking for the truck. There was a trooper in the county that night and Marshtown had two policemen on duty during the week. Rich thanked her for her help and made sure that she had his cell phone number which she had, of course, since he had called her. "One more reason to bless technology tonight," he thought.

Marshtown had a population of about 8,000 so there were many more streets to cover than either Bentley or Grimball. As Andi approached the outskirts of town she quietly asked Rich where she should head first. Rich sounded as confused and scared as she knew he was but he tried to sound cheerful as he instructed, "Let's try Main Street".

They drove slowly up and down the streets of downtown Marshtown with no luck. Before they tackled any residential streets, Rich instructed

Andrea to head out toward the Pamida on the far end of town. They had just made the turn off Main Street when Rich's cell phone rang. Whoever was at the other end of the line must have reassured Rich that his father had been found and that he was okay because Rich's face lit up in a smile that nearly reached the moon that was glowing overhead. As soon as he hung up the phone, he told Andrea with a laugh, "He's in the parking lot at Pamida. We'd have found him ourselves in the next five minutes." The relief in his voice was palpable.

"What happened?" Andrea couldn't help but ask.

"I'm not really sure," Rich admitted as he dialed his mother's phone number. He explained to both Andrea and his mother as she heard him tell his mother, "Mom, the Marshtown police found Dad, he's fine. We're heading there right now. He was sitting in the parking lot at Pamida." He was obviously answering a question from his mother when he said, "I don't know what he was doing there, Mom. Andi and I are on our way there right now, and I'll bring him straight home."

Rich hung up and turned to Andrea, "What I didn't tell her is that the police officer told me that after he knocked on the glass, Dad rolled down the window and asked where he was."

They spotted the location of his dad and the officer easily as Andrea pulled into the Pamida parking lot. Of course, the Marshtown police officer chose to run the red lights on his squad car. Andrea pulled up beside the officer and put the car in park. Rich opened his door and then turned to Andrea and asked, "Can you call the others to let them know what's up?"

"Of course, I will. They'll be very relieved." She reached for his hand to give it a squeeze. "It's going to be all right," she assured him. He smiled as he squeezed her hand back.

As he approached his dad's silver pickup truck, he saw that despite the cold, the police officer continued to talk to his dad through the window. He suspected it was to keep his father distracted until Rich could arrive and take over the situation, which is what he had to do right now, whether he wanted to or not.

He thanked the police officer for finding his father and asked him to pass on his family's thanks to the other officers who had been looking as well. The officer assured him that he would do that, and they shook hands as the young officer headed toward the red lights of his police car.

Richard took the police officer's place at the side of his dad's truck. "Well, Dad, you gave all of us quite a scare."

His father shook his head sadly and spoke the saddest words Richard had ever heard, "Son, I think you'd better drive me back home. I don't think I can remember the way."

Richard quickly explained to Andrea that he would be spending the night at his folk's house and asked her to call Craig Seeley to tell him to get a sub for his classes the next day. "I'm calling his doctor's office as soon as it opens and insisting that Dad be seen sometime tomorrow."

Andrea touched his hand as she assured him that she would take care of all that he asked her to do. He shook his head as he watched his father who was getting out of the driver's door and slowly walking around to the passenger side of the old truck; "Oh, Andi, I'm so scared," he admitted.

Chapter Thirty-nine

Andrea Hogan

Not long after the frantic search for Richard's father had ended in confusion rather than disaster, Andrea found herself with a giant pot of chili that needed some hungry souls to eat it. She emailed her fellow apartment mates and received a return invitation to move the supper up to Richard's apartment so that everyone could sit around Verna Lee's old kitchen table and enjoy some elbow room. He promised to fetch the chili right after school, warm it up and even make a pan of corn bread to accompany the meal. A supper time of 6:30 was established to give Scott time to get back into town after basketball practice, and as the streetlights twinkled through the trees in Rich's sky high apartment, the four friends gathered together and held hands, while Andrea said a simple grace for the meal they were about to partake.

As Rich ladled chili into everyone's bowls, he asked Andrea the question that he knew the answer to. "I take it Verna Lee and Oscar turned you down when you invited them to join us?" Andrea laughed. It was their running joke. They could not seem to roust out their elderly neighbors if the event threatened to conflict with the sacred Wheel of Fortune tradition. "You're right;" she admitted, "Verna Lee thanked me kindly, but said they were 'eating light' tonight. What a hoot those two are. They go a mile a minute while the sun is up, but their internal clocks seem to run out of steam as the sun goes down."

Speaking of their senior citizen neighbors; reminded Scott that he had not heard much about the aftermath of Richard's Dad's episode from the previous week. He turned to Rich and asked, "What did the doctor have to say about your dad when you took him in last week?"

Rich was quick with his answer, "Boy, did I get a lesson in geriatric medicine last week! I called the doctor's office that next morning. Dad hadn't said much when we got home, and he stayed in bed the next morning way past his usual O' Dark 30 waking time. I finally went out and did chores for him. When I got back in, he was eating breakfast and just seemed very sad and quiet. Not like him at all. Scott knows that he's usually a pretty good talker, so I was really concerned, and I insisted that the doctor's office work us in right away. To her credit, Dr. Lottes' nurse never even questioned my insistence that Dad be seen right away. We were at the Doctor's office by 9:30, and Dr. Lottes was examining him a few minutes later. He was in the examining room a long time and after they took blood and urine samples he called Mom and me back into the examining room.

Dr. Lottes said that he and Dad had talked about the symptoms that Dad had been experiencing and that based on the Functional Assessment Staging Test (FAST), he did feel that Dad was showing some of the early signs of Alzheimer's. He assured us that new medications would help slow down the symptoms, but that Alzheimer's was a very tricky diagnosis, and he couldn't absolutely predict the path of the disease. What was really wild was that he said these current symptoms that had so suddenly appeared weren't even related to the Alzheimer's diagnosis. He predicted that the urine sample that was being tested even as we spoke would show that Dad was suffering from a lower gastrointestinal infection and that after a round or two of strong antibiotics, we would see a return to the more normal Richard Senior.

He said it was equally hard to explain, but that this certain type of infection actually caused mood changes and behaviors that might be mistaken for Alzheimer's. He said the driving to Pamida and not being able to get back home was an Alzheimer's symptom, but the moodiness that mom had reported was most likely due to the infection. He started Dad on a strong antibiotic that day and by the weekend he was a lot more his regular self. He also started him on a new Alzheimer's medication so we are hopeful that between the two treatments, we'll see a much better prognosis for him." Rich took a deep breath and reached for more cornbread, the long story clearly was hard for him to tell.

Richard had stopped by Andrea's classroom soon after he had gotten back from the doctor's office that day, but this was the first that the Scott and Trish had heard the ending to their search of the previous week. They were both taken back. While their parents were much younger than Rich's parents, they both had elderly grandparents. Rich was eager to change the subject so he brought up the subject that he had been thinking about for several weeks. "OK, guys, enough sad stuff, here's something I have wanted to talk to all of you about. Actually, I got this idea from Verna Lee and Oscar and their crowd of gray haired eaters from downstairs.

I think the four of us should plan to eat together Monday through Thursday." He got mostly dear in the headlight looks from his supper companions so he went on to explain, "Look, I know Andrea fixes something decent to eat every night; Scott, you grab fast food on the way home from some practice; Trish, I don't know what you eat...and frankly I usually just open a can of soup and make a peanut butter and jelly sandwich, not very nutritious." He saw nods all around the table. My idea is that we pool our money and each of us would fix dinner one night a week. Scott, you'd have to take Wednesday night since that is the only night you're not at practice until 6:00." Rich could see their minds begin to click.

Trish was quick to agree to the idea. "I'm finished with my stained glass class. I think it would be a great idea. I'm not much of a cook, but I'd like to try some new recipes that I'm always reading in my grandmother's cookbooks."

Scott was next to give his ringing endorsement. "I'm all for the idea. Home cooked meals trump fast food any day! I can cook on Wednesday nights. I know how to cook spaghetti and tuna noodle casserole—I get dibs on those two dishes."

Rich turned to his old friend Andi, remembering briefly all those dinners they had cooked together in the year they had shared their lives in that bright apartment in Cedar Falls, Iowa. "So what's your vote?"

Andrea's answer sealed the deal, "I get dibs on meat loaf!"

Chapter Forty

Richard Knight

The very next Monday night found them once again gathered around Richard's old oak table enjoying their first family meal together. Of course, Oscar and Verna Lee had been invited to join them, but the late hour of their dining prevented the dear old friends from joining them. At least that was their excuse. Richard knew for sure that Oscar had refused to give up his Wheel of Fortune tradition, but he could also concede that 6:30 supper hour was an hour and a half later than when his own folks ate!

Richard had volunteered to make the first meal. He had put a beef roast from his folk's freezer into the crock pot on Monday morning along with carrots, celery, and onions. By 6:00 p.m. the meat was fork tender, and he poured off the rich broth to make delicious gravy that his mother had taught him to make. He smiled as he stirred the water and flour into the broth and thought how through all the years of their marriage, he had been the gravy maker of the house. He felt his heart give a lurch, and he thought once again that when a marriage dies, the memories must die with it. If you happened to mention a pleasant time from your previous life, you'd get the "You can't dwell on the past" lecture from someone. Maybe they were right.

His life right now wasn't that bad. He loved teaching back at BGM. There was continuity from his childhood that felt wonderful. His young face smiled back at him from photos around the school, and he found himself wishing his two children could have grown up with that kind of solid educational background. Not that they hadn't had a wonderful education, he and Sally had taught in some of the finest international schools, but they didn't really have a place to call home. The closest thing to home for them had to be their grandparents' house, and there had been too many summers when commitments and vacation plans had kept Richard from bringing the kids home for part of the summer. He shook his head and concentrated on his gravy. It would be inexcusable to serve lumpy gravy to a wonderful cook like Andi.

Andi, now there was a memory he was happy to dwell on. What an odd and wonderful coincidence to have her back in his life. Or was she? That crazy kiss a few weeks ago still haunted him. Where did she fit? Did she fit? Did she want to fit? She had been on her own for more years than he had been married. Did she want someone in her life? She seemed so together, and his life was still a shattered shell of its former self. To outward appearances he looked like he was adapting to his new life back in his home town, but there were still those sad nights as he climbed into a bed now empty of affection and warmth.

He pulled himself from his reverie as he heard a knock on the door, and Andi and Trish arrived with a gallon of milk and extra ice which he had requested they bring. His gravy was perfect and as they all dished up the meal into serving bowls and platters, Scott rushed through the door, his hair still wet from the shower.

"Wow is this ever better than coming home to a cold burrito from the gas station!" he cried. "We should have been doing this from Day One!" He took his place at the old dining room table and was quickly joined by his other friends.

Rich spoke as they all settled in, "I'm not much for saying 'Grace,' but I think this occasion certainly calls for one—Andi, would you lead us?'

Andi was a little startled, but as she looked around the table she felt her heart leap just a little to be with these good people so she stretched out her hands; at her gesture the others joined with her and bowed their heads. "Our dear Heavenly Father, we thank you tonight for bringing all safely together to this table. Please bless this food that has been provided that we may be nourished and continue to do your work on this earth. Amen." She squeezed Richard's and Trish's hands and hoped they had done the same for Scott. "Let's eat!" she declared.

It wasn't long before the meal was devoured, the dishes rinsed and stacked into the dishwasher. As the four friends were drying their hands and thinking about moving along to their own apartments, Rich announced a surprise. "Hey, I didn't want to have us end up watching TV through dinner, but I did DVR Wheel of Fortune, any takers?"

The friends laughed and headed into Rich's living room area to guess consonants and buy vowels for 23 minutes, Rich was very good at fast forwarding through the commercials. When they had all failed to come up with the final "thing", Serendipity, they all headed to their respective homes in the big old school house that now seemed as friendly as an old school chum. They each smiled as they thought about the Walnut Chicken that Trish planned for Tuesday night's dinner. Scott hoped there would be Fortune Cookies!

Chapter Forty-one

Scott Samuels

Scott arrived back in his apartment a few minutes after 7:30 that Monday night, a smile on his face and his stomach full of wonderful homemade food. It sure beat gas station burritos! Tomorrow night he would need to head out to Marshtown after supper to buy the ingredients for his famous Tuna Casserole. He knew he wouldn't have time to bake brownies as Rich had done, but some Rocky Road Ice Cream would make for a nice dessert. He had to remind himself to double the recipe since he was so used to cooking for just himself.

He decided to jump in the shower before he called Mary, Gladys Millen's granddaughter. As he lathered up, he recalled with pleasure the time they had spent together this past weekend. He had had a great time with her on Friday night, so much so that they had gone to brunch after church on Sunday. She went to the Lutheran Church in Marshtown, and he had certainly surprised Andrea when he showed up for the 9:30 service with Mary. He had found the Lutheran service very nice and peaceful, not all that different than his Methodist upbringing. A few more hymns maybe. There was something called the Kyrie that he especially liked. A lay person had stood up at the altar and sang one part while the congregation sang the next part and so on and so forth. The pastor had preached a good sermon on the Good Samaritan, and they had headed to the Country Kitchen for the "All You Can Eat Sunday Brunch" by 10:45 a.m. That included all of the farmers and little old ladies who insisted on saying, "Hello," to Scott as they left the church. That had caused a momentary odd look from Mary. "Do you know absolutely everyone in this county Mr. Samuels?" she had queried.

Scott had blushed and admitted that he just about did. "You've got to understand," he reminded her. "All of these folks have followed my career since my peewee football days. They're real glad that I saved the Bentley School House from becoming a warehouse for Schearer Heating and Cooling...and I've got half of their grandkids on my athletic teams."

"So, I'm dating a celebrity, am I?" Mary had asked coyly.

"Well, get me ten miles out of Van Buren County, and nobody knows my name, but here in this community, I guess I'd have to admit that I'm just a little well known. But I don't know a soul in Burlington, how about we head down there for dinner next Saturday?" he asked.

"Sounds like a plan," she agreed. "But I'm not making any wagers that you won't run into someone you know there either."

Scott stepped out of the shower, pulled on some sweat pants and an old BGM T-Shirt and settled into his recliner to call Mary. She answered on the first ring, and he quickly checked to be sure she and Gladys had finished supper. She laughed, "Grandma finds it hard to wait until I get home from school at 5:00 p.m. before she has supper on the table. She's firmly convinced that I should apply at BGM next year so I can cut my commute down from thirty to ten minutes!"

Scott smiled himself at the other end of the phone, "I have to admit, that seems like a good idea to me too!"

Mary seemed intent on changing the subject as she asked, "What do you have in mind for our sojourn into a foreign county this Saturday?"

Scott realized that he had sounded just a tad too eager and was glad to move on to another topic as well. "Well, they actually have a cinema with six different screens so I thought we might find a movie that we can agree on, I'd even see a chick flick if you want to."

Mary laughed, "I'm not much of a fan of chick flicks myself, give me a good action/thriller anytime, and I'm a happy girl."

Scott could not believe his luck in finding this Renaissance Lady. "I think *Ironman* is opening this weekend, how does that sound?"

"It sounds like, you buy the tickets, and I'll spring for the popcorn and pop...and Milk Duds, of course."

"That sounds great," Scott agreed. "Ask some of your teacher friends about a good place to eat after the movie, and we'll make a day of it." He decided to go for broke. "Ah, I'm not sure if you would be interested, but we do have a home basketball game this Friday night, and my friends from the apartments that I told you about, they usually go together to cheer us on, and then after the game we congregate back at the Principal's office and have a few beers and discuss the game, good or bad."

Mary was silent for several moments, and Scott feared he had pushed too hard. It was just that he really liked her, and he wanted her to meet the people who had become so close to him in the last few months and... Scott's reverie was interrupted by Mary's astonished question. "Are you telling me that Principal Seeley actually lets you bring beer to his office after the game?"

Scott was equally silent for a few moments as he processed her odd question. Then it hit him, he had called their getaway in the old school house by the name that the apartment dwellers always used: The Principal's Office. He was quick to clear up the confusion. "Oh, no, Mary, this is a different Principal's Office—it's at the apartment house that I restored from the old Bentley Schoolhouse. I guess you'll just have to come for the Fifth Quarter party and see for yourself."

Mary laughed and decided she had better check out this Principal's Office even if she didn't have the foggiest notion what a Fifth Quarter was! "OK, I'm game," she told him. "How will I recognize your friends?"

That made him think, "How about if I call you later in the week and find out what you're going to wear and have them look for you? I know for certain that one of them noticed you at the Thanksgiving Dinner, and I wouldn't be surprised if the rest did as well. I think they'll be able to spot you pretty easily."

"OK, I'll figure out my wardrobe for the weekend and let you know later in the week. I'm looking forward to seeing more of this renovated schoolhouse of yours, my teacher friends were very curious when I told them about it."

"You'll get the royal tour, I promise," Scott assured her.

"I'd better get busy grading spelling tests," Mary admitted.

"And I need to plan my shopping list for the community supper I'm cooking on Wednesday night."

"Scott Samuels, you are an interesting man," Mary acknowledged.

"I hope so, because I think you're a very interesting lady." He rejoined.

They both blushed, though neither could see it.

Chapter Forty-two

The Principal's Office

Mary Millen made her way into the BGM gymnasium through throngs of teenagers and basketball fans. She stood just inside the doorway and looked around the busy corridor and wondered what she was supposed to do now. Before she could devise a plan, she saw a pretty young woman walking toward her, waving enthusiastically. "Ah," she thought, "this must be Trish". She had talked to Scott the night before and told him that she would be wearing a bright orange sweater, the better to find her in the crowd. It was indeed Trish who approached her and extended a hand in welcome and introduction. "Hi, Mary, I'm Trish Wilkins. I'm so glad you could join us tonight. Scott made me promise to be here early so you wouldn't be left wondering what you should do next. We've got seats in the parents' section so it shouldn't be quite as noisy as the student section. This is a big game tonight; both teams are undefeated and tied for first place in the conference."

Mary followed the young lady through the hallway ringed with giggling teenage girls and shuffling groups of boys, each checking out each other, but neither group admitting it. They climbed up through the bleachers until they reached nearly the top where scattered groups of parents, grandparents, teachers, and fans had staked out their territory. Seated together was a couple who looked like they had been married for years. They laughed easily at something the woman said, and the man squeezed the woman's hand just before Trish and Mary approached.

As they approached, the woman spotted them and waved to indicate where seats had been saved for them. Trish made the introductions, "Mary

Millen, these are the folks who occupy two of the other apartments at the Bentley Schoolhouse apartments, Andrea Hogan and Rich Knight."

Mary was momentarily nonplussed as she reached to shake each of their outstretched hands. "I'm sorry, for the look on my face, but I had just been thinking that the two of you looked like you have been married for years." There was a definite pause until Andrea laughed and remarked, "Oh well, that's just because we both have so much gray hair." They all laughed, and the tension was broken as Mary took her seat next to Andrea with Trish next to her.

The game was every bit as exciting as Trish had promised it would be. There was never more than a six point difference in the teams' scores in the entire game. When one team would get up by six, the other team would come storming back to tie and go ahead by two or three points. Finally, BGM got a six point lead in the last thirty seconds, and the opposing team had no choice but to foul and hope that BGM would miss its foul shots. They missed a few, but made enough to win the game by two points. The team was understandably happy with the win but showed good sportsmanship by not rejoicing too much until the losing team had slunk dejectedly to their locker room. As Scott's friends made their way down the bleachers, Scott broke away from the congratulations of fans and families to meet them at the first row and reach for Mary's hand to help her down to the floor. Trish and Andrea both stood there and looked at Scott until he reached for their hands and helped them down as well. "Sorry, ladies," he apologized. The two friends smiled at him in understanding. Tonight Scott only had eyes for Mary Milden.

The group quickly decided that the ladies would all head to Bentley with Mary following behind while Rich would wait for Scott to grab a quick shower. Trish and Andrea had appetizers waiting, and they would be popping some popcorn to go along with the beer and wine that was on ice in Andrea's refrigerator. This Fifth Quarter party had only been going on for three weeks, but they had a good routine down and had been enjoying re-hashing the game and winding down after a busy week in their own classrooms. This was the first time that someone other than the four of them had joined in the festivities. Since they didn't get back to the Schoolhouse until after 9:30 p.m., it had been declared way too late for the Swenson's. When the group had worried that they may get a little loud, they were assured that Verna Lee always slept on her "good ear side" and that once Oscar started snoring, nothing on this earth short of a fire alarm would wake him up.

The group adjusted nicely to the new member of the group. Rich, Mary and Scott sat on the couch and Andrea and Trish sat comfortably in the wing back chairs. There was a roaring fire in the fireplace, good food for snacking, and cold adult beverages to enjoy. Mary was careful to switch to Diet Pepsi after one beer since she would still need to navigate the gravel roads to her Grandmother Gladys' house yet this evening.

As the conversation about the game seemed to be winding down, Scott decided to bring up the topic he had been thinking about for some time. "OK, guys, I've got an idea, and I don't want you to say, 'NO,' immediately."

Trish, Rich, and Andrea all looked at each other with curiosity. "What's up?" Rich asked.

"Well, I've been thinking, so many people have been curious about the renovations here and when we had all those folks here at the melodrama and Thanksgiving, I could tell they were all really curious about what the apartments looked like, and mine was certainly in no shape to share with visitors since it was the height of football season, but now, well, it looks pretty good, and I thought I would throw a Christmas Open House. I was just wondering if the rest of you would like to join in, and we'd have a School House Christmas Open House, maybe start another tradition here!"

Andrea was the first to recover from this massive announcement, "You are talking about this Christmas, right? The very same Christmas that will be occurring in twenty three days?"

"Yea, I know it is very short notice. But really, we can pull it off; a few decorations, some cookies, punch. It will be a cinch," Scott assured the astounded group.

"Scott," Rich prodded, "I don't happen to own any Christmas decorations."

Scott laughed, "You may not own any, but I'm guessing your mother has an attic full of stuff that she doesn't use anymore." Rich had to agree that that was probably exactly the case.

"Well," began Andrea, "I did pack a few decorations, and I could always purchase a small Christmas tree."

"I think my grandmother still has some decorations left as well," Trish enjoined. "But how will we invite people. Do we send invitations to everyone in the county?"

Scott assured them, "I'll take care of the invitations. A call to the Van Buren Times and the promise of a photo of my apartment will get us a story, and I'll take out a small ad to boot."

I've already talked to Verna Lee and Oscar, and Verna Lee loves the idea and Oscar says as long as it's over by the time Wheel of Fortune comes on, he's good to go.

Trish, the numbers person of the group, asked what everyone was wondering "…When is this Open House happening then?"

Scott thought a second, and thinking out loud he said, "OK, Christmas is on a Thursday this year so let's have the Open House on Saturday, December 20th from say 3-6 p.m. How does that sound?"

"Like lots of fun," Andrea acknowledged.

Mary spoke up for the first time, "I have about 2000 sheets of red construction paper that was donated to my classroom, what would you think about if my second graders made lots of paper chains to decorate the large foyer in front of your apartments?"

Scott was quick to accept the help, but posed another question, "Where do you think we should have the refreshments?

That caused Trish to ask, "How many people are you expecting at this shindig?"

Scott thought for a moment, "Oh, I don't think we'll have more than two or three hundred people"

All three women gasped audibly. Andrea was the first to recover her voice. "Scott," she said, "I don't know whether to hug you or hit you, but we'll pull this party off somehow!"

Chapter Forty-three

Andrea Hogan

Andrea called an emergency ladies only meeting early the next morning. She and Trish headed for Verna Lee's kitchen table shortly after 8:00 a.m. knowing that Oscar would be up and out already...and that Verna Lee would have toast and hot coffee to fortify their planning activities. Trish expressed all the ladies' opinions as soon as she had a steaming cup of coffee in front of her, "I can't believe that Scott thinks we can pull off a party for possibly 300 people with just three weeks planning time!"

Verna Lee laughed and gave them her insight, "Well, I've had a few more days to think about all this since Scott sprang it on me last Wednesday night, but he swore me to secrecy since he did not want to spoil the surprise! She went on to tell them her ideas about how they could pull this off with so little time. "As you've probably figured out by now, living in a small town is a lot different than even a medium sized city like Marshtown. A few well-placed phone calls can do a world of good. While all of you were cheering on the basketball team last night, I called Sherrie Hodge, the Home Economics teacher. She agreed to give extra credit to any of the girls, she doesn't have any boys in her class this year, who would want to come here next Saturday morning and bake cookies. I figure we only need to make seventy or eighty dozen, and they don't all have to be decorated."

"Actually, that sounds like a great idea. We can even commandeer Scott's and Richard's kitchens as well as yours, mine, Trish's and the one downstairs," Andrea agreed.

"I've already started clearing out the freezer space downstairs and if we all decide to eat out of the freezer this week, we can probably find space in all of ours as well. Not to mention, the trunk of my big Mercury," she reminded them.

Trish asked the next obvious question, "Won't it get kind of expensive for the ingredients? Should Andrea and I buy flour and sugar when we go to Marshtown today?"

"No, dear," Verna Lee explained, "I've got that figured out as well. As you know, we charge the old coots $5 each for their noon meals that we ladies cook for them. Well, since each and every one of us is a whiz at stretching a dollar, we never spend that much money, not even the day we decided to splurge and serve steak, so we have quite a little kitty built up. I think this would be a great reason to spend some of it!"

"Don't you at least need some help getting the ingredients here?" inquired Andrea.

"That's covered, too. Gertie Stuve's grandson works for Cyclone Foods out of Keokuk. Roger has been stopping here every week and helping me figure out what to order for the meals, and then he just has one of his drivers swing by on Friday with my order. I even have an account set up. I'll let him know what we want to make, and between us we'll figure out the ingredients and have everything here Friday afternoon."

Andrea came up with another idea, "What if we assign a certain cookie to each apartment, and then next Friday night we'll distribute all of the ingredients around and be ready to roll on Saturday."

Verna Lee agreed and added, "Why don't we do the decorated cookies in the cafeteria, and once everyone has finished their assigned cookies, we'll have everyone gather downstairs to frost and pack."

Trish expressed all of their sentiments when she declared, "It's a plan."

Verna Lee had even more surprises in store for this little planning meeting. "I also talked to the quilting group, the Comfort Makers, who have been meeting here on Tuesdays and Thursdays, and they want to have a display of their quilts. These are the quilts that will be sent to Camp Ewalu for their fundraising quilt auction on Valentine's Day. This will give folks a sneak peak and get their pocketbooks limbered up to bid on their favorites at the auction."

"How will those be displayed?" asked Andrea.

"I wondered the same thing myself, but the Comfort Makers tell me that all we have to do is string clothes line along two walls of the cafeteria, and they will hang the quilts using clothes pins, lots of them! Oscar and the guys are already figuring out the best way to accomplish all this."

Trish could not hide her admiration of this well organized new friend of hers. "Verna Lee, I think the President should ask you to run his next campaign for office, you've thought of everything!"

Verna Lee laughed, "I don't want to seem like an overachiever…but I'm not done yet!"

"What more could you possibly have up your sleeve?" Andrea laughingly asked.

"Well, the ladies and I were discussing this on Thursday while we ate lunch. Several of them have craft items, and several of them have friends who have craft items, so we sort of have twelve tables of crafts that will be on display and for sale here in the cafeteria that day."

Trish and Andrea burst out in laughter and couldn't think of a thing to add, except, "I'd say we're going to have quite a party here two weeks from today!"

Chapter Forty-four

The Great Baking Day

The Christmas Open House quickly took on a life of its own. Before the weekend was over, the Drama Club had volunteered to decorate Rich's apartment, and the cheerleaders had taken over complete control of Scott's apartment. The basketball team volunteered to serve refreshments along with the cheerleaders, and the football players who weren't on the basketball team volunteered to park cars.

When Mrs. Hodge put the word out about the extra credit for baking cookies, no fewer than forty girls from freshmen to seniors signed up. Mrs. Hodge went one step further and assigned the girls to the various kitchens and assigned them all to bring measuring cups, spatulas, and hot pads!

Saturday morning dawned bright and cold. Andrea, Verna Lee, and Trish were up before dawn and were busy organizing their respective kitchens and the cafeteria kitchen before the men folk of the apartment had even thought about getting going. And going they were! The three men had conferred at one point in the week and decided that being overrun by forty high school girls was not something they wanted to be involved in. Oscar had been meaning to take a trip over to Keokuk to check out the new sporting goods store at the mall, and Scott and Rich quickly accepted his invitation. They had been told to have lunch in Keokuk and to take in a matinee at the 6plex. They were not to set foot back in the building until at least 4:00 p.m. They intended to give them an extra hour just in case!

By 10:00 a.m. the kitchens were humming. Verna Lee and Gertie were in charge of the big kitchen in the cafeteria, and Trish and Andrea supervised the other five kitchens. Very little supervision was actually needed as everything had been laid out the night before with Mary Milden's help. The basketball team had played an away game, and they had all listened to the game in the various apartments they were working in. While cheering the BGM Bulldogs on to victory, the four women had managed to organize this cookie making operation to within an inch of its life. By 11:00 a.m. the aromas that were emanating from the various ovens in the building were so delightful that it felt as if the building had been wrapped in cookies.

It was just about then that the photographer from the Keosauqua Times arrived for some final photos to include with the story about the Christmas Open House. He told everyone that even if he had not already known where he was going, he could have found his way by following his nose. He took dozens of photos of the girls in various stages of cookie assembly. The decorated cookies were just beginning to pile up on the tables set up in the cafeteria. Before the afternoon was over, they planned to have over one thousand decorated cookies and an equal number of other delicious cookies from Verna Lee's cookbooks.

By 2:00 p.m. the cookies from the apartment kitchens were completed, a crew stayed behind in each to clean up, and the rest of the girls descended on the cafeteria to help decorate sugar cookies shaped like Christmas bells, reindeer, candy canes…whatever cut outs came from the various homes of the girls. The frosting had been tinted green, red, blue, pink, purple, and yellow. Some pretty combinations had been concocted with those basic colors, and the cafeteria was a rainbow of colors and designs. While some girls iced cookies, others packed the hardened cookies into plastic containers which quickly filled all of the freezers in the building. Verna Lee's trunk, as well as Trish's and Andrea's were also pressed into service as refrigerators.

They would all have to make plans to go for a week without a trunk. Verna Lee also gave up her back seat as well. By 4:00 though, the cookie baking marathon was beginning to wind down. The girls did a wonderful job of cleaning up and combining the leftover ingredients. Thanks to Verna Lee's careful planning, everything came out pretty close, and she was relieved that they had not run out of anything. A few extra chocolate chips and coconut would be put to good use feeding the old coots.

By 4:30 all three women were seated in The Principal's Office with their feet up and a glass of ice tea cooling their weary throats. It had been a hectic day with lots of instructions to forty plus eager young bakers. In the end, the cookies were finished and safely tucked away into freezers, or very cold automobile trunks!

Trish asked Verna Lee if she had thought yet about the location of the refreshments at next week's gala event. She should have known better, of course, she should have known that Verna Lee would have all of the details worked out to a tee. "Why, yes, dear, I have given it some thought," she modestly admitted. She went on to detail a plan that could have won the War for the South if she had been a General in the Confederacy. While Andrea and Trish weren't quite clear on the details, they did know that it involved massive amounts of powdered hot chocolate mix, basketball players, borrowed coffee pots and cookie platters from every church in the county. There would be refreshments at the Open House. No doubt about it!

The ladies talked and planned and commiserated for the next forty five minutes until they heard the front door of the big old school house swing open and felt the chilly entrance of the men folk at the apartment building before they actually saw them. One look at the three tuckered out women resting their sore feet on the coffee table in the middle of the room, and it didn't take long for the men to realize that if they wanted to eat any dinner tonight they would be the ones responsible for it. Scott felt a moment of remorse when he realized how hard the women must have worked today to prepare the cookies for HIS Christmas Open House. He was quick with an idea though, "Bundle up everybody. We're all heading to Marshtown for Chinese Food, my treat." Oscar started to protest that Chinese food was not his favorite and that he would miss Wheel of Fortune, but Verna Lee threw him a "do not say another word" look, and he was quick to change his tune, "I'll warm up the car, who wants to ride with us?"

His bride of over fifty years started to laugh, and the other two women in the room joined in with chuckles. "Sorry, Oscar," Andrea explained. "Your back seat is off limits until next week, we turned it into a storage facility for Christmas cookies."

"Something tells me, she isn't going to trust me when I try to take her car into town for nuts and bolts next week!" Oscar rejoined. Now everyone laughed as they departed The Principal's Office to bundle up for the trip to Marshtown and a Saturday night supper that none among them had to cook.

Chapter Forty-five

The Great Christmas Open House

There was no sleeping in at the Bentley School House on the morning of the Open House. Students began to descend on the old building shortly after 8:00 in the morning armed with decorations and good intentions. The cheerleaders and the drama kids were in a friendly competition to see which of the two large apartments could be transformed into a winter wonderland with many pilfered decorations from many homes in the county.

Rich and Scott gladly turned their homes over to the young people as they had been enlisted by Oscar to hang the quilts for the quilt show and to set up tables for the craft show. As usual, Oscar and the old coots had worked on a plan the previous week over coffee and Verna Lee's banana bread. As Rich and Scott entered the cafeteria, they saw that industrial sized hooks had been drilled into the walls and Oscar was at the top of an eight foot ladder attaching heavy duty clothes line to the first hook. Scott sprinted over to his friend and suggested that Oscar supervise and he and Rich take over the high wire act. Oscar reluctantly descended and Scott took his place while Rich went up the other ladder. The knots were quickly tied, and the clothes lines stood ready for the quilts to be displayed. They had barely tied the last knots when the Comfort Makers arrived with the beautiful quilts that were to be displayed. Friendly arguments quickly broke out about which quilts should go where, but, of course, they all knew that Gladys Millen would have the last word, and she did.

Scott, Oscar and Rich had barely gotten the clothes line hung before the ladies with the crafts arrived. Each lady was to have two eight foot tables which could be placed in an "L", lengthwise. Verna Lee had drawn a map, and Oscar was under strict orders to not allow seepage into other crafters space.

Amidst the tubs of crafts for sale that were streaming into the space, Mrs. Anderson the art teacher at BGM arrived with even more tubs of supplies that would become decorations that the little ones would create. Mrs. Anderson had been given the entire stage to set up her crafts station for the little children. There was now officially not one square inch of unused space in the entire gymnasium. Each child who came to the open house today would leave with a cardboard cutout of the old school house that they would be free to decorate with the many colors, glitter, and goodies that were stored inside her tubs. The girls from 10th grade art class were coming to be her helpers.

Verna Lee had given her marching orders to Oscar for the traffic plan in the cafeteria and was fully engaged in organizing the refreshments. All of the various tubs and containers of cookies had been taken from cars, trunks, and freezers and were now resting on the counter of the cafeteria kitchen. The basketball team had hefted six eight foot tables up to the first and second floor foyers, and the cookies were soon to follow. The 100 cup coffee pots were filled from the apartments nearby and each apartment also had back up pots to brew coffee and hot water to make the cocoa mix. The cocoa would be served from "coolers" that would keep the beverage nice and hot with plans to replenish the cocoa from nearby apartments as needed. Verna Lee was sure that if everyone followed their printed instructions, all would be well in refreshment land.

At noon the building emptied as quickly as it had filled as all of the planners headed home for a bite of lunch and a change of clothes before heading back to be ready and set up well before the 3:00 start time. Verna Lee fixed sandwiches for the apartment residents and actually served them on paper plates, she was serious about keeping her apartment ship shape for the open house! Oscar was even dispatched to the dumpster as soon lunch was finished so that there would not be even one unseasonal smell in the apartment.

The Football players arrived at 2:00 p.m. to be sure to have plenty of time to plan out their parking strategy before the first of the guests arrived. The first thing they did was to borrow the car keys of each of the residents, and Mary Millen who had come early in the morning to string red paper chain garland, and moved all of their vehicles into the outlying grassy areas and used each vehicle to start a row so that folks would have a better idea of where to park. They even set up an area for Valet Parking for anyone who felt they could not walk from the parking area. The ten or so spaces nearest the building were reserved for elderly visitors who did not want to give up their cars for Valet Parking. Fortunately, the brown grass was rock hard so there was little worry of the parking area getting mucky. The high for today was predicted to be 28 degrees, with a good solid cloud bank that would make the lights in the apartments twinkle even in the mid afternoon.

The cheerleaders and basketball players arrived on the heels of the football players and began to execute Verna Lee's elaborate plan to keep the guests plied with cookies and hot drinks. By the time the first guests arrived at 2:45 p.m. all was in place both upstairs and down. Verna Lee had even borrowed a clicker from the athletic department and assigned one of the cheerleaders to greet folks at the door and discretely keep track of the number of visitors! The greeter was also given instructions on guiding people to various floors to start their tours so that the numbers would be evenly distributed...until critical mass would be reached and gridlock would ensue. Verna Lee had had enough experience with crowds to know that the best laid plans of mice and men, and little old ladies, would disappear when more people than there would be space arrived.

For now though, all was well. Richard, Andrea, Trish and the Swenson's were all in their places. Scott had invited Mary Millen to be his hostess since he fully admitted that his hosting skills were right up there with Millard Fillmore. Scott disappeared just as the guests were about to arrive, but all was forgiven when they heard gentle Christmas music being piped through the old audio system that had originally been used for announcements and the dreaded "Please send Scott Samuels to the Principal's office." Scott was grinning from ear to ear as he made the rounds of the apartments to proudly announce that the PA system repair was his contribution to the festivities. He re-joined Mary just in time for one quick cookie and cup of coffee before the crowds started to arrive.

And arrive they did. This was clearly the social event of the season. Relatives, teachers, cousins, friends of cousins, complete strangers, friends of complete strangers arrived in waves. The football players worked harder than Coach Samuels ever had worked them in two-a-days in the middle of August. The basketball players got their work out as well transporting pots of coffee, hot chocolate and platter after platter of cookies to the two designated refreshment areas on the first and second foyers. Scott and Rich had strung twinkling lights above the doors to each apartment, and Mary Millen's thousands of red paper chains completed the decorations outside of the apartments.

Each apartment resident was quickly overwhelmed with guests in their modest sized homes. They quickly realized that the best way to greet folks was from just outside their doorways. Trish and Andrea met literally hundreds of residents of Bentley, Iowa, and the vicinity, well, as far as the circulation of the Keosauqua Times stretched. There were raves for the decorations, cookies, hot chocolate and even the German Chocolate flavored coffee that Verna Lee ordered especially for the event.

Rich met lots of people, too, but re-connected with many more from his childhood and growing up years here in the area. They were fascinated to hear about all of the exotic places he had called home, especially since most of them had not moved more than ten miles from the hospital where they were born.

For Scott it was also old home week as his friends, his parents' friends, and more than a few relatives stopped by to see what he had created from the old school where so many people had gotten their elementary education. He was amazed though at the number of complete strangers whose curiosity brought them out on a cold winter's day to see what was certainly the most unique housing in the county, if not the State of Iowa.

The cheerleaders at the door kept a keen eye on the traffic flow and directed as many visitors to the downstairs cafeteria to view the quilts, shop the crafters, and help their youngsters make a Bentley School House Ornament at Mrs. Anderson's craft tables. They quickly also took on the duty of keeping track of shopping bags so that guests did not have to trek upstairs with their purchases from the crafters.

Verna Lee and Oscar both delighted in saying, "Hello," to old friends who had come to admire their new digs. For many of their friends it was their first chance to see how it would work for them once they decided to downsize. They exclaimed over Verna Lee's miniature kitchen that really did have everything they needed. They peered into the Cloak room that served as an extra bedroom in Andrea and Trish's apartment to see that a stackable washer and dryer had been installed. In Verna Lee and Oscar's bedroom they admired the old antique bedroom set that had followed them from rented home to their farmhouse and now to another rented home. They all decided that it looked just as nice here as it had at the farmhouse.

In Trish's and Andrea's apartments they admired the decorations that had appeared nearly out of nowhere as students and friends offered bits and pieces to make the two small homes festive and fun. An HO Scale train ran around Trish's living room, and many young people were needed to keep it running on time.

Upstairs in Rich's and Scott's apartments the air was equally as festive, but slightly fewer folks made the climb all the way to the top so the men had a little more time to visit with the folks who had braved the stairs. Both men's families encamped on the couches and chairs and were constantly jumping up and down to give seats to others who joined them from time to time.

Of course, the most interesting aspect of Scott's apartment was Mary Millen in her appearance for the first time in her new role of girlfriend. She was not new to everyone as she had often visited her grandmother through the years. She was still new enough to cause quite a stir. All of Scott's family met her for the very first time that day. In her green wool sweater and matching skirt, her auburn hair that she wore in the old fashioned page boy style shined in the twinkling lights. Her smile was infectious, and Scott's mother would later tell him, "I met the girl you're going to marry today," and Scott did not disagree.

It wasn't until 5:00 p.m. that the crowds began to drift away. Cookies and hot drinks would only hold these farmers and sons of farmers for so long. There were suppers to prepare and dishes to wash. At 5:00 per Verna Lee's instructions all refreshments were consolidated on the first floor landing, and the basketball players and cheerleaders began to dismantle and clean up the second floor station. Combined together the cookies looked more than adequate to handle the last of the crowds; the hot drinks were consolidated and pots and coolers washed and set aside in the cafeteria kitchen for return to various churches on Monday.

As if on cue the crowds stopped arriving at 5:30 p.m. It would have been rude to arrive late so they gave themselves some leeway and were sure to be there before 5:25 p.m. These last minute guests were careful not to tarry beyond 6:00 p.m. as one should not wear out one's welcome.

As the magic hour approached, they all looked around and realized that it was only themselves and the helpers who were left. Suddenly they all burst out laughing and began congratulating themselves on a wonderful tradition begun.

As all hands came together to clean up the spaces, re-pack the few crafts that had not been sold, and sweep up the glitter from the great art project, Trish and Andrea made the rounds of the volunteers and the crafters with small gift bags they had put together to thank each and every one of them for their contribution. It was just a few pieces of candy and a couple of small stocking stuffers but they each saw the delight in the faces of the workers, young and old, as their hard work was recognized.

One of the last tasks of the clean-up process was to take down the quilts and count the coins that had been placed in each fishbowl that had been stationed in front of the quilts. To no one's surprise, Gladys Millen's Wedding Ring Pattern won the People's Choice award, and all together an additional $532 would be sent Camp Ewalu, and this was before even one quilt had been auctioned off!

As the last of the helpers and crafters headed to their cars and to their suppers, Verna Lee had one more surprise for the apartment residents. Way in the back of Oscar's shop where no one would notice or smell… was a huge crock pot full of chili which the residents set upon as if they had not been munching on cookies all afternoon. By 7:00 p.m. they were all heading to their respective abodes for an evening of feet on the couch and soft and loud snoring. As Rich and Scott headed up the stairs to their second floor homes, Andrea finally remembered to ask the question that she had been pondering all day. "Scott," she exclaimed. "How many people were here today?"

"Well," Scott answered, "that's the funny thing, do you remember how much money was raised at the People's Choice for the Quilt Show?" In their weary minds no one could come up with the number immediately. "It was $532," Scott reminded them. "And that was the exact number on the clicker when the cheerleaders handed it over to me at the end of the Open House."

"Well, I'll be," they all said in unison. Laughing, they all made their way to their home.

Chapter Forty-six

Andrea Hogan

Andrea could barely get out of bed on the morning after the Christmas Open House. Every bone in her body ached. She painfully made her way to the bathroom, found some extra strength something, took the max, and crawled back into bed. She was definitely going to the new 11:15 Contemporary service today, and Trinity Lutheran just might have to deal with her unwashed hair! She fell back into bed and promptly asleep for two more hours. When she awoke the second time, she felt slightly more human and decided to spare Trinity Lutheran the fright that could be her hair unwashed and headed for the shower. There would be no leisurely reading of the Des Moines Register for her today.

She sat down just as the rest of the congregation stood up to sing the Praise Songs that always came at the beginning of the Contemporary Service. She looked around this new congregation and was happy to see a number of young families in attendance and even a few of the high school kids who had worked so hard to help make the Christmas Open House a success. She would have to remember to thank them again when the service was over. The guitars, drums and piano certainly added a different feel to the service, but while it was very different from the organ led liturgical service she was used to, she had to admit there was a joy that was almost palpable. She'd have to consider attending this service more often, and inviting Trish to join her as well. She wondered if Rich would ever be open to an invitation to join her at church. It was clear that he was the only one who did not attend church among the apartment dwellers at the Bentley School House. His car was often the only one left in the parking lot when she left for church on Sunday. She had to remind herself to concentrate on the sermon and keep her thoughts about her old friend at bay.

The afternoon did find her on her couch with the Des Moines Register, and she was pleased to hear the familiar ring tone from her cell phone alerting her to a call from her favorite Christmas present ever, her son, William Roger Hogan. His first question was about the Open House. "So did you survive the great onslaught yesterday?" he inquired.

"Barely", she admitted.

"I know that Trish was pretty bushed by the time she texted me last night," he acknowledged.

"It was an exhausting day, but I loved it," Andrea told him. "It was just so much fun meeting the parents of my students, and their grandparents, and the friends of their grandparents! This is such a close knit community that almost literally everyone knows everyone, but they also welcomed me with open arms which was nice to see."

"I'm glad it was a success. Before I forget, fill me in on the details of Christmas with the rug rats at Aunt Dorothy's house in Dallas," he requested.

"You're right about the rug rats," she acknowledged. "All of Dorothy's grandchildren will be in attendance this year, even the Brenner's are flying home from England for the holiday." Andrea had to smile when she thought of how patient Will had always been with the multitude of cousins that he encountered at his aunt's house. Andrea's older Sister Dorothy and her husband Wayne had three daughters who had all married and produced multiple heirs. Until recently they had all lived within thirty minutes of their parents. Last year though the wheel was broken slightly when the middle daughter's husband, Adam, had been given the opportunity to start up a division for his company in London. Adam and Shari with their two kids, AJ and Jordan, had packed up their lives and headed for an adventure. Fortunately for Dorothy and Wayne, they had the resources to fly to London with some regularity.

"Are we still going to Cousin Michelle's church for Christmas Eve?" Will asked.

"Yes, that's the plan," she told him. "We'll start with tamales at Michelle's and head for the early church service so we can get the little ones in bed at a decent hour."

"As usual I'll get there just in time to devour the tamales. I have to work until 2:00, and it's a three hour drive from Whole Foods to Michelle's door," he reminded her.

"I'm just glad you can make it at all," she assured him. "My flight gets in at 10:08 a.m. on Christmas Eve Day so Dorothy and I will have time to do last minute shopping before we head to Michelle's house."

"How long are you staying?" he asked.

"Well, with Dorothy and Wayne, just until Friday night. Then Connie will pick me up, and I'll spend the rest of my time with her in Fort Worth."

"I'm glad you're going to get to spend time with Connie. You guys have really worked hard to maintain your friendship through the years. How was it that you met her?"

"She worked at the Legislative Service Bureau for a few years in the 90's, we just clicked right away. I've always said we were kindred sisters," she explained. "So, back to Christmas, how long are you going to be able to grace us with your presence?"

"Not long, Mom. I'm sorry—you know I wish I could be with you longer, but I have to be back at Whole Foods for an evening shift on Friday night," he explained.

"That's OK," she assured him. "I'm just happy to spend Christmas and your birthday with you again this year."

"Well, there's one more reason I need to get back kind of early...Trish is flying in to Austin on Saturday morning." He told her a bit apprehensively.

"She is?" Andrea could not hide her surprise.

"Mom, I really think she is someone special, and we want to spend some extended time together to see if we think this has a future," he explained.

"But you've only seen each other a few times," she pointed out.

"I know it seems sudden to you, Mom," he tried to re-assure her. "Trish and I have spent a lot of time the past few months talking on the phone and texting."

"Of course, you know I love Trish, Will," she told him. "I just don't want to see either of you hurt. It's a really difficult situation, if things don't work out between the two of you; I'm the one who has to face Trish on a daily basis."

"Look, Mom, I know I've had a dubious history with girls in the past, but I've grown up a lot since then, and I promise you, whatever happens, Trish will not end up hating me in the end."

"Listen, Will, I do appreciate that you've been a lot more serious about a lot of things these past couple of years. I trust you. I love you. I know you'll do what's best for your heart, and Trish's."

"I appreciate that, Mom," Will told her. "Let's enjoy our time together and see what the future brings for all of us, agreed?"

"Agreed," she said.

"OK, now I'm going to call Trish and tell her she can talk to you about the trip—she was afraid you would object."

"No objections," Andrea assured him, "Just plenty of caution!"

Chapter Forty-seven

Coming and Going

It was Andrea's turn to make supper on the Monday night after the Christmas Open House. On Sunday night she had assembled her famous Chicken Enchilada Casserole. Tonight, all she had to do was warm up some canned re-fried beans, make instant Spanish rice, put the casserole in the oven for an hour and call it dinner. There were even leftover Open House cookies for dessert.

As the group settled in around Rich's big dining room table, the conversation quickly turned to everyone's plans for the holidays. Rich knew that Andrea was heading for Texas, but he wasn't sure which route she was taking so he asked, "Andi, are you flying out of Des Moines or St. Louis?"

Andrea replied, "Turns out it's about six of one and half dozen of another. Its four hours to St. Louis and almost the same to Des Moines from way down here in southern Iowa. But I want to spend some time at my house in Des Moines when I get back from Texas so I'll trek up to Des Moines tomorrow after 4th period. Craig is taking my last two Freshmen English classes so I can get a head start on the drive and darkness. I still have to pack tonight."

Trish wasn't sure she wanted to have the conversation dwell on Andrea's trip to Texas since neither of the guys knew that she, too, would spend time in Texas over the holidays. She quickly asked Rich about his plans. "What about you Rich? When do your kids get here?"

Rich couldn't help smiling when he told the assembled group that Scott and Sandy would arrive in town tomorrow night. Scott was flying to Des Moines from Boston around noon. Sandy would drive over from Grinnell to pick him up from the airport, and they would head south from there. He told the group about the travel plans and added that Sandy had told him that she was particularly looking forward to spending time with her dad. The divorce had been hard on both of his children, but girls usually wore their hearts on their sleeves, and her mother's betrayal of not only Rich, but the family was very hurtful to her. She had spent some time in counseling at her dad's insistence and was just beginning to talk about her mother when he called to check up on her. Sandy had not even had the chance to see her dad's new home as she had been involved in sorority activities during the whole month of August. Scott had at least seen the place when he had helped his dad move in.

After Scott and Sandy's plans were reported and analyzed by all in attendance, Trish shared that her mom and stepdad would be flying into St. Louis tomorrow and after renting a car for the trip to Bentley would arrive sometime in the late afternoon. They would be staying at Andrea's place, and Trish would be hosting Christmas activities since her grandmother's apartment was even smaller than her own.

When everyone else was finished relating their travel plans they all turned to Scott to hear what he had in mind for the Holidays. Trish was the first to ask the question that she knew at least Andrea was wondering about, "What did you get Mary for Christmas?"

Scott's face became animated, "I got her the best gift!" he exclaimed. "She had told me how when they have potlucks at school she's always messing with her grandmother's ancient crock pot and while I was at Pamida in Marshtown last week, I just happened to walk past a display of crock pots that not only have removable pots, but the lids lock on so the food won't spill on the way to school. I snapped one up immediately and even had it gift wrapped before I left the store. I am all set for Christmas."

His three dinner companions looked at him in stunned silence. Trish, never one for mincing words was the first to break the silence. "Scott, I know you don't have much experience in buying Christmas presents for girls, but crock pots aren't real high up there on our wish list usually."

Scott looked crestfallen. "But I was so sure it was a great present," he protested. "Well, I guess I'm going to find out pretty soon, she's coming over in twenty minutes so we can exchange Christmas presents before she flies back to Ohio for the holidays."

Andrea was quick to come to his defense, "Scott, dear, it a very thoughtful gift, and frankly, her reaction to the gift will tell you a lot about her character." With that their little gathering broke up so they could all get busy with their own holiday plans.

Just a few minutes after Scott arrived at his apartment, feeling like a giant fool for buying a crock pot for such a wonderful girl as Mary, there was a knock at his door. He opened it to find Mary Millen in a dark blue winter coat and a beautiful ice blue sweater and skirt set, struggling with a large box which was the exact replica, down to the wrapping paper, of the box that awaited her under his Christmas tree. He took one look and burst into laughter. She was taken aback until Scott took her box from her and set it next to her present. She looked from one gift to the other not once but twice, and then it suddenly made sense. Mary joined Scott in hilarious laughter and could barely remain upright. She shed her coat and flew into Scott's waiting arms. Through her laughter she explained, "When I saw that crock pot at Pamida's, I thought how well it would work on the Wednesdays that you cook for the building, and that surely you wouldn't mind if I borrowed it once a month for our Friday potlucks at school."

"Well, it must be true what they say, 'Great minds do think in the same direction'," he assured her. "Quick, let's unwrap our presents and make a tour of the apartments to show the others how much in sync we are." Before they unwrapped their gifts though he pulled her tenderly into his arms and kissed her deeply. His next words were all the Christmas present she really needed. "Mary Millen," Scott began somberly, "I love you."

Mary smiled and looked into his soft brown eyes as she told him, "Well, that's handy because I love you, too."

Chapter Forty-eight

Andrea Hogan

Andrea pulled into the driveway of her painted lady Victorian home in Des Moines and sat for a moment looking through the windshield at the house that had been her home for nearly twenty-five years, and now suddenly seemed like a Bed and Breakfast that she was visiting for a brief time.

She felt like it had been five years rather than five months since she had left this spacious home that had been the site of many family gatherings, bon fires in the back yard, and teenage boys sleeping in every possible bed, couch or floor space. Her home had been the mecca during Will's teenage years. She had always believed that life was too short to not keep ice cream treats in the freezer and pop in the refrigerator. Early on she had also invested in one of those Fire Pits, and Will's friends had gathered in his backyard throughout all their teenage years. When they weren't in the backyard, they were in the basement Rec Room that she had carved out of the old cement block basement. It wasn't a fancy room, but she had done the best she could on a limited budget, and it held its own well stocked refrigerator, a TV that increased in size through the years, two comfortable couches and three bean bags that had seen lots of use through the years. Will, for his part, had added to the Rec Room décor with three old time video games that he had gotten for next to nothing at the Auction at the State Fair Grounds. It wasn't fancy, but the guys in Will's group loved it with fervor. They had especially liked the Saturday night tradition of baking Mrs. Bishop's Chocolate Chip Oatmeal Cookies. Whenever Andrea had not had plans on a Saturday night, and that was most Saturday nights, she had begun to make her mom's famous cookies for the guys. They went through an entire gallon of milk in one evening and almost always polished off a batch of cookies before the evening was over. She felt herself smile at the memories of raising Will in this house. It had always been a struggle financially since she had chosen this big old house rather than a tiny bungalow for those growing up years. She had felt that a boy needed room to roam and through the years Will had explored this old house. From finding letters written during WWI to old milk bottles hidden in the basement cubby holes, Will had explored every square inch of home and yard. She knew he loved this old house as much as she did, yet it had not kept him from exploring new areas of the country to live, work and play. Was she now beginning to cut the ties that had held her to this house for so many years? It was definitely a question to ponder.

Just as that thought popped into her head, she saw the front door swing open and her tenant, Sue Thompson, poke her head out of the massive front door and look quizzically toward her car. Suddenly Andrea realized that she had been sitting in the car for at least five minutes and certainly Sue would wonder why someone had pulled into the driveway and then just sat there.

Before she thoroughly scared the young woman, Andrea jumped out of her car so that Sue could see that she was not being stalked by a mass murderer, just a slightly worn out first year teacher coming home to enjoy at least one night in her big King Size bed.

Chapter Forty-nine

Richard Knight
The New Year

Andrea realized that Richard must have seen her pull into the driveway of the old schoolhouse turned apartment house because she saw him walking out the big double doors and zipping his jacket just as she pulled into her usual parking space in the lot to the side of the building. It was the first Tuesday of the New Year and school was scheduled to begin again the next day. Andrea was surprised not only to see Richard approach her car but was just as surprised by the bear hug that he gave her as she stepped from her vehicle. "I've missed you," were the first words out of his mouth. It made Andrea pause a moment and wonder if she had missed him in the past two weeks; well, maybe a little, she thought.

Richard insisted on carrying in her bags while she struggled along with two shopping bags full of Christmas presents and a plastic tote containing items from her home in Des Moines that she had decided needed to be in her new home in Bentley, mostly kitchen items, of course!

Richard went on into her bedroom to put her suitcases on the bed while Andrea put the tote on the counter and the gifts on her tiny table. As he came out of the bedroom, Andrea asked him about the other residents of their building. He reported that Oscar and Verna Lee were doing very well. In fact, they had decided to take a quick trip to Kansas City to spend some time with Oscar's brother and his wife so they would not be back until next Monday. Trish had arrived yesterday but was spending the evening with her Grandmother. Scott was having supper with Mary Millen and her grandmother Gladys. As if it had just occurred to him, he informed her, "That just leaves the two of us at the old homestead!"

"Funny, this really does seem more like home than my house in Des Moines," she told him. "So how was your visit with the kids?" she asked.

"Oh, the visit with the kids went fine…everything else got a little complicated," he told her. At her look of consternation, he quickly came up with a plan to explain his whole disconcerting holiday season. "Why don't I whip us up some supper, and I'll tell you all about it?"

"Sounds good to me!" she just as quickly decided. "Same time, same place?"

"I'm not promising gourmet, but we won't starve," he assured her.

"As long as I don't have to cook it, I'll be happy," she assured him right back.

At 6:00 p.m. Andrea left her apartment for the short trek up to Richard's place. It really did seem very quiet. While the walls were thick and the big old Victorian doors kept out most of the sounds from the apartments, she realized that she had gotten used to the hum of the television from Oscar and Verna Lee's apartment and the rhythmic thumping of the Christian Rock Bands that Trish liked to listen to. The twinkling rope lights that Scott and Richard had strung for the open house cast a pale shadow on the steps as she moved upward to Richard's home in the sky. She knocked and heard Richard invite her into his home. She realized that he, too, had added a few new things to his décor. Maybe the kids had gotten him to go shopping for accessories when they were home. There were framed photographs of his family on the wall and a new table centerpiece on Verna Lee's old oak table. Andrea walked to the photos on the far wall to admire Richard's children. She saw a number of framed photos of his children at various stages of their life, but she was most surprised to see a large framed photograph of Richard, his ex-wife, and Scott and Sandy that appeared to be only a few years old. She turned with a questioning look on her face just as Richard was walking out of his kitchen with a steaming platter of spaghetti and meat balls. Richard gave her a rueful smile and just said, "Let's eat first, and then I'll give you the run down on my strange Christmas. Tell me about Christmas in Texas; is it super-sized like everything else down there?"

As they enjoyed his improvised but delicious meal, Andrea told him about eating the traditional tamales Christmas Eve dinner at her niece's house and Will showing up right on time to devour his usual dozen. From there they had headed to the Baptist church where they watched a beautiful Christmas pageant complete with a rubber baby Jesus and a beatific Mother Mary.

She went on to explain that Christmas morning at her sister's house was a mad house of too many toys and plenty of cousins for Will to enjoy. She had always regretted that she had such a small family for him to enjoy. He relished spending time with his Texas family. Living in Texas, he had grown very close to his cousin Michelle and often made the three hour trip to Plano for their family celebrations whenever he could. Because of that, Michelle's children knew Will better than they knew their Great Aunt Andrea.

Andrea told Richard that after a brief but pleasant visit with her sister Dorothy and her husband Wayne, she had been picked up by her dear friend Connie who lived in Fort Worth. Richard had not known that Andrea had originally planned to spend the winter in Fort Worth with Connie until her life had changed so radically when she accepted the position of English teacher at BGM Community School District.

They finished their meals and carried the dishes into the kitchen where, as usual, Andrea washed and Richard dried. They refilled their wine glasses when the last dish was dried and headed back to the couch in Richard's living room. "OK, my friend, time to tell your story," Andrea informed Richard.

"I'm warning you: it's pretty bizarre!" Richard cautioned her.

"Spill the beans!" Andrea commanded.

"Well, everything started out just fine. Sandy picked Scott up from the Des Moines airport, and they got here right when I expected them. We headed out to the farm to be with the folks on Christmas Eve. Dad was having a really good day and seemed almost his old self. He teased Sandy and offered to arm wrestle Scott for the last chicken leg on the platter. We were meeting my younger sister and her family at the Methodist Church in Grimley for the 8:00 Christmas Eve service so we all piled into the big old Oldsmobile that Dad bought new in 1986 and away we went. Dad even let me drive, and Mom and the kids were in the back seat. It was really very nice. In the past when we came for Christmas, it was always based around what worked best for Sally's family in western Iowa. We rarely had Christmas with my folks and usually arrived a day or two after the festivities to leftovers and unwrapped presents under a tree that had seen better days!"

Andrea took a sip of her wine and looked quizzically at Richard. "So far, so good," she observed.

"I'd have to agree with you," Richard replied. "It wasn't until late Christmas afternoon that things got strange."

"Richard Alan Knight," Andrea began.

Richard interrupted her, "OK. OK. I know I'm in trouble when you use my middle name, and I promise I'll get to the interesting part soon, but I did want to tell you what a nice Christmas Day we had."

"I'm all ears," Andrea assured him.

"Anyway, we went back to the farm late Christmas morning. The kids and I knew to have a light breakfast because when Mom says she is serving dinner around noon, you'd better be in line for the drumstick at 11:59 or you'll be out of luck. We had exchanged presents and sat around here watching the parade in the morning. I just felt like we were clicking as a family for the first time since Sally's announcement at the Lake two summers ago."

"When we got to my folks house there were already loads of people there. My two sisters and their teenagers, husbands and even one foreign exchange student were there along with my brother and his rug rats. It was great fun to watch the little ones open their presents, and we absolutely gorged ourselves at the dinner table. We all bundled up after the dishes were done and took a walk around the farm which, of course, led to a snowball fights with the girls versus the guys. The guys held their own even though they were outnumbered two to one, and we finally all fell into the living room to snooze or watch TV."

"Sounds like *It's a Wonderful Life* so far," Andrea interjected.

"Yeah, so far so good," Richard agreed. "At about 5:00 people started to depart so they could get back home or to the in-laws before bedtime. Mom naturally sent tons of food home with everyone, and I was helping to get it all organized and out the door. My brother was just driving out of the farm driveway when a car pulled in and came down the drive toward the parking area by Dad's big garage. It was pretty dark already so we couldn't tell who it was, and we were all standing at the door wondering, Who in the world? when Sally stepped out and started running toward us."

"Sally, as in your ex-wife Sally?" Andrea asked for clarification.

"The very one," Richard assured her. "Before I could stop her, she had flung herself into my arms and started crying uncontrollably. My folks were understandably stunned and didn't know what to do. We finally got her into the kitchen and sat her down at the table while Scott and Sandy bent over her, trying to figure out what was wrong. I asked my folks if they could wait in the living room while we sorted everything out, and they were more than happy to escape this woman whom they had been bad mouthing in their Lutheran way for the past year and a half or so."

"I agree, this is pretty high drama for Lutherans," Andrea told him.

"Anyway, I got her sat down at the kitchen table, and she began to babble out her story, and it was quite a story! It seems that she had gotten involved with a man back in Frankfort. However, it turned out that he had been a little more than sketchy about his former involvements. Two days before Christmas the guy broke up with her even though he was supposed to come home for Christmas to her sister's house. I'm not quite sure how things transpired after that, but since Sally had already purchased two tickets to fly to Omaha to visit with her sister's family in Denison; instead of catching the flight from Chicago to Omaha, she rented a car, arrived at my parents' house, and broke down."

"Oh, dear!" Andrea exclaimed.

"I was just flabbergasted," Rich explained. "I really didn't know what to do, but I knew I had to get her out of my parents' kitchen so I told Sandy and Scott to take her and the rental car here while I tried to explain everything to my folks."

"What did your folks say when you told them all this?" Andrea asked.

"They were very shocked and just didn't know what to say. Sally had never been real comfortable with my folks, but, of course, they had treated her very kindly, that's just what my parents do," Richard explained.

"So what happened when you got back to the apartment?" Andrea wondered.

"Well, this is where it gets even stranger if you can believe it," Richard began. "When I finally got back to the apartment after numerous trips to the car to pack up gifts and leftovers, Sally was sound asleep in Sandy's bed. Scott explained that she had fallen asleep almost immediately when they started driving the eight miles back to Bentley and that he could barely wake her up enough to walk her into the building and up the two flights of stairs to my apartment. Sandy had turned down the sheets and barely gotten her into bed before she was asleep again."

"Awkward!" Andrea added.

"Ya think?" Richard retorted. "Here was this woman who had destroyed our family, broken my heart and cost me a sizable chunk of my retirement, and she was asleep in the new home that I had created with the sole purpose of forgetting her!"

Andrea was a little surprised by the wrathful irony in his voice. He had always been so stoic about his divorce. She knew little more than what he had just repeated in that statement, well, the information about the retirement was new, but really she couldn't remember much more that he had shared. Mostly he talked about his kids when they talked, and he could talk about them for hours, it was one of the things she liked most about him.

"Sandy insisted on sleeping on the couch so Scott and I dug around and came up with a sheet and an extra blanket, and we all just headed off to bed figuring we would deal with all of the drama in the morning. I'm not sure how much sleep I got. I was just so ticked off at Sally for ruining what was supposed to be a great holiday with my children. I suppose I finally fell asleep because the sun woke me up around 8:00 a.m., and I realized that I smelled coffee."

"There could be worse smells to wake up to," Andrea interjected.

"Unfortunately, the coffee had not been made by one of my loving children, but by Sally. She had woken up early and sent Sandy to sleep in her own bed and had proceeded to take over my kitchen. By the time I woke up, she had found the canned cinnamon rolls in the refrigerator, baked those and made coffee. She was sitting at my table reading the copy of the Keosaqua paper that had the write up about the Christmas Open House, complete with half a page of photos; you probably haven't seen it yet, have you? I'll dig it out before you go home."

"That's OK, I have the papers being delivered tomorrow. Go on. Go on!" Andrea urged.

"I get weary just thinking about all the drama," he said. "I have never been one for making a scene, you know that. I can't think of a time during the year that you and I lived together that either of us raised our voices."

"Not once," she agreed, patting his hand.

"So, the long and short of it is that the guy she was involved with had turned out to be a total jerk. They were looking forward to spending Christmas break at her sister's house in Denison. This was to be the big reveal to the family, and she said they had hoped Scott and Sandy would join them in Denison for New Year's. Forget that the kids had planned to be with me that whole time and that we were going skiing in Dubuque for two days. Forget that she had not gotten around to talking to the kids since their birthdays in September. Forget everything except what is convenient for Sally."

"Oh, Richard, I'm so sorry. This had to be just awful for you to go through," Andrea told him.

"It wasn't fun I'll admit that right away, but I've got to say my anger did mellow out a little bit as I saw how devastated she was by all this. She was very depressed and went on and on about how sorry she was for breaking up our family and how she never should have left me, it got to be pretty melodramatic after a while. In the end I just told her that she needed to straighten her life out for the kids' sake if nothing else. I told her that the fun years were coming where the kids would get married and produce grandchildren for her to spoil and then send home."

"She finally seemed to settle down a little, and then she asked if she could spend the day with the kids before she went on to Denison to her sister's house. I told her that I had plenty to keep me busy out at the folks' farm and that she could spend the day with the kids, but that she needed to be headed to Denison the next day. I pointed out that this was my time with our kids and that I had already paid for hotel rooms in Dubuque. She agreed and asked if she could make dinner for us all that night. I agreed and got out of there. When I got back from my folks, and believe me it wasn't easy explaining all this craziness to them, she and the kids had put up all these photos, and there were candles lit everywhere, and there was a feast of roast beast on the table." He paused to take a breath and continued, "The weird thing was that the kids had seemed to completely forgive her for the past two and a half years and in many ways I seemed to be the one on the outside. It was just all very strange, and it was capped off by family movie night where Sally dug out all of our old home videos that I had had dubbed onto DVD's a few years ago."

Rich sighed heavily, "All in all it was terribly awkward and just really put a damper on my time with the kids. Sally cleared out on Saturday as promised, and the kids and I took off for Dubuque. The ride to Dubuque was pretty quiet, but the kids perked up when we got to the slopes, and we really did end up having a nice time together. The kids had never been to Dubuque because we had always flown in and out of Des Moines and had not had much time for side trips when we rented our cabin at Lake Redfern."

"Did you come back to Iowa every summer?" Andrea asked Richard.

He thought for a moment and then replied, "We didn't before we had kids. But once Scott and Sandy arrived on the scene, I wanted my folks to have some connection with them, and I knew they would never fly to where we were living so that's when we started renting the cabin."

There were a few years as the kids got older though that their busy schedules prevented them from coming to Iowa so in the past decade, we only made it about every other year. We had actually talked about buying a vacation home on Lake Redfern, but Sally was never very comfortable there with all the vegetation, mosquitoes, and those ever present flies!"

"I take it she put up with it for the sake of the family?" Andrea asked.

"She was a pretty good sport most of the time. She spent a fair amount of time at her sister's house in Denison, and, of course, we all spent time with her folks while they were living."

"When did they die?" Andrea realized she was getting more information about Rich's life before BGM than she had ever known before.

"Sally's folks died within about seven months of each other about ten years ago. They both had heart conditions; her dad died in April, and her mother died in November," he explained.

"That's very odd," Andrea offered. "That's the exact same time frame in which my folks died, only twenty five years ago. They barely got to know Will before they died, and he doesn't remember them at all."

"Well, knowing you I'm sure you handled the whole situation far better than Sally did, she was a basket case for several years after their sudden deaths," Rich added.

"It's a terrible thing to go through, but I had my faith to keep me strong," Andrea told him. "Of course, I was also busy with a toddler at the time so I had to just keep putting one foot in front of the other."

"Were you still married when your folks died?" Rich inquired.

"No, the divorce had been final for a few months when my dad suddenly died around Easter. I have to say that Will Senior was very supportive through that time, emotionally at least, don't get me started on financially!" Andrea warned.

"A conversation for another time," Rich agreed.

"Or never," Andrea added.

"So your mom died around Thanksgiving that same year?" Rich asked.

"Actually, it was on Thanksgiving," Andrea explained. "We were making the adjustment to life without Dad, and she just suddenly felt very ill around 6:00 p.m. I called the ambulance, but I think she was dead before she got to the hospital. I remember tugging Will into a snow suit and shaking as I drove to the hospital which was fortunately only a few blocks away. They came out to the waiting room after only a few minutes and told me there was nothing they could do."

Rich took her hands in his and squeezed hard, "Oh, Andrea, I'm so sorry you had to go through all that by yourself."

"They say what doesn't kill you makes you stronger. It was a rough time, but I came through it with my faith in tact and at peace with the ways things turned out," Andrea agreed.

"As I recall, you've only got the one sister so you didn't even have a big family to help pull you through."

"Yes, I was a surprise late in my mother's life when she had given up any hope of having another child," Andrea explained. "My folks were the same age as some of my classmates' grandparents, but none of their grandparents ever chaperoned a school wide slumber party like my mother did," Andrea smiled at the memory. "Of course, I was horribly embarrassed when one of my friends spotted her out on the battle ball court!"

"She sounds like quite a character, like mother, like daughter I might add," he teased.

Andrea glanced at her watch and saw that it was almost 8:30 p.m. They had talked and consoled each other for almost two hours. "I'd better get a move on it. I've still got a load of laundry to do before I can go to bed."

Rich walked her to the door and took her in his arms before she walked through to head back to her apartment. She wrapped her own arms around him and gave him a long and loving hug. Rich suddenly pulled away and looked in her eyes. "Hey," he declared, "You've got a birthday coming up."

Andrea laughed and asked how in the world he had remembered her birthday after all these years.

"Actually I've always thought of you on your birthday, after all, you share it with 'The King, Elvis Presley.' Whenever there was a news story about one of his landmark birthdays, I would think of you, and your Aunt Dorothy, who also shared the King's birthday."

"You have a remarkable memory, my friend," she told him.

"What do you say we go out and celebrate your birthday in style this Saturday?" he asked.

"Great, I'll let the others know," she told him.

"We'll have a celebration here Sunday night, and I'll invite everyone then, but let's make this just the two of us. Let's call it a date."

Andrea smiled up at him and agreed, "Yes, let's call it a date. I'll wear a dress."

Chapter Fifty

Trish Wilkins

Trish's whirlwind Christmas travels had left her exhausted. After a fun few days with her mom and her stepfather, she had flown to Austin on a Delta flight that was short on comfort but long on affordability. She had thoroughly hashed out Will Roger Hogan with her mother, and they had both agreed that while he seemed great on paper, it was worth the $199 e-ticket to spend more time with him and get to know him better.

She admitted that she was slightly skeptical that this man could be as decent and upright as he seemed to be in their conversations, emails, and texts over the past four and a half months. She had told her mother as much and was surprised that her mother had been the one to tell her to believe in Will, and to believe in love. After all her mother had been through with her dad, she told her mom that she was surprised that she still had faith in romance. Her mom had smiled and told her that while she knew it had been a mistake to marry Trish's dad, they had been terribly unsuited for each other, she had always hoped to find her own knight in shining armor. She told Trish that she had found her knight when she married John Reynolds. "He's not your typical idea of a dashing leading man," she told Trish, "but his spirituality and kindness more than make up for his lack of hair."

They had laughed together, and Trish's mom had pulled out her checkbook and written a check for $199 and handed it to her one and only daughter. "Find out for yourself," she advised Trish.

So Trish had jumped on the Delta flight to Austin and found herself running into the waiting arms of Will Roger Hogan.

186

Their few days together were everything she could have wished for and more. They had explored every inch of Austin from thrift stores to amazing nightlife (How amazing was it to find a man who was as thrilled by a bargain as she was? She credited her friend Andrea with passing on that handy trait.) They took hikes in the nearby parks and river valley. The weather had been wonderful as well, rising to between 70-75 each day with clear blue skies and gentle breezes. She felt her body relax, and she nearly forgot the frozen tundra that was Iowa at this time of the year. The late nights and early mornings had caught up with her though, and she had slept for nearly fourteen hours when she arrived back in her apartment on Sunday. She had roused herself around noon on Monday and headed to Marshtown to spend some time with her grandmother. She reminded herself that she needed to cherish each visit with her dear Nana; she seemed active and healthy now, but Trish knew that could change at any moment.

Will had told her how his grandmother on his dad's side had died unexpectedly, and it had seemed to age his grandfather almost immediately. His grandfather had only lived another fifteen months, and Will had hated that the last three of those months had been spent in a nursing home. He told her how he and his mother had had an ongoing argument for years because he was sure he would never allow her to be in a nursing home, and she was just as adamant that if it came to it, she would not want to be a burden and would want to be in a nursing home. Trish smiled when she thought of his sincere look whenever he talked about his mother. She was pretty much convinced that you could tell a lot about a man from the way he treated his mother, and Will could not be matched in that category.

Her grandmother had been anxious to see her, and they had chatted about Trish's busy Christmas traveling schedule. She was anxious to hear news of Trish's visit with Will in Austin. She was surprised when they were finishing up the supper dishes and Trish realized it was already after 7:00 p.m. "Goodness, Nana," she began, "I've been enjoying your company way too much. I've got to get back to Bentley and put a load of laundry in yet tonight. I've run out of socks after all my travels!"

Her Nana kissed her goodnight and sent her off into the darkness to her cozy little home in the old school house. Trish waved to her grandmother as she pulled away from the little one story apartment building. She shivered and wished she had taken the time to warm up her car before she had headed out into the night. She also couldn't help thinking that the temperature in Austin had been in the high 50's when she had left there yesterday. What a difference a few states made! She smiled again when she remembered Will holding her in his arms at DFW where he had driven her so she could catch a flight directly to St. Louis. He had been reluctant to let her go, and she had been equally reluctant to go. He had smiled down at her and told her that their time together had been magical. He also said he was beginning to have a difficult time thinking about life without her. She had stayed quietly in his arms until she had decided to be bold and say what was on her heart. "Well, then Will Roger Hogan, you're going to need to decide what the next step will be for us." With that she had kissed him quickly and dashed into the terminal. When she had looked back through the thick layers of glass, he was still standing there, but she could see that there was the hint of a smile on his face.

Chapter Fifty-one

Oscar and Verna Lee Swenson

The old school house was quiet when she and Oscar arrived home on that early January Monday. All the other residents were back into their routines of classes and extra-curricular activities. They had had a lovely visit with Oscar's brother and wife, Elmer and Agnes. She smiled to herself as she thought of the tiny couple. Neither one of them more than 5'4" and with names like those, she had always felt that they had been fated to marry each other. Oscar and Elmer had had a great time picking through Elmer's fifty years of accumulated junk. They were planning an auction in the spring and a move to a beautiful retirement community just outside of Kansas City. Agnes had thanked her several times for setting the example for them in their downsizing. Elmer had been reluctant to consider the move, but had agreed when he realized that his younger brother had already taken the plunge and gotten rid of his years of accumulated junk. (Oscar did not share with Elmer that a goodly amount of the junk had accompanied him to the school house and was now safely tucked away in his basement shop, far away from the prying eyes of his lovely bride).

As Oscar headed to his workshop to secret away a few items from Elmer's barn that he had hidden in the trunk of the Lincoln, Verna Lee sorted laundry and was reminded once again what a good idea Scott had had when he put the stackable washer and dryer in what had been the cloak closet in the classrooms. It was certainly a better use of space for her than a tiny bedroom.

As she was putting in the detergent, she was somehow reminded that tonight was the first meeting of the Community Theater group, the

Bentley Players, they were being called. A steering group had been meeting during the fall and early winter to plan for the organization and to decide their first production. Carl Wells was onboard as the Director, and they had decided on the old classic *Arsenic and Old Lace* as their first endeavor. It was sure to be a crowd pleaser and had just the right size cast for their first play. Now tonight there would be a meeting of anyone interested in helping in any way, acting, sewing, building, baking treats for the evening fellowship. Both she and Oscar would be there, and she knew that many others in the county were also planning on attending. She smiled as she thought about how much had happened since that big old tree had fallen on the BGM auditorium. The Bentley Players would be sharing the stage with the high school production of *The Fantastiks* that Rich Knight would be directing. Fortunately, Rich always held rehearsals right after school, and the Players would take up residence after supper and would rehearse for a couple of hours before enjoying de-caf coffee and treats and heading home around 9:00 p.m. It was wonderful to think that between the old coots, the quilters, and the actors, the cafeteria/gymnasium would be hopping from morning to night.

She put the kettle on the stove and when the water had heated, she made herself a cup of tea and sat down at the kitchen table to go through the mail and the newspapers that had accumulated during their brief vacation. Most of it was junk mail, of course, but there were a couple of delayed Christmas greetings and a note from one of the cheerleader's mothers saying how much her daughter had enjoyed helping out at the Christmas Open House, and volunteering her PEO group to do a Festival of Trees in the nooks and crannies of the old schoolhouse next year. "What a nice addition that would be," Verna Lee thought to herself. She set the note aside to add to the file folder that she was already keeping in anticipation of next year's event. It helped to be organized! As she slipped the note into the folder, she wondered what things would change between now and next year? Would Scott marry the dear Mary Millen? Would Trish leave to be with Andrea's son in Austin? For that matter, would the loving looks between Rich and Andrea ever blossom, or was it too late for love for those two old friends? Would she and Oscar be in good health? She quickly dismissed this last thought and got busy putting supper on the table, of course, they would be in good health, she was sure of it.

Chapter Fifty-two

Scott Samuels

It was his night to cook for the group so he rolled himself out of bed extra early on that frosty January morning. He reached into his cupboard and pulled out his excellent Christmas gift from his darling Mary, his five quart crock pot with snap on lid. He'd even snap the lid when he transported supper to Rich's apartment, even if it was just across the wide hallway from his own apartment. He was very happy that the evening meal tradition had begun again after the Christmas break. It was a wonderful way to unwind from the day, or grab a quick bite to eat without having to prepare it on game days. Wednesday was his night because BGM held with the old tradition of not scheduling extracurricular activities on "church night." He wondered how many of the young people were heading to church tonight, probably not many and certainly not enough!

He shook his head and reminded himself that he'd better pay attention to his recipe or his Company Chicken Casserole would not be fit to eat when he arrived home this afternoon. In a few minutes of intense concentration, he was able to put the whole recipe into the crock pot, and he even remembered to turn it to "Low"…and at the last minute he even remembered to plug the crock pot in. "Close call," he thought as he headed for the shower.

He found himself singing in the shower and smiling as he toweled dry and jumped into sweats and a T-Shirt to head out the door on time. He was once again very glad to have a career that did not require a suit and tie, except on the rare occasions of sports banquets!

As he drove toward BGM, he thought long and hard about the decision that he had been contemplating for the past several weeks. The ten days that Mary had spent in Ohio with her folks had felt like ten weeks. It was funny how sure he felt about his feelings for her. He had dated lots of girls when he had been in the NFL and even in his late 20's, but now in his 30's there was a decided shift in his emotions. He wasn't interested in former cheerleaders as much as in current Christian. He had never considered himself very religious. Sometimes he felt like he attended church more out of habit than for inspiration, but he surprised himself by admitting that he could not be serious about any girl,well, woman, who was not a Christian.

In his heart he knew that Mary was the right woman for him. He smiled as he remembered the athlete's definition of love that he had once read, "A feeling down deep that you can't quite itch." Certainly he had a special feeling down deep for Mary, and he had recently come to define it as love and not just lust. So, the next logical step was marriage, wasn't it? He was surprised that it made him more excited than fearful. He felt sure that Mary loved him as well. How should he ask her though? A romantic dinner? A walk along Indian Creek? Suddenly he had an idea. He grinned broadly and decided that he needed to make a trip to Burlington this weekend and go ring shopping. This would be a proposal for the ages! He'd have to talk to Mr. Frye in the new Communications Department…this proposal was going to be worthy of taping!

Chapter Fifty-three

Andrea Hogan

January was tearing by. In her old life at the Legislative Service Bureau, January had been relentless with the work that needed to be done for the Senators and Representatives. Now, fresh young teenage faces replaced the faces of seasoned lawmakers, but their demands seemed to be no less fearsome. The new semester had brought with it the dreaded *Hamlet* and *Romeo and Juliet* units that all of the freshmen seemed to dislike with equal relish. She remembered reading them in Miss Arnold's English class in the 1960's at East High in Des Moines; she herself had dreaded them as well.

She had been working on a lesson plan in front of the fireplace in The Principal's Office last week when Richard had happened by and seen her consternation, as well as thick volumes of Shakespeare's plays and commentaries as she struggled to find a way to make the age old words meaningful to this new generation of students who could barely spell, let alone speak in iambic pentameter.

"Don't tell me," he exclaimed as soon as he saw her layered in heavy books, "The dreaded Shakespeare unit!"

She laughed as she realized he was putting into words just what she had been thinking.

"Oh, Richard," she queried, "How did you handle this stuff when you taught Freshmen English?" Probably not very well," he conceded. "But through the years I did come up with some tricks that I can share with you."

"Share away," she encouraged.

He went on to describe in great detail about how he would have the class read a certain section and then translate the basic message of the lines into languages teens could understand such as "Hip Hop", "Rap", "Truck Loving Country Western" and the always popular, "Bugs Bunny." He explained that while you could not do this for every single verse, it did give the students a fun way to understand the material and still relate to the old Bard. He also suggested showing West Side Story, Hamlet with Richard Burton, and even a couple of cartoon versions just to break up the heavy stuff a bit.

She had felt immediately relieved and just a little more prepared than before he had entered the room.

He had continued to hang out in the doorway even after his mini curriculum lesson so she had invited him to join her by the fire. He seemed to come up with an idea and told her he would be right back. Within a few minutes he had returned with two piping hot cups of hot chocolate complete with Peppermint Candies for stir sticks. She laughed as she accepted her cup and inquired, "Leftovers from the tree decorating?"

"Waste not, want not," he advised.

"I wanted to tell you how much I enjoyed our time together for your birthday dinner," he began.

"I had a wonderful time too Richard. It was really special. It's not every day that a girl turns 59!" she agreed.

"It's been such a crazy few months. I don't feel like we ever get a chance to just sit down and talk. We covered more ground in those few hours that we were together than we did in the six months that we've lived in the same building," he acknowledged.

"It was good to hear about your life in Mons and Frankfurt and the kids growing up," she agreed. "You and I lost touch so quickly after college that all those years are just a blur to me."

Richard laughed, "You should have seen the look on your face when you saw that it was me grabbing the end of that couch from you last summer!"

"I admit I was taken aback, especially since I had never mentioned anything to Will about our time together, and I was deathly afraid you would say something like, 'Why, Andrea, I haven't seen you since we used to live together in Cedar Falls'."

Richard shook his head and admitted, "I wouldn't have put it past me. Have you told him about us yet?"

"No, it's just not the kind of a thing you want to talk to your son about. We're friends now, and that's all he needs to know. I told him we went to college together, and he accepted that without any questions. The only person who knows we lived together is Trish. She immediately saw that something was up that day and made me promise to tell her the whole story."

"It was a pretty good story, the kind of thing you see in novels more than in real life!" he added. "Do you ever wonder what might have happened if we'd been able to Skype instead of depending on Uncle Sam and answering machines to stay in touch.?"

"Actually I did wonder about that for a long time after my divorce," she told him. I even tried to find you once, through the UNI Alumni Association. I learned that you were married, and I decided that I'd better stop imagining what might have happened and get on with living my life and raising my child. That was solely my focus during Will's growing up years. His dad wasn't around much so I felt like I needed to do double duty, and there wasn't any room for regrets." She looked up at him then and realized she had said far more than he was prepared to hear. She laughed and waved him away with, "Be gone with you now. I've got lessons to plan!"

He laughed then, too, and jumped up from the couch, but he paused at the door and told her softly, "I wish you had looked harder." He was gone before she could reply.

Chapter Fifty-four

Scott Samuels

As Valentine's Day approached, Scott began to put his terrific plan into action. He caught up with Kevin Frye who had recently been hired at BGM to start an on-air television station for the school. It was designed to provide better communication among the students and the faculty, as well as teach valuable skills in the field of electronic communication. He explained his entire plan to Kevin who immediately told him he was in!

On Valentine's Day, a Saturday, fortunately, there just happened to be a home basketball game scheduled. It had become tradition rather quickly for Mary to attend all of the games with Trish, Rich, and Andrea. She had actually arrived at Scott's apartment in mid-afternoon, and they had watched a silly movie until Scott had had to leave for the team meeting. Trish and Andrea had invited Mary to share a soup supper with them before the game so Mary had kissed Scott good-bye at the landing and gone immediately to Andrea's cheery apartment.

Trish and Andrea were waiting for her with Andrea's famous Potato Dill Soup and after a brief grace; they set to the eating of the soup with relish. Mary asked where Rich was, and Andrea told her that he had spent the day at the farm with his folks and would join them at the basketball game. What she did not tell Mary was that Scott had told each of the apartment dwellers not to miss the game under any circumstance. Rich had been clueless as to the reason for the command appearance, but both Andrea and Trish smelled a romantic moment brewing, but neither of them was about to spill the beans to Mary.

After some good natured debate about the relative merits of each of their vehicles, they decided to go to the game in Mary's car since she claimed to have a heater that would blast them out if necessary, and the thermometer was hovering around 10 degrees on this Valentine's Day.

As they drove the eight miles into Marshtown, Mary asked the question that she had been pondering all day, "Do you think Scott may have forgotten it was Valentine's Day? He hasn't said a thing about it so I just kept my gift for him in my purse, it's a new stop watch, and I really want to give it to him, but I can't if he's totally forgotten the day!"

Trish looked at Andrea and at Andrea's stern look, she decided to just reassure Mary that Scott had probably planned to do something for her after the game, after all it was a sub-state regional match, and Scott was probably just wrapped up in the strategy to get his team to State.

Mary seemed to accept this explanation and seemed eager to hear about the flowers that she had seen in Andrea's apartment. Andrea explained that Will always sent her flowers on Valentine's Day, ever since he had first started working and had funds of his own. "But there were two bouquets in your apartment, weren't there?" Mary inquired.

"It was a surprise to me, but the other bouquet is from Richard, Rich." I haven't even had a chance to thank him yet, he must have left his cell phone in his apartment since I could hear it ringing above me when I called to thank him." What she did not share with her young friends was the sentiment on the card that had come with the flowers, "For all the Valentines I've missed your presence in my life." What in the world did that mean?

Before they knew it, they were pulling up in front of the gymnasium at BGM High School. All of the women looked toward the construction project that was the new auditorium. "It looks like they're making good progress despite the weather," Andrea remarked.

"I'd hate to be up on those steel beams," Mary added.

"Let's just hope it gets finished in time for next fall's play," Trish chimed in.

As they made their way toward the gymnasium entrance, they could clearly see that Valentine's Day was in the air. In honor of the day the school had declared this a "red-hot" basketball game and to a person everyone was decked out in red attire. It looked amazing, and Andrea could see that the folks running the newly acquired cameras for the Communications Department were having a field day catching all of the colorful clothing, and the people filling the stands.

Even the basketball players had gotten into the spirit of the day and were wearing their red "away" uniforms rather than their usual black uniforms with red accents. It truly was a fired up atmosphere in the old gym. The game proved to be just as hot with the lead trading back and forth all through the first half. Finally in the last two minutes of the half, the BGM boys were able to sink two three pointers and steal the ball and run the length of the court for an easy lay-in at the buzzer. Score at Half time: BGM, 35. Keota, 30.

Andrea was surprised to see the pep band come out at half time to give a mini concert while the cheerleaders did several routines while the band accompanied them. Andrea was even more surprised when the band stayed put as the two teams returned to the floor. Instead of warming up on the full court, the players from both teams took a spot on the far side of the court and were just standing around dribbling and talking to each other. All of a sudden she heard a familiar voice on the PA system, and she saw a larger than life shot of Coach Scott come up on the newly installed giant screens at either end of the gym.

Scott began, "Good evening, ladies and gentlemen. I'm sure you are all anxious for us to get back to the action in this great high school basketball game, and I assure you we will be shooting hoops within just a few minutes. But for the moment, I would like to ask all of you to indulge me while I give a very special lady her Valentine's Day present. I'm sure she has been wondering if I have forgotten this very special day, and I assure her I have not. But, I wonder if Ms. Mary Millen would mind joining me at center court so that I can give her this gift I have in person?" At this the camera panned toward the area where the group of friends was seated, and the camera began to follow the progress as Mary ventured toward the middle of the basketball court.

The crowd boisterously began calling, "Mary, Mary, Mary." Mary looked around at Trish, Rich and Andrea who were all equally dumbfounded at this turn of events. She shrugged her shoulders and made her way to the center court with the camera following her every move.

When she had nearly reached the BGM emblem on the middle of the floor, she looked into Scott's eyes with a very questioning look. In answer to her look, he dropped to one knee, took her hands in his and for all the world, or at least those around the BGM television network, said those most precious of all words, "Mary Millen, I love you, and I would like to ask you to do me the honor of marrying me." For a split second there was silence as the entire gymnasium waited for her reply.

They did not have to wait long as she began to laugh and cry at the same time as she replied, "Yes, oh yes. I love you, too." With those words Scott rose from his knees, produced a ring box and two dozen long stemmed red roses while the Pep Band played "The Hallelujah Chorus." As the audience began to recognize the strong cords to this beloved piece of music, they all rose to their feet and began to applaud in earnest. Scott kissed Mary and held her for a long moment. He slipped the ring on her finger, amazingly it fit perfectly, and they both began to walk back to the bleachers where Scott deposited Mary next to Andrea and the other friends. The Pep Band jumped up from their chairs and quickly moved them to the side, and the players began to warm up in earnest.

Everyone around her admired the ring, and it was quite some time before the four friends were able to turn their attention to the game in front of them. As if inspired by the love in the air, the BGM team started to pull away from their opponents and went on to a ten point victory and a trip to the Regionals in Iowa City.

After the game more people came up to Mary to admire her ring and tell her what a good man she was getting in Scott Samuels. He was after all the young man who had gone from this small town to play in the pros and rather than abandoning his past, he had returned to it to restore the old Bentley School House and to teach a new generation of young people.

Mary smiled and agreed with all of the folks singing Scott's glory. She agreed that it was a really romantic thing to do and assured all of them that "No," she had not suspected a thing. It was not until much later that night did she realize that one of the reasons for the entire production was so that she could share it with her grandmother Gladys. Scott handed her a DVD as they met after the Locker Room Rituals and told her that the video had already been uploaded to U-Tube. "I told your dad when I talked to him last week that they would be able to see the proposal, and hopefully your acceptance, before he went to bed tonight."

Mary was astounded, "You talked to my dad?"

Scott smiled and told her, "I may be impetuous, but I'm not stupid. I asked your dad for your hand in marriage, and he told me it was completely up to you, but from what he had heard from you, he thought I was worth taking a chance on. I just prayed that you would agree with him!"

"Oh, I do. I do," Mary assured him.

Chapter Fifty-five

Andrea Hogan

She heard the familiar Vivaldi ring and knew that her boy was calling from sunny Texas. She looked out the big old schoolhouse window and saw the bare trees buffeted by a brisk breeze and for a moment wished she was in Austin with Will!

He could barely contain himself as she answered the phone. "Mom, oh, Mom, I can't believe it!" he cried in delight.

"What in the world?" Andrea began to ask, but Will interrupted her.

"Mom, I'm the new Program Director for WMPG in Portland, can you believe it?"

Andrea was truly speechless. Finally she uttered, "Will, I didn't even know you had applied for the job!"

Will laughed, "I'm sorry, Mom. It was such a long shot, I didn't want to get everyone's hopes up and then not even get an interview."

"When did you interview?" she asked incredulously.

"During the National Public Radio Conference that was held in Dallas last month. They asked about ten of us applicants to come up with a year-long format, and then they set up a series of interviews during the conference. Can you believe it? They loved my folk show, and when I told them I want to expand it to reach European artists, they loved that idea, too!"

"So, I heard you say Portland, but I didn't catch if it was Maine or Oregon?"

Will laughed again, "It's the one in Maine. Do you remember how much I liked the city when I was working for the Spine Moving Company?"

"Oh, I do, Will. You almost moved there and started an east coast branch of the company," she remembered.

"Actually, Eric did move back there, it's his home town, so I have built in friends. Did I tell you that he married Erika?"

"Yes, I think I remember a very big party that lasted a couple of days," she recalled.

Will seemed giddy with anticipation and laughed his reply, "Well, it seemed to go on for days, but probably didn't last much more than eighteen hours! Wow, Mom, I can just barely wrap my head around all this. What a difference a few months makes in a person's life. Just a little over six months ago, I thought I'd be in Texas forever, and I wasn't sure if I'd ever find my dream job, or my dream girl, and now I have both."

Andrea's reply was quieter and much more serious. "I take it you're referring to Trish?"

Will's reply was equally as serious, "Yes, Mom, I mean Trish. How do you feel about that?"

"Will, if you're sure, then I'm thrilled. I love Trish as a friend, and I know I'll love her as a daughter." Andrea hesitated, "That is the direction you're heading, right?"

"Yes, Mom, I plan to make an honest woman of her," he assured her. "Actually, I also want to talk to you about Trish"

"I'm all ears," Andrea replied.

"Well, there are a couple of things that she and I have been talking about. As you already know, Miss Trish is a very practical person. So, she and I have been talking about a future together even though I haven't actually asked her to marry me, which I fully intend to do, when we are in Europe this summer."

"You and Trish are going to Europe this summer?" she asked in surprise.

"I've been saving my hard earned dollars for a couple of years now, and I have enough to spend a month backpacking in Europe, living my usual super cheap lifestyle, of course! I negotiated with WMPG to work via the internet during that time in exchange for recording new artists and looking for unique recordings in European record shops."

"Trish is planning on going with you?" Andrea asked

"Yes, Mom, she's dying to talk to you about it, but I wanted to talk to you first."

"Honey, as long as you have long range plans, I'm perfectly happy for you and Trish, I just didn't want either one of you to end up hurt," Andrea explained. "So does Trish know about the Portland job?"

"Yes, I did tell her about it once I got the interview. What she doesn't know is that I'm going to ask her to go there with me."

Andrea found herself speechless one more time.

Will cautiously asked, "What's your reaction to that little time bomb of information?"

Andrea thought for a moment and sighed, "Oh Will, I only want the best for both of you, but that's such a commitment on both of your parts. Are you sure about your feelings for her?"

"I'm sure, Mom," he told her quite solemnly. "As a child of divorce, I have always held myself to a different standard with women, I will not repeat past mistakes, and my feelings for Trish are true and sure. I don't mean to hurt you or bring up bad memories, but you've got to know that I don't ever want to put anyone through what Dad put you through."

Andrea felt the tears running down her cheeks, and she could only croak out an "I love you."

Andrea could hear the smile in his voice, "I know you do, Mom, and I love you, too. Now stop crying and go see your friend Trish and hear all about our plans for Europe. But not a word about my plans for Portland, that bomb shell needs to come from me, and it will soon. I know Trish will have to sign a new contract in March if she is going to stay at BGM, but I hope I can tempt her to leave small town Iowa."

Andrea bid her only child farewell and started for the front door to have a long visit with her neighbor, and future daughter? As she walked through the door, she remembered that she had completely forgotten to talk to Will about her own plans.

Chapter Fifty-six

Trish Wilkins

Trish opened the door to her apartment even before Andrea could knock. Will must have texted her to expect the knock on her door. Trish greeted Andrea with a hug. Andrea hugged her back and asked, "What's this about a trip to Europe without me?" Trish looked suddenly stricken so Andrea was quick to assure her, "I'm kidding. I'm kidding!"

Trish smiled and led her dear friend to her couch while she headed to the stove to start some water for tea. They had a lot to talk about.

Trish told Andrea all about the plans that she and Will had made for their great adventure in Europe. They would depart on June 8th and return on July 15th. That would mean just a little over a month for them to explore as many countries, and record shops, as their time and money would allow. Trish pulled out the map of Europe that she had been using to plot their itinerary.

"We're planning on flying to London and staying there for five days, and then we'll take the Chunnel over to Paris and train it or rent a car from there. I'm checking out every hostel between London and Madrid. We'll probably spend most of our time in France and Spain, but I'd love to try and get to Greece as well. The idea of seeing where mathematics was born is fascinating to me." Trish could barely hold in her enthusiasm.

"It sounds like the trip of a lifetime," Andrea agreed. "I know I fell in love with Spain when my friend Quinna and I travelled there to celebrate our 50th birthday year."

"I've been investigating the prices for rail passes and car rentals. I'm not sure yet which would be the cheaper route to go, but I'll figure it out," Trish assured Andrea.

"I tell you what: when you get it figured out, let me know, and the transportation within Europe will be my gift to the both of you," Andrea informed her.

The hug that Trish enveloped Andrea in and the lovely laughter coming from this young woman who seemed to be heading into her very own family was a huge down payment on what she would eventually pay for a couple of rail passes or a sub-compact vehicle to race around Europe.

Trish pulled out her cell phone and speed dialed Will so he could hear this piece of good news from his generous mother.

Will's enthusiasm was equaled to Trish's and his closing comment made Andrea smile an even broader smile, "Mom, you, of course, once again, win World's Coolest Mom." With that endorsement Andrea headed to her own apartment and Trish sat down to write a long email to her own mother. She wanted to tell her about this newest development in the Trish and Will saga. She also wanted to tell her mother that she had fallen hopelessly in love with this quirky young man who loved listening to old fashioned folk music and finding ways to reduce his carbon footprint.

As she began typing, she couldn't help but wonder why Will had said he planned to call her tonight after *"The Amazing Race."*

Chapter Fifty-seven

Scott Samuels

The four friends sat back in their chairs after polishing off a delicious supper of Andrea's Dilled Potato Soup and crusty French bread. They had all enjoyed seconds, and Scott had even had a third bowl of the hearty fare. He reasoned that it was all vegetables so it couldn't be that bad for his waist line!

Always curious, Trish asked the question that she and Andrea had been debating since Valentine's Day, when would Scott and Mary set the date? "So Scott," Trish began, "When's the big day?" He looked at her blankly. She tried again, "You know, your wedding day, you are planning on fulfilling that promise you made on Valentine's Day, aren't you?"

Scott laughed, "Oh, the wedding, I thought you were talking about the basketball sub-state game next week. I guess I can only handle one important date at a time!"

"Men!" Trish exclaimed. And they all laughed.

"I guess I do have news about the wedding," Scott admitted. "Mary and I talked last weekend, and we both agreed that we don't want to wait a long time. This is her second marriage, and I've never wanted a big wedding to begin with. So, we're thinking of having the ceremony, here."

"In the gymnasium?" Andrea asked.

"Well, not the ceremony," Scott explained. "We're actually thinking of having the ceremony on the first floor landing."

His three friends stared at him dumbly so he went on to explain. "The ceremony itself will be pretty small so Mary was thinking about filling the area with candles and, of course, we still have the rope lighting up that we used at the Christmas Open House. We'll rent a few chairs, and then we'll invite more people to come to the reception afterwards. Actually, we'll offer an open invitation like we did for the Open House. When he saw the look of consternation on Andrea's and Trish's faces, he was quick to assure them, nothing big, just cake and punch."

Andrea and Trish both breathed a sigh of relief.

"So, when are you thinking of doing all this?" Trish asked once again.

"Well, we decided we could either wait until summer, or get married just before spring break, and the winner is….spring break!" This announcement was accompanied by appropriate applause and congratulations by his friends.

"So, we are talking about this spring break, aren't we…the one coming up in, oh, let's see…thirty-seven days!"

"The very one," Scott assured her. "Now don't try telling me that you all can't pull off one little wedding, I've seen what you all can do when you put your minds to it."

Trish and Andrea smiled and agreed that, yes; they probably could pull off one small but memorable wedding in thirty-seven days.

"I'll call Mary, and we'll have a planning session on Saturday morning," Andrea decided.

Trish nodded and added; "Now we can add Wedding Planners to our resumes."

Chapter Fifty-eight

Andrea Hogan

Andrea had decided that no matter what the weather was like on the first day of March, she was taking her walking regime out of doors. As a New Year's resolution, both she and Trish had been walking at least one half hour each day on a tired old treadmill that they had purchased second hand at the Stuff Etc. store in Keosauqua. They had placed the behemoth in the far corner of the gymnasium and had maintained a rigorous schedule of good intentions throughout January and February. Andrea noticed that her slacks were a little looser, and she definitely noticed that she had more energy as she climbed the many stairs at BGM. But she was thoroughly tired of listening to Peter, Paul and Mary on her iPod and longed to see something other than concrete walls. She set her alarm for 5:00 a.m. when she went to bed in February and resolved to get up and out by 5:15 a.m. when the calendar turned to March.

When the alarm did go off on that first day of March, Andrea groaned and rolled over to hit the snooze button. But she was awake. It was just her way. She could rarely go back to sleep once her eyes were opened. She turned off the alarm and stumbled toward the bathroom to get ready for her first foray into the early morning streets of Bentley, Iowa.

She was surprised to find Richard waiting for her as she pulled on gloves and arranged her floppy hat over her curls. "Goodness," she whispered, "I didn't think you would really take me up on my offer to accompany me on my early morning jaunt!"

"I've always been an early riser anyway, as you remember, so I thought I might as well get some exercise, my doctor keeps telling me I'm not getting any younger. Even though my mind feels like it's still twenty-three, he insists my joints are getting close to 60 and need some lubricating."

As they left the building together, Andrea recalled, "Actually, I hadn't thought about those Sunday mornings in years. You were always willing to get the paper and make coffee."

Richard nudged Andrea as they turned the corner, "As I recall, I was always well rewarded for that paper and coffee." Andrea slapped him playfully on the arm, but he noticed that she was smiling as she took his arm and increased their pace.

They fell into easy conversation, as they always had. They talked about the progress of the spring play and his father's health. Richard told her that his dad was doing better on the new medicine, but Richard's mother was more determined than ever to get off the farm and into a more controlled situation. "In fact," he told her, "Mom and Dad have decided to hire Scott and Sandy to work at the farm this summer and organize a sale at the end of August. They want to build a house in Marshtown and rent out the farm land. It will be quite a change for them, but with Dad's health so tenuous they've decided to scale back and slow down."

"That's really sensible," Andrea agreed. "I've seen so many of my friends' parents refusing to give up their homes and then going straight from that home to a nursing home. You just have to know when to pack it in."

Richard laughed and acknowledged that he wasn't sure his dad was ready to "pack it in," but his mother certainly was and that was enough to get the ball rolling. "It will be wonderful to have both kids in the same place for at least a couple of months," Richard acknowledged.

"You can always escape to my apartment if their music gets too loud," Andrea offered.

"Aren't you going to be here this summer? I always forget this isn't your real home. It just seems like you've always lived here."

"Funny you should mention that," Andrea began. "I've been thinking about my house in Des Moines. I've talked to Will, and I've decided to sell it."

"Really?" Richard seemed surprised.

"I've been thinking about it since Christmas. It just doesn't seem like home anymore," Andrea began. "I haven't shared with you, or anyone here, that my decision to seek a big change in my life didn't just come from a lifelong desire to be a teacher. You see, the year before I was eligible to retire, a very dear friend of mine was killed in an accident in Des Moines. He was crossing a busy street in downtown, and some woman, talking on a cell phone, turned a corner too quickly and hit him while he was crossing the street. Doug was killed instantly. We had been dating for a little over a year, and we were starting to talk about a future together and suddenly he was gone."

"Oh, Andrea, I'm so sorry. In a small way I think I know a little how you feel. When Sally left so abruptly, I felt like I had been widowed."

"Yes, that's how I've felt these past few years," Andrea agreed. "But its way past time to move on with my life, and certainly changing careers and moving to a small town is evidence that I'm trying!"

"And succeeding," Richard added. "So are you planning a major down-sizing, or are you going to try and cram an entire house into your miniature home?"

"Well, it will be a major down-sizing, but still I'm planning on looking for a small house here in Bentley, or Marshtown," Andrea admitted.

"Wow, you're full of news today, my dear," Richard laughed. "I'll be sorry to see our gang break up. Trish's announcement last week that she's leaving to carve out a life with your son was shocking enough, now this!"

"At least I'm not moving to Maine, yet!" Andrea laughed.

"I couldn't take that much change in one fell swoop!" Richard protested.

"Oh, I'm happy enough here for now, but if those two start having babies, I cannot guarantee that I won't pick up and leave again. Surely it can't be as hard the second time!" Andrea laughed.

"Let's hope they wait for a while on those babies. I'm just getting used to having you in my life again, and I like it." Richard added.

Andrea laughed again, "Oh, you, I know you only like me for my lasagna!"

"That's a big part of it, I admit," Richard teased her, but then he got serious. "It's a lot more than that."

Before Andrea could think of a comeback, she was startled by the sound of a large truck rumbling up the quiet residential street that she and Richard were walking down. As the truck passed, she noticed a For Sale by Owner sign in front of the house across the street from where they were walking. She stopped so abruptly that Richard almost stumbled. As he caught himself, he looked down at her startled face, "What in the world?" he asked, and then he saw it, too. Across the street, sitting in a beautiful shaded corner lot stood a small brick bungalow with dormer windows in its second floor. From the look on Andrea's face Richard could tell that love at first sight also referred to small brick bungalows with dormer windows on the second floor.

When Andrea finally spoke, he knew she would be buying that house in the very near future. She looked at him intently and said, "Richard, look at the address on that beautiful house, its 1951, the year I was born."

Chapter Fifty-nine

Trish Wilkins

Trish sat on the couch in her apartment with a teaching contract in her hands and marveled at the way her life had taken such an amazing turn. She, who had not dated anyone for more than a few months all through college, was suddenly planning a life with a man that she had not known at this time last year. The amazing thing was that she felt no fear, only excitement. She would be moving to Portland, Maine, in just a few months, and the time before that move held the romance of a trip to Europe with the love of her life.

The trip to Europe was enough for her mother and grandmother to absorb so she had not mentioned the impending move back East yet. However, she had not had the luxury of keeping her principal so uninformed. Contracts had to be signed by the last day of March so she had made an appointment with Craig's secretary, Linda Alexander, to see him as soon as Will had asked her to move to Maine with him.

As she had walked into Craig's office and taken a seat in front of his giant, messy desk, he looked at her and began the conversation with, "Why do I have the feeling that I'm not going to like what you're about to tell me?"

Trish was dumbfounded. How did he know? Was he psychic?

Before she could reply, Craig laughed and explained, "It's a very small world that we live in here in the greater Bentley, Griswold, Marshtown metroplex. First I heard that you were planning on backpacking through Europe with young Mr. Hogan this summer, and then I overheard Andrea telling one of the other teachers that her very talented son would soon be programming music for Down-esters…and even though I'm not the math whiz here, I can still put 2+2 together and come up with 'My very talented first year math teacher is leaving'." Fortunately, he spoke these words with his usual kindness and concern that had instantly made him her favorite boss of all time.

Trish had still felt terrible telling him that, yes, he was right. She had assured him that she loved working for him and teaching at BGM…it was just that…

Craig had stopped her before she could complete her well-rehearsed apology. She had certainly been surprised by his next comment. "You, just happen to be a very lucky young lady."

Her look of confusion was enough to keep him explaining, "My college roommate just happens to be the Superintendent of the Portland, Maine, school district. He has at least three math positions opening up, and he's expecting an email from you at your earliest convenience."

Her look of confusion had slowly but surely turned to a look of pleasure and extreme gratitude. He had smiled at her and responded, "I'll consider myself hugged."

Trish had left Craig's office with a smile in her heart and her hands reaching for her Blackberry.

Now, less than a month after that fateful conversation, she found herself about to sign the second teaching contract of her young career. Craig's friend in Portland had barely interviewed her after she had sent her transcript and credentials. He had said, "If you're good enough for Craig Seeley, you're certainly good enough for me." "Good enough" was good enough for now, but she knew that she would need to start working on her master's degree sooner rather than later. She was relieved that she would be able to attend an actual university rather than the virtual one that living in a small town in southeast Iowa would necessitate. Still, she would miss this little town and all the wonderful people who had enriched her life over this past year. She was spared feeling the guilt of abandoning her grandmother by the knowledge that she would be moving to Arizona over the summer. Trish's mom and her grandmother had come to the mutual decision that they needed and wanted to live closer to each other so Nana herself was Arizona bound and looking forward to new adventures.

So, it was time to break the big news to both of the loved ones in her life…oh, yes, and her father as well! She reached for her Blackberry…she supposed she would start with her mom. After all, she had been the person who encouraged her to go to Texas and see if Will was for real, and he most certainly was.

Chapter Sixty

Verna Lee and Oscar Swenson

Verna Lee looked around the gymnasium of the old Bentley Elementary School house and marveled at how busy it was today, well, most any day! Gladys Millen was hard at work on her sewing machine, working on Mary's wedding dress. She noticed that she had plenty of helpers each with their own opinion of how it should look. She wasn't worried that they would sway the way that Gladys would construct the garment. Gladys had been sewing longer than any of them, and they all respected her talent. She was glad that Mary had chosen a simple pale blue fabric that would set off her eyes and had not tried to re-create her first wedding. This would be a special, but low key, event marked with good friends, close family members…and a few hundred friends who would join the festivities after the ceremony. She laughed and thought, "Scott and his invitations in the newspaper!"

She wondered if this open invitation would bring as many as the open house at Christmas time had, surely not, but they would be prepared just in case. Thankfully, it was an easy menu of wedding cake, punch, coffee and homemade cream cheese mints, made by the Home Economics students. The cake was being ordered from the Hy-Vee store in Marshtown, but since she did not like to take any chances she would supplement the store-bought cake with cakes that Scott's family would provide. His mother, sister, sister-in-law, three aunts and two cousins had all been recruited to provide two cakes each. That should be enough to cover all of the guests even if the entire town of Griswold decided to show up…and they just might. After all, this was Coach Samuels who was getting married!

She was distracted by the sound of a power saw across the room and noticed that her husband and best friend for the past fifty some years was equally busy working on the set for the Community Theater production of *Arsenic and Old Lace* that would be the debut production of the fledgling Bentley Community Players. He and the other old coots were constructing multiple sets that would swivel into place with the help of a few hardy stage hands. Fortunately, the set for the high school production of *The Fantastiks* was very simple, although it did somehow involve cutting a hole in the floor where a secret compartment would be utilized by one of the characters. She shook her head and realized that she might be mixing up the two productions!

In any event the men were not lounging around eating banana bread and discussing politics today. The skills that they had learned through many years of Do It Yourself and Honey Do projects were holding them in good stead today. But speaking of banana bread, she realized that she had better get some coffee going as they would all soon be gathering around for their mid-afternoon break, and then they would all head to their own homes. Many would return to an empty house filled with memories but no voices to keep them company. She looked around at the widows and widowers around her and wondered, not for the first time, if she should do a little match-making on the side?

Of course, not all of the old folks who filled this room had had the happy marriage that she and Oscar enjoyed. She remembered husbands and wives who had not been kind to their spouses, and she further wondered if some of her friends were just as happy to be at home with the television rather than a spiteful spouse. She decided that she did not have the time to worry about the romantic needs of seventy and eighty years olds as she gave herself a shake and headed for the fancy new coffee system that she had purchased with the proceeds from the Old Coot lunches. It was a wonderful system that brewed a pot of coffee in four minutes and had a warmer for the first pot while a second pot was being brewed. A long ways from her glass percolator that she used each morning when she was first married and her new husband needed some encouragement before he headed out into the cold to do morning chores. While she set out Banana Bread, Pumpkin Bread and her own Chocolate Chip Oatmeal Cookies, the first pot finished, and she started the second one brewing. Gradually the noises in the room diminished, and she saw that men and women alike were putting their respective work away and would soon be heading to the tables set up in the middle of the gymnasium. As she arranged treats she remembered, "Ah, its Yoga night." The old coots would have one more task after their break; the tables would need to be put away so that the class would have room to contort into their strange poses. She was just glad that hosting a yoga class at the Community Center did not also require her to attend.

As she moved the treats and coffee pots to the front counter, the Old Coots shook off the dust and headed to the Boys Room to wash their hands before coming up to the counter. They knew better than to try and get away with dirty hands in Verna Lee's house…or The Bentley Community Center.

Chapter Sixty-one

Richard Knight

"You want me to do what?" Richard asked incredulously.

His landlord and now friend laughed at his usually unflappable tenant. "Rich, you can do it, you're an actor… just pretend you're playing a minister in a play."

"Let me get this straight: you want me to pretend to marry you and Mary?"

"Oh, no, it will be an actual ceremony, you'll just be in charge instead of a person with a clerical collar," Scott tried to explain.

When Rich looked no less confused, Scott tried to explain in a little more detail. "Listen, the Pastor who has been at my folks' church for the past twenty years just retired, and I don't know the interim pastor at all since I've been going to church with Mary at Andrea's church. The pastor at Mary's church plans to be in Mexico when we want to get married. We both of us thought that rather than ask someone that we don't really know…we would ask you to perform the ceremony."

Rich wasn't much clearer and so he reminded his new friend of one small problem, "But I'm not a pastor!"

Scott smiled and reassured Rich, "Oh, don't you know you don't have to be a pastor to perform a wedding ceremony in Iowa? All you have to do is become ordained by The United Life Church, it's free and you can even do it on line."

"You can?" Rich was practically speechless. "Okay, let me get this straight, you want me to become ordained and perform your wedding ceremony? What do you want me to say?"

"Well, say whatever you think we should hear. Mary and I are going to write our own vows so I'm hoping you'll kind of fill in with kind words and maybe a little advice."

Rich grew serious. "I'm not sure I've got too much advice to give, but I think I can come up with a few words of wisdom about staying friends through thick and thin. I think that's what happened to Sally and me, we stopped being friends. Sorry, I didn't mean to get maudlin on you! Hey, I'd be honored to do your wedding. Let's get on the internet and get me official. I take it you and Mary have already figured out the stuff that needs done at the Court House?"

"Yup, we've already gotten the license and after the ceremony, we'll all sign the marriage certificate, and we'll be legal".

"Legal is good," Rich agreed. Then he thought to ask, "Who's standing up with you?"

"My brother will be the Best Man, and Mary has asked Trish to be the Best Woman."

"Best Woman? What happened to Maid of Honor?" Rich asked

"Don't ask me," Scott declared, it's all Mary's idea. She always hated being the Maid or Matron so she figured if there could be a Best Man, there could be a Best Woman. Mary's best friend from her high school days is about nine and a half months pregnant so there's no traveling for her. Mary and Trish have really hit it off since that first night that Trish waited for Mary outside the gym before the basketball game."

"Well, that's great. I assume Andi, Andrea, will have some role in this shindig?"

"Absolutely, we'd like her to read some scripture. I thought the two of you could kind of work on the ceremony together."

"Well, it sounds like we have a plan. Now let's get me some credentials!" Rich declared.

Chapter Sixty-two

The Wedding

Fortunately, the Friday of the wedding was a half day for school because even the awesome women of the Bentley School House apartments needed a few hours to transform the first floor vestibule into a wedding chapel. Because Mary had wanted to be married surrounded by soft lights and candlelight, the wedding had been scheduled for 7:00 p.m. The rest of the world would be invited to come to the reception at 8:00 p.m., and Richard had assured everyone far and near that this would not be a long drawn out ceremony.

The plea had gone out the week before for candles from friends and family, and throughout the week Verna Lee had been collecting candles that had literally been left at her doorstep. Trish and Andrea carried boxes home from school with every conceivable scent and size. This wedding would not only look good, it would smell tremendous as well. On Thursday night the ladies had commandeered every conceivable candle stand and object that would put the candles at different heights around the space. Fortunately, there were wonderful nooks and crannies all around the foyer.

Richard had generously offered the use of his large apartment for the ladies of the wedding party. They gathered there around 4:00 p.m. after the florist had arrived and the white calla lilies had been strategically placed between Andrea's and Trish's apartment doors to form a defined space where the ceremony would take place.

The men-folk, Scott, Rich, Mary's dad, and Scott's brother were all busy in the gymnasium helping Oscar and several of the Old Coots to set up dozens of tables and chairs that were being decorated just as quickly by Scott's and Mary's mothers as well as various aunts, cousins, friends and, of course, Verna Lee. The decorations, like the ceremony, were simple yet elegant. Verna Lee had put out her feelers and borrowed twenty five tablecloths in various hues of white and ivory. In the middle of each table stood a small bunch of brightly colored Shasta daisies. Flanking the daisies were tea lights that Verna Lee planned to light just before the guests were set to arrive. She also knew that any self-respecting citizen of Van Buren County would be home in bed by 10:00p.m., exactly two hours after the reception was scheduled to begin.

The cake had been delivered from the HyVee in Keosauqua, and it looked quite lovely. Simplicity reigned again, but the brightly colored daisies around the layers were charming and the couple on the top of the cake was smiling broadly. The additional cakes were surrounding the larger cake, and she quickly saw that the women she had asked to provide extra cakes had also gone the extra mile to decorate lovely miniature wedding cakes. She wondered how many had dug out their cake decorating supplies for the occasion. This would be the main cake station where the happy couple would cut the cake and feed each other the traditional first piece. As she loaded additional cakes onto the big brown cart she usually used to collect dirty dishes from the old coots she looked to see that the cake stations on either end of the gymnasium were ready to receive their fair share of the treats. There would be coffee, punch and mints at each of these stations as well. She smiled at her own ingenuity. This reception would be lovely, but also efficient.

Upstairs in Rich's apartment, both Mary's mother and her grandmother fussed over the last minute adjustments to Mary's dress. Gladys had put the finishing touches on it yesterday, and they all agreed it looked like a designer piece from a fancy Paris shop. It was a light blue linen dress that came to just below her knees. The bodice was tightly fitted and scalloped along the neck line. The blue of the dress set off the blue of her eyes, and she wore three inch high heels that helped her make up her height deficit when she stood next to Scott. Next to Mary's dress hung the pale pink sheath that Trish would wear as the Best Woman. Simplicity was the key here in all ways. The guys would be wearing their good Sunday suits and a small blue daisy in their lapels.

Across the hall in Scott's, soon to be Scott and Mary's, apartment were cold cuts, salads, and soft drinks for the residents and wedding party. Scott and Mary had decided that they would avoid each other for the entire day of the wedding so that their first sight of each other would be as she was coming down the wide stairway that led from the landing between the main floor and the upper level. They were practical people, but still, they wanted to uphold at least a few traditions.

One of those traditions would be something old, something new, something borrowed, and something blue. The something old was an antique handkerchief that had come from Mary's father's mothers wedding. Fortunately, Mary's mother was an organized person who had found the handkerchief on the first foray into their attic. The something new would be the beautiful gold heart shaped pin her mother and father had given her just before the whole dressing process began. The something borrowed were the earrings that Andrea had owned for quite some time. They were pearls, but with a very slight hint of blue. For the actual something blue, Mary proudly wore her grandmother's blue amethyst necklace that she had worn in her own wedding. The mirror that had been hauled up from Trish's apartment revealed a beautiful bride, grateful for a second chance at love.

By 6:30 p.m. everyone had been fed, dressed, and was ready for the twenty or so guests who would attend the actual ceremony. Thanks to Kevin Frye and the new AV equipment purchased by BGM, the rest of the well-wishers would see the ceremony on a continuous loop that he would set up after he recorded it from his precarious perch near the entrance to the Principal's Office/Library.

Everything was set. At a few minutes before 7:00 p.m. Trish, Rich, Scott, and his brother Steve took their places in front of the calla lilies. The High School Band Director Charles Carnes played background music while he waited for his cue to begin the very untraditional wedding march. This part had been all Mary's idea. She had not had the nerve to do this when she had been married the first time when she was a young girl of just twenty-one, but this time she would do things her way. She had no intention of being given away a second time by her adoring father. This time she would walk alone into this marriage, well, Scott planned to meet her half way down the aisle that had been created by the folding chairs.

She would not walk down the stairs to the traditional wedding march, or even an instrumental version of an old classic song. Instead, at a signal from Andrea, Charles Carnes began to play and sing the Kingston Trio version of *The First Time Ever I Saw Your Face*. As Mary walked slowly down to the landing, Charles sang, *"The first time ever I saw your face I thought the sun rose in your eyes, and the moon and stars were the gift you gave to the dark and the empty skies, my love, to the dark and the empty skies."*

She stood at the landing and looked out over the loving crowd as he sang,

"The first time ever I kissed your lips, I felt the earth move in my arms like the trembling heart of a captive dove that was there at my command, my love that was there at my command." As Andrea stood, the rest of the crowd stood, and Mary walked to the middle of the aisle where Scott was waiting for her. As they finished the short walk to the front of the foyer, Charles finished the beautiful song with the final verse, *"The first time ever I held you near and felt your heart beat close to mine, I felt a joy to fill the earth and last until the end of time, my love, and last till the end of time. Our love will last till the end of time."*

Richard smiled broadly as he faced his two new friends who were grinning and holding on to each other's hands for dear life. He began the ceremony by welcoming everyone, "Dear family and friends of Mary and Scott, first of all they have asked me to welcome all of you here on their behalf, so, 'Welcome'".

A slight bit of laughter floated over the assembled group. He continued, "We've come together on this early spring night to celebrate with Mary and Scott. We've come to celebrate their decision to marry and to wish them well on this new life that they are about to navigate together. Our most important task tonight though is to be witnesses to the solemn vows that they are going to make to each other. These vows will form the foundation of the life they will live together. Before we hear their vows, they have asked their friend Andrea Hogan to read a few passages from the Bible because they want to be sure that their marriage is blessed by and formed by the love of God that they both share."

Andrea stood up and moved to the music stand that had been set up in front of the keyboard. She opened a well-used Bible and turned on a reading light that was clipped to the stand. She smiled at the happy couple and began by saying, "Mary and Scott, you've asked me to share my favorite bible passages with you today, but I hear that Verna Lee wants to get the reception started by 8:00,tonight, so I think I'd better limit this to just a few of my very favorite verses. I know that you're expecting me to begin with the love chapter in the Bible, First Corinthians: Chapter Thirteen, and I will get to that, but the verses that I want to begin with are from the letter that the apostle Paul wrote to the church at Philippi, "Rejoice in the Lord always; again I will say, Rejoice. Let your gentleness be known to everyone. This Lord is near. Do not worry about anything, but in everything by prayer and supplication with thanksgiving let your requests be made known to God. And the peace of God, which surpasses all understanding will guard your hearts and minds in Christ Jesus…I can all do all things through him who strengthens me." Just change that last verse from "I" to "We" and I think you will find that advice will hold you well in your marriage. "The second reading that I would like to share with you is from Colossians: Chapter Three."

She read, "As God's chosen ones, holy and beloved, clothe yourselves with compassion, kindness, humility, meekness, and patience. Bear with one another and if anyone has a complaint against another, forgive each other; just as the Lord has forgiven you, so you must forgive. Above all, clothe yourselves in love, which binds everything together in perfect harmony. And let the peace of Christ rule in your hearts."

"Finally, no wedding would be complete if we did not hear those beloved verses from First Corinthians: Chapter Thirteen, the Love Chapter. "Love is patient, love is kind, love is not envious or boastful or arrogant or rude. It does not insist on its own way; it is not irritable or resentful. It does not rejoice in wrongdoing, but rejoices in the truth. It bears all things, believes all things, hopes all things, and endures all things."

Tears were running down Mary's face, and Scott quickly wiped away a stray tear as Andrea finished her reading and turned to speak to these two young people who had come to mean so much to her in a few short months. "Mary and Scott, May the God of love bless your marriage and keep you bound together through the love of his Son, Jesus Christ, our Lord and Savior."

As Andrea took her seat, Charles began to sing a lovely song that Mary had found in a CD that she had borrowed from Andrea. It was by a duo known as The Shaffer Brothers.

Come stand with me, be my one and only.

All my days to come, stand with me, be my one and only, one and only love.

Stand with me, share my life, my hopes, and my dreams for all eternity.

Stand with me, be my one and only, one and only love.

Give me your hand and with this ring I will be always here for you.

Give me your hand and hand in hand we'll journey always me and you.

Give me your hand, together we'll go through the years. We'll treat each day as one.

Give me your hand, and hand in hand, we'll journey always me and you.

Give me your hand, together we'll go through the years. We'll treat each day as one.

Give me your hand and hand in hand we'll journey always me and you.

Come stand with me, be my one and only all the days to come.

Stand with me, be my one and only, one and only love.

There wasn't a dry eye in the house by the time he was finished.

It was definitely a hard act to follow, but it was Richard's turn to address the young couple. Like the true actor that he was, he had written a script and memorized it so that he needed no notes as he began to speak to them.

"Mary and Scott, I have to say I was absolutely floored when Scott asked me to officiate at this ceremony tonight. But the astonishment soon gave way to a sense of honor and pleasure. I'm all for helping people marry each other! I believe in marriage. Marriage proves that you are serious about the feelings you have for each other. Marriage also means that you are entering into a covenant, not just a civil contract. A covenant means that you're in this relationship for the long haul. You're committed to working through the bad times and rejoicing during the good times. A covenant is the promise that you will love each other, and God. I will only give you one piece of advice tonight, always be each other's best friend. When you are each other's best friend, you will naturally turn to each other when you are hurt or happy. You'll build love as you build your friendship. I promise."

He looked up from the eyes that had held his and spoke to the assembled guests. "Mary and Scott have chosen to write their own wedding vows so at this time I turn to you Scott and ask if you have anything you would like to say to Mary?"

The smile on Scott's face was infectious, and everyone in the small foyer found themselves smiling, too, as Scott turned to Mary and said, "Mary, I am so grateful that you are going to marry me." With those words all of the guests burst out laughing. Scott and Mary joined in the laughter, but then Scott became serious and continued, "Mary, I pledge to you that I will walk by your side in this life we are leading. I promise to honor you, to love you, and to always ask God for guidance in the decisions that we will make together." Scott turned to Richard to let him know that he had spoken his piece. Rich turned to Mary and said to her, "Well, that was quite a speech for a football player. Now it's your turn!"

Mary took a deep breath and began, "Scott, I'm really glad you're marrying me, too." The audience laughed appropriately. "You know that my heart was pretty much shattered when my first marriage ended. I truly never thought I would love anyone again. I'm so glad I was wrong. When we first met, you happened to tell me the athlete's description of love as being 'a feeling down deep that you can't quite scratch.' At first that seemed like just clever words to me, but as I thought more about it, I came to see that there is more truth than fiction in those words. I know that ever since I met you at the Community Thanksgiving Dinner right here in this building, I've had a feeling in my heart that is unlike anything I have ever felt before. It didn't take very long for me to realize that the feeling was love, and I was so happy to learn that you were feeling the same. Your very public proposal on Valentine's Day was music to my ears, and my heart literally leapt for joy when you asked me to share your life. So, now we have gathered our family and our friends, and we'll be joined by even more family and friends in just a little while, to share in our joy. On this evening my dearest Scott, I promise to love you, to care for you, to walk beside you in good times and in bad, and most of all, I promise to always keep our love for God as the most important tie that binds us together."

She turned to Rich to let him know that she was finished. Rich smiled at both of them and told them and the assembled group. "Well, we're almost done!" At that moment he turned to Scott's brother Steve and to

Trish to recover the rings that both had been holding. He handed the larger of the two rings to Mary and asked her to place the ring on Scott's finger and to repeat, "Scott Eugene Samuels, please accept this ring as a symbol of my love and faithfulness." Mary did as she was instructed. Rich turned to Scott and handed him Mary's ring. "Your turn," he told Scott. "Mary Gladys Millen, please accept this ring as a symbol of my love and faithfulness." Scott repeated his line without a hitch and looked into Mary's eyes with love and admiration.

Rich looked at the newly married couple and declared, "By the powers vested to me by the internet, I now declare you husband and wife. You may seal this union with a kiss." And indeed they did.

As they turned to face their family and friends, Charles broke out with *The Hallelujah Chorus*, and all of the guests rose to their feet and applauded the newlyweds as they walked the few short feet to the back of the foyer. As the guests began to filter out toward the steps, Scott and Mary greeted each one and Verna Lee, Andrea, and Trish slipped down the stairs to light tea lights and take up their places at the cake stations.

It was a good thing it had been a relatively short ceremony. By 7:45 p.m. the headlights began to appear through the glass blocks of the gymnasium windows. All of the guests from the ceremony had made their way downstairs and had taken up their rightful place in the tables nearest the main cake station. They would have a bird's eye view of the cake cutting whenever that ritual began. In the meantime there was coffee and punch and cream cheese mints to keep the partygoers at bay.

At first Mary and Scott greeted each guest as they arrived for the reception. Even though they had requested that any gifts be directed to the Marshtown Habitat for Humanity organization, there were still many cards and a few small gifts to mark the joyous occasion. The cards and gifts were taken by Scott's aunts to the gifts table which allowed the guests to greet the couple with open arms and hearts. Slowly the guests made their way into the gymnasium, and it quickly became apparent that this plan was not going to work. Rich consulted with Verna Lee, went up the stairs and announced to the throng of people waiting in the chilly night air that Mary and Scott would be greeting folks at the tables after everyone had been seated. Rich ushered the friends that he had just married into the gymnasium, and they began immediately to mingle among the guests while the folks waiting to join them quickly found tables and surrounded themselves with family and old friends. Within fifteen minutes the tables were nearly filled with well-wishers, and Verna Lee gave the signal for Rich to escort Mary and Scott to the cake table for cake cutting and speechifying.

Rich used the portable microphone that he had brought from the high school to get everyone's attention and to welcome them all to Mary's and Scott's wedding reception. He reminded everyone to view the ceremony on the television set that Kevin had supplied over in the far right corner of the gymnasium. He then invited the happy couple to say a few words to the assembly of friends and family. Scott took the microphone and greeted everyone with simple but heartfelt words. "Mary and I are so pleased that you've chosen to take time away from hearth and home to help us celebrate this very special day. Most of you have known me since I was a little boy. You've been there for me through good days and bad days. I'm happy to report that this is definitely one of the good days! We are blessed to be able to welcome my new wife to our community, and I look forward to all of you coming to know her in the months and years to come. We are happy to make our home here, and we look forward to a long and happy life among you. Now, I hear we need to feed each other some cake, so let's get to it!"

With that he reached his hand out to his new bride and brought her close to his side while she used her free hand to slice a big piece of the three tiered wedding cake and offered it to her new husband. He took the cake and sliced one for her. Then amid laughter and playful hoots they managed to feed a little of it to each other before giving up and kissing each other instead.

Richard took the microphone from Scott and through his own laughter; he invited the crowd to disperse to one of the three cake stations and to enjoy this time of fellowship. He assured everyone that Scott and Mary would make it to each table before the evening ended.

With that, bedlam ensued. And a good time was had by all.

Chapter Sixty-three

Verna Lee Swenson

Verna Lee suddenly jerked awake and was momentarily unsure of where she was. It was broad daylight, and she always awoke before the dawn. Beside her, Oscar snored softly, seemingly dead to the world at this late hour of...7:45 a.m...good heavens! She smiled, after all it had been nearly midnight before she and Oscar had snuggled under the covers after last night's late night festivities. She moved quietly out of bed and slipped into her slippers and robe and made her way out of the bedroom in hopes of having a few minutes with a hot cup of coffee before Oscar awoke.

"Another great event," she thought to herself as she added coffee grounds to the trusty old Mr. Coffee and poured water into the reservoir. Last night had been a study in cooperation and good organization. By 8:30 p.m. everyone had been served cake, mints and a beverage of choice. Mary and Scott made the rounds of the tables to greet and meet the many friends and relatives that had responded to Scott's open invitation in the Keosauqua and Marshtown newspapers and had joined them in celebrating their wedding day.

There had been so many folks for Mary to meet. Even though Mary's grandmother, Gladys, had lived in the community for over twenty years, she was still considered a newcomer to the area, and Mary's mother had married and moved to Ohio long before Gladys had married her second husband Rollin and taken up residence on the farm outside of Bentley, so Mary would need to begin at the beginning in making friends and establishing her home here in Bentley. Fortunately, she would be able to give up the long commute to Keota after this school year as Craig Seeley had been happy to hire her to fill the 3ʳᵈ grade position that had opened up in the elementary building in Marshtown.

As Verna Lee was puttering around her kitchen waiting for the coffee to brew, she heard the sound of muted voices and luggage being knocked against the old marble steps that led from the second floor apartments. She distinctly heard Mary shush her new husband as they made their way down the steps toward the front doors of the old school house. She pulled her robe tighter around her and opened her apartment door to greet the newlyweds.

"Happy first day of your life together!" she called in a stage whisper.

Mary and Scott both grinned and came forward to give Verna Lee a quick hug. "Thanks again for the wonderful reception, Verna Lee. Everything was perfect!" Mary assured her.

"I'm so happy we could help to start your married life off right, do you have plenty of time to get to the airport?" Verna Lee inquired.

"Yes," Mary replied, "We don't have to be in St. Louis until 2:00 p.m. so we'll have plenty of time to get there, park the car, and have a little lunch before we have to board the plane to Mexico."

"When will you return?" Verna Lee asked in her quiet voice.

"We fly into St. Louis a week from today and depending on the weather we'll either drive back here or spend the night in St. Louis," Scott explained.

Just then Trish's door opened, and she slipped into the hallway to join the departing party.

"Don't tell me you're going on the honeymoon with the newlyweds!" Verna Lee asked laughingly.

"No, I'm just tagging along to St. Louis," Trish explained in a whisper. "I'm catching a plane to Boston where Will is going to meet me, and then we're heading to our new home in Portland, Maine."

"That sounds very exciting, dear," Verna Lee assured her. "Will you be able to meet back in St. Louis next weekend?"

"We're hoping it all works out," Scott concluded.

Verna Lee reached up to give each of them a kiss on the cheek and wished Scott and Mary a very happy honeymoon and Trish a wonderful Spring Break. They all made their way down the steps and into the chilly spring air.

Verna Lee turned back to the Mr. Coffee that had just finished brewing her morning coffee, and it did look like she would have a few more minutes to herself, she could hear Oscar snoring from the bedroom.

She poured her coffee and marveled at what a different life it was these days. She and Oscar had ventured all the way to Lake Darling for their honeymoon all those years ago. As for making plans to move across the country …well, it wasn't for her, but certainly seemed to make Trish happy.

She smiled as she heard a muffled sound coming from the bedroom, and she rose to fetch a cup of coffee for her beloved. Weddings always made her sentimental, and she decided that she would make the old coot his favorite French toast with cinnamon and vanilla. He really was a pretty good husband…and friend.

Chapter Sixty-four

Andrea Hogan

Andrea sat at her kitchen table on the day after the wedding, got out her calculator and began once again to put numbers on paper to determine if purchasing the house at 1951 Maple Street was a wise investment or a foolish dream. She had to admit that because of her wise investments through the years and her extra principal payments that had paid off the Des Moines house several years ago; she could well afford this somewhat impulsive move. Will had been very supportive of her idea, wanting only her happiness, as always. Now, it was ultimately her decision.

She smiled as she thought about the first time she had been inside the house. The realtor must have thought she was crazy when she and her entourage had shown up to look at the house. She had contacted the only Realty Company in the county as soon as she had gotten home from school that day that she and Richard had first spied what she had immediately thought of as her next home. The realtor that had been on duty that night assured her that no one would be snatching up the 1951 property anytime soon. It had been on the market for nearly a year, ever since its owner, Myrtle Ritland, had gone into the nursing home after falling and breaking her hip. Andrea had made an appointment to see the house the very next Saturday and had begun immediately to assemble her support system to determine if the house was worth the effort it would be for her to sell her home in Des Moines and settle more or less permanently in Bentley, Iowa.

Of course, she had asked Richard to accompany her. She valued his opinion and perhaps more than she cared to admit, wanted his approval of this purchase. Next she had explained the situation to her landlord and

232

friend Scott. She had thought that he would be disappointed that she would not be a long term renter. He had quickly assured her that young teachers who were stuck in substandard apartments in Marshtown approached him monthly to see if any of the tenants had decided to move out. He had already secured a tenant for Trish's apartment, though it would be empty through the summer as the young teacher was stuck in a lease until August 1st. It had been Scott's suggestion to bring along his brother Steve who had been the driving force in the renovation of the Schoolhouse. Of course, Trish had insisted on coming…and Oscar and Verna Lee looked pleased when she had asked them to come and take a look as well.

"Of course, I've been in the house many times," Verna Lee reminded her. "The Dorcas Circle used to meet there at least three times a year, back when there was a Dorcas Circle." Andrea had been eager to find out about the layout of the house, but all Verna Lee could remember was that Myrtle had purchased some horrific blue, red, green and yellow shag carpet in the 1970's and covered up her gorgeous hard wood floors. Verna Lee decried her old friend's bad taste and did mention that the downstairs was one nice big living and dining room, but that the bedrooms on the first floor were, in her word, dinky.

The Saturday of the appointment was sunny, and the Schoolhouse friends decided to walk the few blocks to Maple Street. Steve would meet them there and the realtor promised to be there at 10:00 sharp. They were an amusing looking group. Verna Lee and Oscar set the pace while Rich, Andrea, Trish, and Scott, and Mary followed behind, linking arms and singing, "We're off to see the wizard" with varying degrees of harmony and key.

Fortunately, they had run out of steam by the time they stopped in front of 1951 Maple Street because Steve and the realtor were waiting for them; Steve was already finding out the basic information about the house.

Andrea introduced her troop to the realtor and tried to explain why she had so many folks along with her. The realtor just smiled and assured her, "I'm just glad someone is finally serious about this little gem. Let's go inside."

They first entered into a lovely screened porch complete with wicker furniture and a glider at the far end of the porch. "Oh my goodness," Andrea exclaimed, "that glider is just like the one from my folks' house."

"The glider and the wicker furniture are included with the sale price. The rest of the furniture got divided up when Myrtle moved to the nursing home. Nobody in the family wanted these pieces."

He started to open the front door, but before he did he turned to the group and warned, "Now, you need to look beyond this carpet that you're about to see, I promise you there are wonderful hardwood floors underneath."

Andrea patted his arm and assured him, "It's OK, and I've already been warned."

Even with Verna Lee and the realtor's warning, she had to admit that the carpet had been something to behold. A basic royal blue shag, it contained specks of red, green, and yellow throughout. It was also, everywhere! A sea of speckled blue stretched as far as the eye could see, and Andrea had the horrible suspicion that since it was also in the hallway, it must have also been in the bedrooms as well. She was right. Verna Lee put the best possible spin on the entire situation. "Just think: you won't have to worry about drop clothes when you paint."

Leave it to Verna Lee to have an optimistic outlook. The walls would certainly need painted. They were a pale pink, but the beautiful walnut trim had not been painted, and walls could easily be painted. Andrea had been immediately drawn to a built in cupboard all across the back wall of the dining room area. It had leaded glass in the doors and miles and miles of shelves that would hold every piece of china and crystal that she owned, and maybe even someone else's collection as well. The walnut doors under the buffet area would be wonderful storage space for linens and her other serving pieces that she was always regretting that she had left in Des Moines.

Behind the dining room was a very nice sized kitchen. The cupboards were original to the house, and the appliances looked like they were from the early 70's, avocado to the max. Trish burst out laughing as she walked around the corner. "That's avocado," she laughed, "I've heard it existed but I've never actually seen it in an appliance!"

Rich came up behind her and declared, "Then you've lived way too sheltered of a life! My folks had to have the newest color in their kitchen when they remodeled after I left for college."

Steve had taken one look at the kitchen and declared, "Total gut job." He was probably right.

They had moved on to the two small bedrooms and the hall bath. Andrea had felt mixed emotions, they were both about the size of her bedroom at the schoolhouse, but far smaller than her master suite that she had lovingly created out of two rooms in her old Victorian in Des Moines. She remembered, with a little bit of longing, her Jacuzzi tub and separate shower.

Steve had ventured an idea. "Why not," he had mused "make this bedroom to the left a walk in closet, expand the bathroom, and make an entrance from the bathroom to the closet and another entrance from the other bedroom into the bathroom?"

"Would guests have to go through my room to get to the bathroom?" Andrea asked.

"I think we could actually carve out a small half bath under the stairs that lead to the second floor. All you really need is a stool and a tiny sink. I'll have to check out the basement to be sure we can get plumbing to that area, but I'm thinking it's doable," Steve had advised.

They had headed upstairs at that point and found three nice sized bedrooms and a perfectly acceptable bathroom; fortunately with hardwood floors intact and no tacky carpet anywhere in sight. All of the bedrooms needed a new coat of paint, and the rose colored wallpaper in the front bedroom would have to go, but all in all, perfectly acceptable.

Steve had been pleasantly surprised, "I wouldn't do anything up here except paint and give it a good cleaning."

Andrea had agreed, "This floor will be for Will and Trish, she had added, for when they visit, so some paint and elbow grease will certainly suffice. Don't you think, Trish?"

"Let me choose the color, and I'll even do the painting," Trish had agreed.

"Let's not get ahead of ourselves," Andrea had cautioned. "I don't even know how much they're asking for this place!" They had all turned to look at the realtor, and he had held up his hands sheepishly and advised them, "Well, they're asking $48,000...but I think you could get it for $40,000."

Oscar and Verna Lee nodded their approval at the price, and Rich and Andrea exchanged knowing glances. Both had been expecting to hear a figure thousands higher, housing prices in small towns certainly were more reasonable than the large cities they were used to living in. Andrea turned to Steve and asked, "Ball park figure for renovation?"

"Conservative estimate: $25,000; I looked at the foundation, and it really looks great, but you need a new roof and that includes the one on the garage as well. But once you've done those things, you'll have a house that will last another eighty years."

"When would you be able to do the work?" Andrea asked.

"I've still got about six more weeks on the restoration of the Hughes' house up in Marshtown, and I promised to take my wife to Colorado for a week when we finish up so I'm guessing mid-May."

Andrea had laughed and asked all of her friends to pray for her while she made the decision. "Now I'd better take some pictures of this place so I can send them to Will and get his opinion!"

She had snapped away while the rest had walked outside to enjoy the soft warm air of the spring morning. Richard had walked in a few minutes later and found her staring around the living room and dining room. She had been startled when he had said, "I can see you living here, Andi."

"So can I Richard, so can I," she had said.

Chapter Sixty-five

Richard Knight

To an outsider the activity going on at the old Bentley Schoolhouse gymnasium must have looked like total chaos. Rich looked around and was heartened to see all of the activity. Oscar and his friends were putting the finishing touches on the scenery for *The Fantastiks* and the ladies were busy fitting costumes on young people. Andi was running lines with the two main love birds of the play, Matt and Luisa, well, Tony Shaw and Jill Brooks. From the looks of things, they knew their lines quite well; they needed to, they opened in a little over a week. Richard never tired of this production. He had discovered *The Fantastiks* while he was in college. The Theater Department at UNI had done it his junior year. He had worked as a stage hand and could sing every song and recite every line by opening night. That had come in handy when the actor playing Mortimer had fallen off the stage and broken his foot before the last performance. Rich had stepped into the role and pulled it off without a hitch. The director had been very grateful and since he was also his Acting 101 professor, Rich was assured that his final grade would indicate his gratitude. And it had.

Not that Rich had needed much extra help in the classroom. He had been a good student and knew since high school that he wanted to be a high school English and Drama teacher. He had gone on to graduate school right after college because he knew he wanted to be the best in his field. As it turned out, he had learned far more in the first few years as a teacher in the Framingham, MA, school system than he had ever learned in graduate school.

Rich was shaken from his reverie by Oscar's booming voice. "Hey, Rich come and take a look at this trap floor we just finished. We need to do more plays that need a trap floor, its great!" Rich headed off to see the handy work of the old coots, he had to stop thinking of them as such, but Verna Lee's pet name for these old fellows was too catchy to chase out of his mind! The trap door truly was a thing of beauty. The fellows had constructed it so that when the hatch was raised, a small set of steps led down to the dark and spooky area under the stage. They had taken pity on the young man who would need to hide down there during much of the musical and installed a light bulb so the creepy crawlies would at least be seen. They were still working on the giant trunk that would cover the trap door and allow the actor to emerge at various times during the production. It was a small part, but an endlessly entertaining one that could easily steal the show from the regular characters.

Verna Lee and Mary's grandmother, Gladys, were fussing over the length of Luisa's dress. Gladys was definitely opting for a shorter skirt while Verna Lee was voting for a length that was a little closer to the middle of the knee cap. The debate was vigorous but friendly. Clearly Verna Lee had won when the pinning was finished and Jill was practicing her "flouncing." The hem was firmly pinned at the knee. Rich smiled and turned away from the ladies and blew his whistle that he found was just as effective in getting the attention of actors as it was football players.

"OK, thespians, let's get started. We've only got six more rehearsals before opening night!" A collective sigh came from the young actors, but they hurriedly took their places to begin rehearsing those lines they had worked so hard to learn.

Chapter Sixty-six

Andrea Hogan

Andrea stopped momentarily to survey the chaos around her, and distinctly had a feeling of *de ja vu* all over again. Her apartment had once again been overrun by teenagers as the ever expanding cast of characters and production assistants (as Richard liked to call the volunteers who did everything from applying makeup to moving chairs) vied for space to create the magic that is, was, and ever will be…theater. Make up application was in full swing for all of the actors. Young women were working hard to make teenagers look elderly. Young men were bearing up under tons of make-up, and three different actors were singing three different numbers in the small space that was her living room, dining room and kitchen. Finally, someone kicked the singers into the hallway and closed the door on them so the chaos at least got a little quieter. She wondered what it would be like to get ready for next fall's play when they would be in their newly built backstage area for the auditorium. Richard had shown her plans that looked like the space would be a lot more efficient than that of her kitchen table.

She smiled to herself, as she often did, when she thought about what a change her life had taken in the past few years. First the tragedy of Doug's untimely death, then her decision to go back to school to get her teaching degree, and now this totally new life among new, and old, friends. She wondered what new adventures would await her as she sold her home in Des Moines and took up permanent residence in, of all places, Bentley, Iowa.

She had after all, bought the little house at 1951 Maple Street. The banker in Marshtown, who happened to be Craig Seeley's brother-in-law, had quickly given her a bridge loan to purchase the property and begin the renovation. She would close on the property on May 15, and she hoped to get a head start on the renovation by accomplishing the list of demolition items that Steve had given her. Anything that she and her cohorts could do would reduce the cost of the renovation.

Richard had already told her that he and his son would tear off the old roofs over the house and the garage and re-roof them before Steve and his guys tackled the renovations inside. She had been astounded at this offer and had immediately offered to pay them for their work. His reply had caught her off guard, as usual, because he had agreed that she could pay his son a couple hundred dollars, but his labor was a free gift. He had even offered to give everything upstairs a couple coats of paint before she moved in. She had asked Trish and Will to pick out the colors and through many long skype conversations and text debates, they had settled on a palette of coffee, sage green, and butter yellow. The yellow color would also be in the hallway. The upstairs bath would be a soft green with an accent wall of lime green. "Very hip and trendy," she thought. The paint had been purchased and rested safely in Oscar's work room downstairs.

Steve would begin the renovation in the kitchen. With his help and Richard's input, they had designed a very nice kitchen with plenty of cupboard space and even a small pantry, a feature that even her big eat-in-kitchen in Des Moines did not have. She was not putting in an extravagant kitchen. She well knew that at some point in time this house would be put up for sale and she dare not price herself out of this small town market. It would be adequate, and the cupboards, while not cherry, would hold her dishes and pots and pans just as well as cherry.

After the kitchen was complete, Steve would move to the bedrooms and create the new scheme that would find the second bedroom becoming her closet with an entrance from the bathroom. Her bathroom would include a deep soaker tub with a Jacuzzi and a separate shower with one of those rainfall shower heads like she had always wanted. The entrance from the hallway would disappear and a double vanity would be installed where the entrance had once been. Again, she wasn't sure if she would ever need a double vanity, but undoubtedly the next owner would expect one with a renovated home.

One of the demolition tasks that Andrea and her friends would tackle was pulling up the horrid blue rainbow carpet. Despite Verna Lee's idea that it would make a good drop cloth, Steve wanted to see what they were facing before he began the renovations.

Andrea's reverie was interrupted by the plaintive cry of a young amateur hairdresser as she tried to make Jill Brooks' lovely black curls behave in a way that would be the most pleasing for the audience, "Mrs. Hogan," the young girl cried, "I'm all out of hairspray and Jill's hair will just not behave.!"

Andrea jumped up and headed toward her bedroom to retrieve the extra can of hairspray that she knew she had left in there. Unfortunately, no one had told her that the guys had taken over her bedroom to change into their costumes, and she was just about to open the door when a loud chorus of "NO!!!!" rose from the girls in the apartment. Andrea breathed a sigh of relief and speaking through the door asked the guys to pass out the hairspray. One embarrassing moment averted. It was time to get this show on the road!

Chapter Sixty-seven

The Principal's Office

Even Oscar and Verna Lee joined the group in the Principal's office after the opening night crowd had finally departed. Oscar gladly accepted a beer from Scott, and Verna Lee sipped a bit of white wine that Trish had poured for her. Oscar was the first to lift his beer in a toast to the Director, Assistant Director, and right hand helper of *The Fantastiks*, "To a great show, my friends. I understood almost every word!" These few words were high praise indeed from Oscar. They passed another half an hour pleasantly chatting about the show, enjoying some adult beverages and especially the appetizers prepared by Mrs. Mary Samuels. Mary beamed as each and every guest in the small room praised her abilities and remarked what a joy it was to have her as a member of this little group.

"But the group will change so soon," bemoaned Scott. "I'm just getting used to all of you and Trish and Andrea are moving already!"

Andrea was quick to interject, "You're not getting rid of me that easily, Scott Samuels. I intend to show up for Fifth Quarter parties every Friday night when there's a home game."

"And don't forget about bridge on Sunday nights and the yoga class on Saturday morning that Dee Anderson is going to start up in the fall," reminded Verna Lee.

"I'll be here for all of them," Andrea assured her. "I'm even thinking about starting a Bible Study at my house. I hosted one for years in Des Moines, and I really miss it. We'll have to round up all the Lutherans, Methodists and Catholics in town and see if we can't come up with a group."

"Will there be food?" asked Scott.

After the laughter died down, Andrea reassured him, "Yes, there will be food."

"Count me in!" exclaimed Scott.

"Count us in!" corrected Mary.

"Oh, yeah, sorry about that Mrs. Samuels; I'm still getting used to being two instead of one."

"I'm happy to remind you," Mary replied, and kissed her new husband fondly on his slightly balding head.

Scott reached for the beer that Trish was handing him and suddenly he remembered what he had been meaning to tell her.

"Hey, Trish, guess what? I rented your apartment for the months of June and July, now I'm not out any rent before the new teacher arrives in August.

"Well, that's good news, but I've gotta ask…who in the world wants to summer in Bentley, Iowa?"

"I have no idea who it is. It was done entirely through email, and I never even spoke to the person. She just sent me an email out of the blue and asked if I had any vacant apartments for the months of June and July. It was pretty weird; she wired transferred two months' rent to my account from some bank in Frankfurt, Germany.

Rich and Andrea perked up when they heard the name of the city where they both knew that Rich's ex-wife was teaching. Rich was the first to think to ask a very important question, "What's the name of the person you rented the apartment to?"

"Oh, I'm terrible with names, it was something like Suzy, Sandy, something like that. The last name was Stoddard. I remember that," Scott assured him.

Richard groaned, and the entire room turned to stare at him. "Was it, by chance, 'Sally Stoddard'?"

"Yes, that's it, why? Do you know her?"

"Oh yes, I know her, she's my ex-wife."

There was a general chorus of, "WHAT???"

Scott literally went pale. "Oh, no, Rich, I had no idea! I knew you had told me about some drama with your ex-wife over Christmas break, but I didn't ever ask her name, and I just didn't even dream that there was any kind of a connection. Do you want me to contact her and tell her I can't rent to her?"

"No, of course not, Scott. There is no sense in taking money out of your pocket. I'm sure she wants to spend time with the kids this summer; they're both going to be here to help my folks arrange for their big auction in August. I was already planning on hanging out at Andi's apartment to escape the kid's loud music…now I just think I'll plan on camping out at Andi's new house instead!"

"You are most welcome to do that," Andrea assured him.

Richard shook his head in disbelief and raised his bottle of beer to offer a toast, "Well, here's to ex-wives and new lives…may they coexist peacefully!"

Chapter Sixty-eight

Andrea Hogan

Andrea decided to hang around as each of the residents of the school house took their leave after Scott's stunning announcement. Richard certainly did not seem inclined to go anywhere as he reached for another beer from the cooler that was being rolled out of the Principal's office. She already had a full glass of wine so she took a sip and asked her old friend who was looking glumly at his new bottle of beer, "Well, in the immortal words of every television psychoanalyst, 'How does that make you feel'?"

Richard chuckled appreciatively. "I feel like I just fell off a thirty foot ladder and landed on my heart. One minute I'm flying high on the wings of another wonderful high school musical, and in the next minute all the stress and anxiety of the past two years has suddenly descended on me again. I felt like I was just coming out of a long dark funk, and now I get to contemplate spending the summer with the woman who caused it all to begin with. Andi, I don't want to see her. I don't want her to get any ideas about waltzing back into my life the way she did last Christmas. But I also don't want to deny her access to the kids; I don't want to be that kind of a person."

To Andrea's complete and utter shock, her old friend put his head in his hands and began to cry. She stared at him for a few moments, and then, as if her body was acting of its own volition, she moved across the leather couch and took him in her arms. He wrapped his arms around her, and the tears flowed for several more minutes. Finally he let go of her and reached into his back pocket for his ever present handkerchief and blew his nose forcefully. He looked up at her sheepishly.

"Not sure where that came from. It's actually the first time I have ever cried over the end of my marriage."

"Sometimes a good cry can be very therapeutic."

"I guess, but it still doesn't solve my problem. I get to spend two months dealing with the one woman that I can truthfully say I had hoped never to see again. I feel like booking the first flight out of here at the end of school and not showing up until she leaves. But I'm looking forward to being with the kids, and I really want to paint your house and..."

Andrea was quick to interrupt him, "Please don't feel like you have to do anything at the new house. I'll completely understand if you just want to get out of Dodge."

Richard sighed and said, "No, it's just wishful thinking. I want to be with the kids this summer, and I really do want to help you with the house. I'll just have to grin and bear it, I guess."

"I thought you were planning on taking the kids to Canada in late July. Is that plan still on?" Andrea asked.

"As far as I'm concerned, it is," he acknowledged. "I've talked to Dad, and he thinks it should take the kids about six weeks to get everything lined up for the auction so I was planning on a road trip. This will probably be our last chance to travel together for a while. Scott will graduate from Emerson next year, and Sandy will be heading overseas for her junior year abroad."

"So, make it absolutely clear to Sally that she is not invited on the trip and focus on that time that you'll have with the kids." Suddenly Andrea had another idea. "I've wanted to plan some kind of break from all this renovation and house selling. We could plan a long weekend over the 4th of July. Once you come back, you'll only have a couple of weeks or so to deal with the situation."

"That's the best idea I've heard all evening. Where do you want to go?"

"Well, I haven't been to New York for a theater weekend in several years. You remember me telling you about my friend Doug who was killed?"

Richard nodded his remembrance.

"We went one year and saw four Broadway shows in three days. It was great."

"Then let's plan on re-creating the magic one more time," he replied. Then he stopped suddenly and asked, "It won't make you sad to go back to a city where you had such a good time with Doug?"

"You know," Andrea said reflectively, "it might hurt a little, but hurting is also how we grow as a person."

Richard laughed ruefully, "Then I'll surely grow by leaps and bounds if I survive this coming summer."

He stood up and pulled her up with him, "Bedtime for Bonzo," he began.

"And you're Bonzo," Andrea finished.

Chapter Sixty-nine

Trish Wilkins

The school year was hurtling to a close. Trish looked out of her classroom and marveled at the beauty of the early spring in this part of Iowa. The Forsythia around the High School was rampant. A sea of yellow flowers lined the parking lot that was visible from her classroom windows. She realized with a start that she would miss this place when she left to pursue Will's dream in Portland, Maine. She was surprised she could feel so drawn to any one place after less than a year. She had to remind herself that the life she had known this year would not be the same even if she had decided to stay. Andrea would be living in her adorable house that she already referred to as the 1951. She suspected that Rich would be spending much of his free time there as well. Scott and Mary would be busy building their nest upstairs. She also suspected that a two bedroom bachelor pad was not the kind of home that Mary wanted when they decided to have children. So, life changes, and she was making the biggest change of any of them.

Whenever she began to feel even the least bit doubtful, she would take out her cell phone and click her phone on so she could see the shining smile of one William Roger Hogan. Any doubts flew to the highest rafters as she looked on his kind face and funny smile. She was so proud of how hard he had worked to realize his dream to work in public radio. All of the hours he had volunteered while he still lived in Des Moines and Austin had finally garnered him the job of his dreams, program director. He would choose the music that a new generation would come to love, at least the generation growing up around Portland, Maine.

She smiled when she thought about the goals that she had set for herself just a few years ago. She had to admit she was doing pretty well on accomplishing those goals. She had wanted to be a math teacher, and she was one. She had wanted to find a wonderful man and fall in love, and she had. Now, the long term goals of a home of her own and a family also seemed within reach. When she had visited Will at spring break she had helped him get settled into what would be her next home. It was a beautiful apartment in an old Victorian house right in the heart of Portland. It was walking distance to shops and restaurants and just a short bike or car ride to either the radio station or East High where she would be teaching. As they both established themselves in the Portland area, they had talked about purchasing a home sooner rather than later. The apartment would be twice the cost of her current one and home prices out east had taken a nosedive along with the economy so they would not need to add too much more each month to come up with a mortgage payment.

She and Will talked and wrote about their future so often that she had just come to accept that they would be married. Still, she couldn't help but wonder if he would actually ask her to marry him or would they simply begin a life together that would eventually find its way to the altar. She had to admit to herself that it really didn't matter to her one way or the other. She knew that it mattered to Andrea. She had seen the disapproval in her friend's eyes when they talked about this move. She knew that Andrea wanted at least a ring on Trish's finger. She also knew that Andrea had pressured Will to make it legal before asking Trish to uproot her life and follow his dream to Portland. That thinking was for Andrea's generation, not hers and Will's. In their hearts they knew they were heading for the altar; it might just take them a little longer than Andrea would like to get there. She really needed to remind her friend that this was her son whom she had raised to be upright and progressive. She had to come to terms with the decisions that he made, even if they were not the ones Andrea would have made.

The bell rang, and she looked at her classroom clock with a start. She had spent her entire forty-five minute planning period daydreaming about the future. She looked down at the legal pad that was always nearby in case she needed to do some quick figuring, and realized that she had written *Mrs. William Roger Hogan* all over the first page of the pad. She laughed and quickly tore the hopeful writing off before any of her students arrived to find her doodling her future wishes. She had to admit to herself that she liked the sound of the name she had written over and over. Maybe she wasn't quite as progressive as she supposed herself to be!

Chapter Seventy

Verna Lee and Oscar Swenson

The old coots were at it again, and so were her fellow seamstresses. No sooner than the high schooler's had finished their musical, but the new Community Theater Group had ratcheted up their rehearsal schedule as their premier production loomed right around the corner. Not only were the actors busy, but the old coots were pounding and painting several hours a day while they created a 1940's living room for the production of Arsenic and Old Lace.

All around her, sewing machines buzzed as two dozen costumes were being constructed or re-furbished from dresses and suits from the war years that could be found in many an attic in the greater Marshtown, Griswold, Bentley metropolitan area. After all, one never knew when the pencil skirt or trousers without cuffs would come back into style.

The Comfort Makers, as the ladies had come to call their quilting group, were still busy working on several projects even though some of the ladies had been recruited to work on the costumes. Verna Lee noticed that the clock on the wall of the old gymnasium was heading toward 3:00 p.m. so she pulled out the can of decaffeinated Folgers coffee, scooped up three good scoops of coffee and proceeded to make one last pot of coffee for their 3:00 Koffee Klatch. She always offered both leaded and unleaded coffee at this gathering since caffeine seemed to affect everyone differently.

The group had fallen into a very pleasant pattern. They gathered in the Gymnasium around 11:00 each morning. The day's cooking team would have arrived at 10:00 to whip up a nutritious lunch for the ladies and the men as well. After lunch the men did the dishes while the ladies did twenty minutes of Tai Chi each day. They followed a DVD that she had found at her favorite "Stuff Etc" store in Marshtown. She wasn't sure if they were doing it correctly, but she figured the stretching and moving had to be good for them. By 1:00 p.m. they were all engaged in the business of the day. The men had decided that once the set for *Arsenic and Old Lace* was built they would switch to creative bird houses. One of the guys had found the plans for a bird house that was supposed to be squirrel proof and could be painted to look like buildings in the community. They had already come up with a plan to create the Old Bentley Schoolhouse, the Lutheran church in Marshtown, the Methodist church over in Griswold, and the old mill out in the country near Keosauqua. They figured they could sell the houses for $25 at local craft shows and still show a tidy profit for the Community Center.

The ladies were no slouches when it came to fundraising either. They were already making plans to sell cookies, pies, and cakes at the Farmers Market in Marshtown each Saturday during the summer. They had also designated a few of their quilts that they had decided to place in a raffle that would conclude at the end of the summer. All in all they were determined to raise $5,000 in the coming months to assist in the heating and electrical costs that the busy gymnasium must be creating for Scott. Not that Scott had asked for any assistance in the fuel or electric bills. They all knew that he would probably turn them down when they offered him the money, but they wanted to offer it, nonetheless, to show their deep appreciation of the friendship and special times they had all shared in the old gymnasium.

The coffee was ready, and Verna Lee rang her small bell that would bring the friends to the tables set up in the middle of the room. True to form, the ladies would sit at two of the three rectangular tables, and the men would occupy the third. In many ways it truly was just like junior high school. They were enjoying Verna Lee's delicious banana bread with their coffee today, and the conversation flowed among and across the tables. As they all finished the last dregs of their coffee and the men had used their fingers to get the last vestiges of banana bread, Gladys Millen suddenly stood up from the table and used her fork on her coffee cup to get their attention.

"Excuse me. Excuse me," she began. It took another rap on her coffee cup, but she soon had everyone's attention. "I just wanted to let all of you know that I have made the decision to move into Andrea's apartment at the end of the summer." This announcement was followed by a chorus of "Oh's!"

"I'm not ready to sell the farm yet," she informed the curious men and women assembled. "But I think it's time I packed it in and moved to higher ground. There will be a big auction of Rollin's farm equipment and most of the household goods." She turned to her good friend Verna Lee and declared, "I'll need your help to decide what I can cram into Andrea's apartment!"

Verna Lee smiled and assured her, "You'd be surprised how many pairs of salt and pepper shakers you can live without!"

"Well, it's going to be a little strange, but it will be nice knowing that when the winter winds come, I'll only have to maneuver the stairs rather than icy roads to come down here and sew." With that she sat down and the ladies around her all assured her that she was making the right decision. It made every last one of them wonder if they shouldn't be doing something similar in the not too distant future. Too bad there weren't more apartments here at the old school house, they thought. Why, they could start a regular old hippie commune or something!

Chapter Seventy-one

Richard Knight

Rich opened the door to his unlocked apartment and immediately knew that his two children had arrived for the summer. Their car in the parking lot had also been a big clue. The apartment fairly buzzed with teenage hormones. Rich was grateful that Scott Samuels had included the miniscule third bedroom in this apartment so that his own Scott would at least be able to have a space he would call his own. Since there was no closet in his small room, Rich had installed two boards with at least twenty hooks for clothes or gear. He just hoped his son would use them rather than toss everything on the floor as he had done as a child.

He was very happy to be able to sing out, "Hey, kids, I'm home!" as he had done for so many years when they had been growing up. While they did not come running as they had done as little tykes, they did quickly emerge from their bedrooms, and both enveloped him in giant bear hugs. Sandy was the first to speak. "O, Daddy," she cried, "it is so good to be anywhere but my dorm room! I feel like I have been tied to my desk for the last three weeks!"

Scott scoffed at her hysterics. "Try thirty-six straight hours with no sleep and a final at the end of that time!" Scott's first year of graduate school at his father's alma mater, Emerson University, had been rigorous, but Rich also knew that he had gotten straight "A's" the first semester and he suspected that this semester's grades would be right up there as well. His children were certainly smarter than either he or Sally!

"Well, I'm just glad to have you both under the same roof for more than a brief visit," Scott assured his children. "We've got a busy couple of months ahead of us. Your grandparents have taken this moving to town idea to heart. The walls are up on their new house in Marshtown, and they have a take no prisoners mentality when it comes to getting rid of stuff. I had to rescue several boxes from my old bedroom closet that were destined for the dump."

Sandy looked worried. "Grandma hasn't done all of the work already, has she?"

"No," her father assured her. "She is just getting started. She hasn't even touched the kitchen, or the attic."

"I'm sure there will be no shortage of work for me when it comes to going through Grandpa's things either," Scott chimed in.

"You're right there," Rich agreed. "The garage at the new house is only half the size of the one on the farm, and then there's the barn to deal with as well. I'll try to help as much as I can, but I'm also going to be pretty busy with Andi's new house."

His children looked at him blankly. "Who's Andi?" they both asked in chorus and then blushed furiously for having done it.

Rich tried to jog their memory. "You remember Andrea, she lives downstairs. Scott, you met her when I moved in. I guess you haven't met her yet, Sandy."

Sandy was suddenly cautious. "Why would you be helping your neighbor with her house? Is that your summer job?"

"Oh, no, it's not a job. Andi's my friend, and she just bought this really cute little house in town. I just want to help her make it nice," Rich explained.

Both of his children eyed him suspiciously. Scott asked the question: "Is she your girlfriend?"

Rich suddenly felt very tongue tied. "Oh, I wouldn't say that, but she is very important to me, and we've renewed a nice friendship over the past school year."

"What do you mean, renewed?" Scott asked.

Rich hesitated. He did not want to lie to his children. He just wasn't sure how much of the truth to leave out. He decided to leave most of the truth out of the equation, at least for now.

"We knew each other at UNI. We had a class together." There. That was the truth.

Fortunately, his children lost interest quickly, as most children do when confronted with their parent's past. Rich looked at the clock on the wall and realized that he needed to get cooking. He explained to his children that in just about an hour four more people would be presenting themselves at their door, expecting to be fed some semblance of a supper. They both thought it was neat that most of the apartment residents gathered for dinner each evening. Rich told them that it would be "Taco Night," and they both set about slicing, dicing, and cooking up hamburger and chicken for the meal. This gave Rich time to whip up a batch of his famous brownies which brought yelps of joy from his two children.

As they worked together in his kitchen, Rich decided to broach the topic of their mother.

"So, when will your mother be arriving in the greater Bentley metroplex?"

His children looked at each other for a moment before Sandy explained, "She'll be here June 1st, that's as soon as her apartment will be available."

"What is she planning on doing for furniture and dishes?" Rich asked

It was Scott who answered this time. "Mom's moving back to the States, Dad."

Rich couldn't help the slight edge of panic in his voice, "Where?"

"She isn't sure," Scott told him, "She's been applying for jobs in Iowa and Massachusetts. She says she wants to live close to at least one of her children."

Rich could not keep the thought that he was certainly glad there were no openings at BGM from creeping into his mind. He decided then and there to not let Sally's presence ruin his summer with his children. "Who's up for making Spanish rice?" he asked his children.

"You are," they agreed in chorus.

Rich reached for the rice in the cupboard. It was good to be a Dad again.

Chapter Seventy-two

Andrea Hogan

As she sat back to enjoy her second cup of coffee after Rich's fabulous Taco and Brownie celebration, Andrea realized how much she would miss this easy camaraderie that had grown among these new friends over the past nine months. Just in the span of time that it takes for a student to pass from fourth to fifth grade, Andrea's life had completely changed. Here she was the new owner of a 90 year old house in one town and the owner of a 100 year house in another. Hopefully, her 100 year old painted lady in Des Moines would be easy to sell. Certainly she had updated it through the years, and she knew that Jane had kept the house just as immaculate as she always had. Her plan was to spend two weeks boxing up anything that would be moved to the new house and disposing of whatever accumulated detritus that existed. Fortunately, there wasn't much of that since neither Will nor she was a saver. Their rule had been, If you haven't used it in a year, you don't need it.

At the end of the two weeks she hoped to be ready to put the house on the market with her personal items removed so that a family could see themselves living there as they entered the home. After that she could arrange an early or an extended closing; it was nice to know that she still had her apartment in the school house until August. By then her new home should be finished and the Pod she had rented could be transported to Bentley where she would begin the next adventure in this life she had been given.

She couldn't help but wonder what next year would bring. Would the week night suppers continue? What would it be like for Verna Lee to have one of her best friends living just a few steps away? Would Scott and Mary continue to live upstairs or would they eventually buy a home to raise the family that they would no doubt begin sooner rather than later? Too many questions to deal with! One step at a time, she decided.

"Speaking of steps," she thought to herself, "I'd better motor on downstairs and get to grading those freshmen compositions."

She rose from the comfortable chair and spoke to the assembled group, "I'm off to grade freshman comps, anybody want to trade work for the night?"

"Gladly," Trish offered, "I have twenty calculus tests and fifteen algebra tests."

Andrea smiled at her young friend, "No, thanks, I guess I'll take my compositions after all!"

A chorus of good-byes followed her out the door and down the steps to her little home. She turned on the heat under her ever present Tea Kettle and put away dishes that had been drying in her dish drainer. When the kettle began to shake, rattle, and roll, she chose some orange blossom tea from her vast array of choices and settled down to a long evening of reading, correcting, and encouraging her young writers.

Two hours and fifteen essays later, she put down her red ink pen, stretched her sore back, decided to call it a night, and finish the last five before school began in the morning. She rinsed her tea cup and left it in the sink to wash when more dishes had accumulated. She turned and walked to her door and was just about to twist the dead bolt to the lock position, old habits die hard, and she always found herself locking her door each night, when she heard a light tapping on that very door and a voice softly saying, "Andi, it's me, Richard. Can I come in?"

She stopped her locking motion and opened the door to find Richard standing there in a ratty gray T-Shirt and pajama bottoms. She looked at him curiously and motioned him inside.

For a long moment he just stood there looking at her, and she began to wonder if she had a smudge of chocolate on her mouth from her evening snack. Without warning he put his arms around her and kissed her with a passion she had not thought he possessed. There was nothing tentative or confused about this kiss as there had been with that one last fall. This was a kiss. She wasn't quite sure what to think, but her body knew what to do.

She felt her arms wrap around his sturdy body, and he drew her into an even deeper kiss that she found herself responding to without hesitation.

Finally he stopped kissing her lips and began to explore her face with light, happy kisses as he tried to explain this sudden change in attitude. He laughed as he explained, "I was lying up in bed thinking how nice it was to have my kids home. Suddenly the thought came into my head that the only thing better would be to have you next to me right then. Not Sally. You. It was very literally like a light bulb went off in my head. I want to be with you. I want to touch your face, and hear you laugh at my silly jokes. I honestly don't know what the future holds, but I know what the here and now holds. Please let it hold us," he implored.

It was Andrea's turn to look at Richard for a long moment. In answer to the longing look in his eyes, she took him in her arms and kissed him soundly. "I don't know what the future holds either, but I know I want you in it. Now you'd better get back upstairs and get some sleep. I expect you to be waiting for me at 5:00am for our morning walk." They both went back to their respective beds with smiles on their faces.

Chapter Seventy-three

An Old Fashioned Memorial Day Picnic

The Sunday of Memorial Day weekend dawned bright and cloudless. Verna Lee was already busy as the sun began to rise. The Lord would just have to forgive her today because there was no way she was going to be able to get to church and coordinate a potluck picnic lunch for two hundred of her closest friends. She smiled at her own joke. She probably couldn't claim more than one hundred of the guests as friends. When the Old Coots and the Comfort Makers decided to throw an old-fashioned Memorial Day picnic and had put an article in the Marshtown News and the Keosauqua Times, she had been astounded at the RSVP's that had come in through her answering machine and Andrea's email account. She was pretty sure that no one in Bentley would be eating lunch at home today, and quite a few other families from the surrounding area would be joining in the celebration.

She had to admit that she was once again proud of her planning skills as each family would be bringing an essential item for a successful potluck. She was not one of these people who just left a potluck to chance. She had attended way too many where potato salad and brownies dominated the food line. No, she had a plan. Families whose last name fell between A-F would be bringing salads, G-N would be bringing vegetables, and M-S would supply the desserts, T-Z could bring whatever they liked! The Community Center funds would pay for the paper products, cold drinks, hot dogs and brats to grill. She had decided against hamburgers to keep the buns simple.

She consulted her master list to see when the fellows were scheduled to arrive to transport the banquet tables out to the grassy area under the big oak trees in the front of the schoolhouse. She had been sure to pepper this committee with the younger folks to give the old coots a respite from carrying heavy tables and chairs. She even had one more person to add to the list of helpers. That nice young son of Andrea's had arrived last night and had volunteered to help out this morning.

She realized with a pang of sadness that tonight would be the last night Trish would sleep in the old schoolhouse and Andrea would return only briefly to pack up and move to her new little home on Maple Street. Just as quickly though she thought fondly of having her friend Gladys Millen just across the hall from her, and there would be a new teacher living in Trish's apartment in the fall. There would also be Rich's ex-wife there all summer long. That would be strange for Rich she thought, but nice for his children to be with both their mother and their father, even if a schoolhouse floor divided them.

In fact, it had been quite convenient for Trish as the woman-- What was her name? Sandy, Sally, Sue, something like that—would be buying all of Trish's large pieces of furniture, and she would only have her clothes, books and little stuff to put in that shiny silver pickup truck when she moved to Maine. What an exciting time for those two young love birds. They would discover a new part of the country while they grew deeper in love.

She shook her head sharply and told herself to get going. No time to lollygag as her mother would have said. She heard Oscar stirring in the other room, and she pulled the bacon out of the refrigerator. She figured she'd better give him a good breakfast since he would be busy all day, and into the evening, no doubt.

Chapter Seventy-four

The Principals Office

Friends, young and old, were sprawled over every piece of furniture and floor space in the cozy Principal's office that had become their official gathering spot when important matters needed to be hashed out. The Memorial Day Picnic had been an unquestioned success. Cars from miles around began pouring into the old schoolhouse parking lot well before noon. All of the guys in the apartment house, with the able help of Rich's son Scott, and Andrea's son Will, had begun to haul out the heavy wooden tables and the sturdy folding chairs that had seated so many people at the Thanksgiving feast and Scott and Mary's wedding reception. Twenty tables were quickly set up under the giant Oak trees that were sprinkled around the huge front lawn of the schoolhouse where children had jumped rope and played tag just a few years ago. Dozens of tables were brightly decorated with green, yellow and red plastic tablecloths waiting for families and friends to gather around for an old fashioned Iowa picnic.

At the far end of the lawn the guys had put up two funeral canopies borrowed for the occasion from Pedrick's Funeral Home. Fortunately, no one had died in Van Buren County in the past week so the canopies were available to borrow. The large canopies provided ample shade and protection from the elements for the ten serving tables that had been set up in two rows with plenty of room left between them for four lines of folks to go through the serving line. It was always Verna Lee's goal to get everyone served in less than twenty minutes, and she was sure this arrangement would accomplish that goal. The array of food had been amazing. As each new dish arrived, Verna Lee had inspected the contents and sent it to one of the ten tables that had been numbered so that salads ended up on tables one and six. Vegetable dishes were assigned tables two and seven while desserts occupied tables three and eight. Tables four and nine were for overflow, and tables five and nine held the silverware (Verna Lee's rule: always put the napkins and silverware at the end of the line).

The roasters with the hot dogs and brats were the last stop made by the picnic goers.

At noon Verna Lee rang her trusty school bell, and all conversation ceased. Reverend Knudson from Andrea's church walked to the microphone that Scott and Rich had set up for the occasion and offered the blessing for all of the wonderful food and the good folks gathered together to commemorate the lives of all the servicemen who had given their lives to protect our freedom.

And the eating commenced. Verna Lee dismissed tables so that the line was never more than twenty people deep. By 12:30 she herself was sitting next to Oscar, and she had had plenty of choices as the last one through the line. Of course, the deviled eggs were gone, but they always were, besides, she liked her own recipe better than anyone else's. It was the touch of balsamic vinegar that gave hers a special zing.

There had been seconds and thirds enjoyed by many before Trish, Will, and Andrea had gathered the young children to take them to the grassy area behind the school for a series of races, group games, and finally chances for anyone who could recite the Pledge of Allegiance, to pelt Principal Craig Seeley with a water balloon. Needless to say, a change into dry clothing was needed before the good principal was allowed into the family vehicle for the trip home. Now the friends were scattered around their favorite gathering place, and the windows had been thrown open to catch the cool evening breezes that are so delicious in Iowa in late May. They had hashed and re-hashed the picnic and all of the dishes served as well as which families had prepared favorite recipes—and which families had let Sara Lee do their baking for them. Before long Verna Lee announced that she and Oscar were ready to head to bed. Before she could rise from the couch, however, Scott jumped up and asked for everyone's attention.

"Now you guys know that I'm not much for making speeches. But I do know that this will be the last time we will gather together like this, maybe forever, not that I mean to sound maudlin.

I'm sure Trish and Will will visit often, but there will be new friends in Trish's and Andrea's apartments when school starts in the fall and whether larger or smaller, our gatherings just won't be quite the same. I wanted to thank all of you for making this a memorable year for me. Just look at all the changes, in less than a year, we all moved in here, had that wonderful Thanksgiving dinner where I met Mary, celebrated victories and mourned losses, became friends, and really, became family. When I think of all of you, I think of you as my friends-in-law." His speech was interrupted by appropriate groans all around.

"OK, I deserved that," he admitted, "but I do think of all of you as my chosen family. Mary and I are so blessed to have you in our lives." With those words he pulled his bride up from the floor where she had been resting, sipping a soda. With his arm around her waist, he turned to the assembled group to and announced, "Mary and I wanted you to be among the first to know that we are expecting a baby, we don't know which kind yet, around the end of January" Spontaneous applause broke out, followed by hugs, kisses, and general good wishes. Someone asked him if he and Mary would continue to live upstairs.

His reply was only somewhat hesitant. "We've decided to see how it goes. We know we'll be here for the next year or so, but after that we may feel that dragging the paraphernalia of a young family up two flights of stairs is more than we want to do. Mary's Grandmother Gladys has graciously offered us the farm house if we decide we want to move there. It's good to have options!"

As they settled down once again and Verna Lee once again moved toward the edge of the sofa to make a graceful exit to her own apartment and bed, Will Hogan suddenly stood up to face the assembled group. He cleared his throat and began to address the group. "Well, I'm sure you're surprised to see me stand up to make a speech, but Trish and I also have some news to share, and we thought this would be the best place to do it." Curious faces turned toward him, and he burst out laughing when he saw the alarm in the women's eyes and the cluelessness in the guys' eyes.

He went on to explain, "As you all know, I have known Trish for the past couple of years as she and my mom became friends when they were both at UNI, but it wasn't until they both moved here that I really came to know Trish as much more than my mom's friend. She has become my best friend and the love of my life. As you know, we depart tomorrow for an extended trip to Europe. Before we leave though, we would like to share with you the joyous news that this young woman has consented to marry me and has accepted my grandmother's engagement ring." With those words he pulled Trish to her feet and produced her left hand for a thorough inspection of a small but exquisite diamond in an antique setting that seemed to have been made just for the young lady who proudly showed it off.

Another round of hugs and hearty handshakes followed. Before anyone could settle back into place, however, Verna Lee took the floor inquiring, "OK, does anyone else have any other announcements tonight?" When she did not get a response, she smiled at them all broadly and announced herself, "Then my groom, and best friend, I might add, will be off to our bed. It's been a memorable day."

The group agreed, but lingered together for one last round of beverages. It was as if they all knew this night would never be repeated, and they were all reluctant to have it end.

Chapter Seventy-five

Andrea Hogan

Andrea was surprised to see Richard waiting for her at 5:00 the next morning, just as he had been almost every morning since they had begun their morning walks in the early spring.

She smiled as she saw him sitting on the hard marble steps that led up the stairs to the second floor and his, no doubt, sleeping children. She reached out her hand and pulled him to his feet, and he held that hand as they walked out into the clear crisp early dawn. She smiled to herself and spoke only when they had closed the doors of the old schoolhouse carefully behind them.

"Well, I think we made our escape without waking up any of the other tenants and guests," she declared as they continued to walk hand in hand down the side walk of the old schoolhouse out to the deserted street that ran in front of the grand old building.

As if by instinct they both headed toward 1951 Maple to spend a few minutes in Andrea's future home, each of them wondering if it would also be Richard's future home.

As they approached the front porch, she waited while Richard pulled out his key ring to unlock the front door. The action reminded Andrea of something that she had wanted to tell him.

"Don't let me forget to give you the extra set of keys to Will's truck. He actually remembered to bring them all the way from Maine, which is fairly amazing in and of itself".

"I'll remember to remind you" Richard promised. "Hopefully I won't lose the first set that you gave me yesterday, but better to be safe than sorry." It had been decided that Richard would drive Will's truck over the summer while he and Trish were in Europe. They would be departing from St. Louis so they would make one more trip back to Bentley at the end of their vacation to pick up the truck before heading to Maine to begin their new life together.

In fact, Andrea would head out in just a couple of hours to make the drive to the airport and then the long trek back to her home in Des Moines. She fully intended to have Will do the driving to St. Louis so she could cat nap in the back seat and be well rested for the solo drive later in the day. She would climb into her bed at the old house (as she now thought of her home that had kept her warm and dry for nearly twenty five years) just before midnight, if there wasn't much road construction.

Still, she had not wanted to miss this morning walk, and having Richard appear had been doubly nice. They entered the quiet house, and Andrea reached for the switch to flip on the overhead light. It was amazing to see the progress that had already been made. The floors had already been sanded, stained and sealed in two long weekend projects headed up by Richard with plenty of help from Scott, Oscar, and two very helpful football players who had made quick work of the sanding on day one of the project. One had run the big machine that Richard had rented for the day, and the other one came behind with the hand sander for the edges. Richard and Scott had both taken turns on the sanders and had both been happy to turn the jobs back to the two young men. Oscar had stood back, smiled, and swept sawdust. The young men were happy to earn an extra $20 apiece on top of the $100 that Andrea had paid each of them at the end of the day. By mutual assent, Richard and Scott each reached into their wallets to provide the extra tip, with a grateful acknowledgement to what their backs would have felt like if they had had to run the machines all day by themselves.

Now the floors were covered with protective paper so that Richard could begin on the paint in the living room in the next few days. Large patches of sample colors adorned the walls where old lady pink had resided for more years than Andrea liked to count. She had finally decided on a celery color with a darker shade as an accent wall around the fireplace and the built-ins. She thought it would be soothing and go well with her couch and rug that she would move from Des Moines.

They moved through the living room and dining room to the kitchen… which was no longer there. Everything had been gutted to the studs, and she had picked out modest cupboards and countertops from The Home Depot in Keokuk. They would be delivered in a few weeks after Steve had completed the re-wiring and the plumbing project that would bring a new dishwasher into the kitchen. She liked the small but efficient kitchen, and she especially like how it was separated from the living and dining room. She was not in favor of the new styles where every pot and pan was exposed to her guests. She always cooked first and cleaned up later…sometimes much later!

Her bedroom area was still just a plan on paper. The walls had not yet been knocked out, and only the bathroom had been gutted. Fortunately, there would still be the bathroom upstairs for Richard to use when he was here working on the house. She felt somewhat guilty in accepting the wonderfully kind offer of his help; after all he would end up painting every room in her house before the summer was over. She wondered again if he thought of it as his house. Would it be his house by this time next year? Where were they heading with this relationship?

Was she sure she wanted to find out?

As if he had read her mind, he stopped her before she stepped on the first stair tread that would lead them to the upstairs bedrooms. He took her in his arms and kissed her tenderly.

"I can't believe that after today, I'm going to have to wait until the Fourth of July weekend to kiss you again," he said, with a cute little pout on his lips.

"Oh, I'm sure you'll survive," Andrea assured him. "And just think how much fun the reunion will be." She kissed him again, hard, to bring her point home.

They made their way from 1951 Maple up to Walnut and then over to Locust and on to the equally deserted Town Square. Only a few of the storefronts were home to businesses. Others were boarded up or had become storage space for Old Man Schearer's Heating and Cooling business, the fate that the schoolhouse would have shared had not Scott outbid the feisty old plumber.

They had both been quiet as they walked around the town square, but as they headed back toward the old schoolhouse, Richard finally voiced what they had both been wondering.

"Andi, when you get back from Des Moines and are here for the foreseeable future, where do you see me in that future?"

Andi did not immediately answer. Finally, she asked, "Where do you see yourself in my future?"

Richard was quicker to answer than she had been to ask. "I see myself right by your side. Growing old together, celebrating grandchildren, finding the happiness and companionship that I know we can achieve."

Andi stopped walking and turned toward Richard. "Richard, darling, I think I want those same things, too...but I'd just like to get there a little slower than I think you want to travel. Remember, I've been divorced for more years than you were married. I came close to sharing my life with someone a few years ago, and a reckless driver stole that chance from me. I just want to take things slowly and be assured that this is what I and the Lord want for my life. Can you live with that?"

Richard looked down at her lovingly and replied, "Yes, I can live with that; it's you that I don't want to live without. I want you to be sure. I can be patient, because Andrea Michelle Spencer Hogan, I love you."

Andrea leaned back to look into his wonderfully dark eyes and admitted out loud what she had first known over thirty years ago, "I love you, too, Richard Daniel Knight".

The End?